*To Chunky —
And Lila —*

D1414913

LUCKY PUNCH

*Two of the
greatest — and
luckiest —
people I know!

Granny!*

Granville Toogood

ISBN: 1983705578
ISBN 13: 9781983705571

The pages are yellowing now, dappled and frail as a moth's wing. My fingers touch the old leaves in a kind of wonderment, the first contact in more than fifty years. The feel of it brings back swarms of memories, and my fingers linger for a long moment before I gently peel away the fragile parchment and begin my journey in time.

There it is, in my own hand. The hand of a boy not yet a man. A boy from long ago. Even the ink is fading.

I put on my reading glasses.

MY JOURNAL

Random notes…
I need to write this. Not because things are hard for me but because they're easy. Maybe too easy. People say I'm handsome, a pretty good athlete. My friends say I have a way with girls. I'm privileged, I know. I lead a comfortable life. I'm only seventeen, and things are good. I should have no complaints. So why am I down when I should be up? Is there something wrong with me? Am I the only one who feels restless and dissatisfied? If my friends feel the same, they keep it to themselves. All I know is that I need more, want more. It's not money or things. It's something else. And I know I won't be happy until I get it…

Won't be happy until I get it.
I look up and smile. The last light of day slips through the window and melts slowly down the bookcase in the den, a little rainbow of descending color in gathering gloom. I can hear the tick of the clock. The dog, forever asleep on the carpet in front of

the fire, mewls and twitches, lost in canine dreams. The clock and the dog. Beyond that, only deep silence. Outside, the last amber flecks of fast-dying day glitter on what's left of the snow.

I can smell aged paper, the faint odor of the old leather binding, the mustiness of years untouched somewhere up in the stacks of boxes collecting dust in the attic. How many times did I tell myself to find it, retrieve it, keep it safe in a drawer? And how many times did I find some reason not to?

I look down again, turn the page.

Maybe the problem is what's going on with my father. Does every son have trouble with his father? Is it normal to feel this hostility? He never did anything to hurt me. So why am I so angry? Is it just part of growing up? (Mom, on the other hand, is another story). My friend Mike from boarding school has a better relationship with his adoptive father than I have with my real father. I've learned useful things from my father, but most of the time we don't get along. Maybe we just don't much like each other anymore. Sometimes I think he doesn't like what I've become, or what I am becoming. Perhaps it irritates him that I always try to test myself, prove something to myself. I don't think he understands that, and I don't think he understands me. And maybe I don't understand that all this pushing and questioning and testing is all about trying to prove myself to him!

I wonder.

I glance over at the mirror, half expecting to see the ghost of my father. But instead I see my grandfather. I hardly recognize myself. Look at that white hair! For an instant, I see the blond kid that was me. How did everything happen so fast? The old journal leather feels warm, comfortable cradled in my palms. My hand is slowly disappearing from these fragile pages and will someday be gone, along with everything else. But it is strong and sure. It doesn't meander. It's neat, tidy, straightforward, but also a little cavalier and arty in places, perhaps reflecting—or belying?—what I was really feeling at the time. Some of those arty little curlicues look bold. Is that the sign of a big ego? Did I overestimate myself and my capacities? Are these the words of an earnest young man, a seeker?

Or a cocky little prick?

Is that why I have waited so long? Because maybe I really didn't like *myself*? Is that why I was afraid to read these pages, to relive that epic year? Or was it some kind of crazy superstition, afraid that opening the journal might let out some long-forgotten spooks?

No. No. None of that, not that.

Why, then?

I have no idea, and maybe I'll never know.

The dog lets out a dog sigh, like air escaping from a bike tire, opens his droopy, lidded eyes, and gives me a long look, apparently satisfied to see I'm still here.

I like to think I designed my whole life. But maybe it all came down to dumb luck. I started out lucky and pretty much ended up lucky. People always said so. No tragic endings for me. No terrible conflict, blistering clashes, or heart-wrenching drama that brings tears to the eye. Sure, I knew sadness and sickness, remorse and regret like everybody else. But nothing serious enough to wreck the train.

People tell me it would have been a better story if it had ended up a terrible tragedy.

"That's quite a tale," my friend said. "But don't ever try to write a story with a happy ending, because nobody cares."

"So what do they care about?"

"They care about the hard things. Strife and suffering and overcoming unimaginable challenges."

"But that's not what happened."

"Then maybe you're out of luck."

Maybe he's right. A book about luck and I'm out of luck.

But it was one hell of wild ride and quite a story, just the same.

I look down and reread the words.

I know I won't be happy until I get it…

Well, I finally did get it. But it took me a while to figure out exactly what I wanted.

What I wanted was to live my own life.

I have no idea where that driving need for independence came from, but I'm pretty sure I know when it started.

BULLY

As I'm riding home from school on my new bike in sixth grade, a big kid runs into the street and grabs the handlebars. I've seen him before. It's Carl, one of the tough public-school kids who shouts, "Pussy!" every time he crosses a private-school kid like me.

He's at least two years older, half again as big, and a bully.

I'm scared.

But there's no way I'm just going to let him steal my beautiful bike right out from under me.

"Get off the fuggin' bike, Ace!"

"Why?"

"Because I said so, asshole! *Get off the fuggin' bike!*"

I jerk the bars and twist my upper body to try to shake him loose, but his elbow comes out of nowhere. The next thing I know, I'm lying on the street and the big guy is mounting my wheels. I make a desperate lunge and manage to catch him just as he tries to pull away. He swats me again with a backhand cuff, which sends me reeling. But my body bump is just enough to pitch him off balance. He starts to wobble, then the goon and my new bike tip over together and crash.

He leaps to his feet, dazed, and charges, flailing wildly. I can see bright streaks of fresh blood where half his face and one ear met the road.

"*Motherfuuuggggggger!*" he yowls, overwhelming me before I can put a safe distance between us. I throw myself backward, but he still manages to hit me a good clip on the lip. I stumble and fall, expecting him to come down hard, fists flying. I can already feel my lip swelling and taste the salty flavor of my own blood.

I struggle to my feet, so crazy pissed off you could poke a fork through my lip and I wouldn't have noticed. The goon walks right by the fallen bike and keeps on going. Putting his hand to his mangled ear, he shouts back at me: "This ain't over, you fuggin' pussy! I know where you live! *I know where you live!*"

After he's gone, I realize how badly I'm shaken.

I'd hoped that might be the end of it. But a few days later he's standing in my driveway with two buddies in black leather jackets, looking to redeem his bruised self-esteem with a pound of my flesh.

They're right in front of the house, challenging me to come out. My nemesis has maroon scrapes on one half of his face and a bandage on his ear. But he's way bigger than me and has backup. I'm aware of my fat lip, purple as an eggplant and still sore. I feel a sickening wave of fear, and for a long, disorienting moment, my mind teeters between flight and fight.

But then full adrenalin kicks in. I'll fight because I want these three dumb fucks to know that even if I'm scared, I'm not chicken. I don't like the odds, and I know I'm outmatched. But I'm willing to bet a beating that even if he wins, picking on a smaller kid, especially a pussy from private school, could seriously damage his local macho image.

Hearing noise, my father comes up behind me and puts his hand on my shoulder.

"Who are these people?" he asks.

My heart's beating too fast. I hope he can't tell.

"It's the same guy who tried to steal my bike," I tell him.

"Forget the others," he says without hesitation, voice calm, no emotion. "You must make the first punch. Walk straight up to him. Don't say anything. Aim for the nose and hit him as hard as you can. If you miss or if he doesn't go down—or quit—keep hitting, and don't stop until he does."

What about the other two? But I say nothing, open the door, and step outside.

"Pussy!" the goon screams. "Fuggin' pussy! You need Daddy to protect you?"

The door's already closing behind me, and I walk straight at him.

A strange calm sets in. Fear evaporates. Sound mutes, and all I can see is his nose.

He throws up his fists to square off, but I hardly notice. Too late, the big guy can't believe I'm already on top of him, right between his fists.

In an instant, I score a hard blow.

I can hear a gratifying little crack, a twig snapping. It's a direct hit, backed by almost my entire body weight, sending the better part of his nose back into his face.

He staggers two steps in reverse and throws his hands over his face, then stares into the palms. His nose is bent at an odd angle. Blood spurts from both nostrils down his mouth and chin, a gratifying sight.

I feel good. No remorse, no regret.

"Wha' the *fugg*!" he yowls, like a wounded animal, staring at me in shocked disbelief.

"Wha' the fugg! You broke my fuggin' nose...you fuggin' motherfugger! You broke my nose!"

He tries to wipe the blood away with his hands, but it keeps coming.

Just as I'm preparing for all three to launch a counterattack, the goon turns and trots away without a word, gaping into his bloodied palms. The other two follow in silence, heads down.

"Harry."

I turn around, hyperventilating.

"Well done," my father says. "What is the lesson?"

"Don't be afraid?"

"No, son. Fear is natural. Fear can be your friend. The lesson is self-confidence. Never rely on anyone else to do the hard things for you, Harry. To be successful, you will always have to rely on yourself."

━┿ ┿━

Years later, I finally take my father's advice—only to discover that we have vastly different notions of what it means to be independent.

"A summer job?" he says, glancing up from his newspaper. "You're too young for a summer job. Why would you want a job anyway?" he says absently, the paper rattling as he turns the page.

"I want to work. I want to earn some money."

"You don't need to earn money. You don't have to work. You have your allowance."

He's listening with only half an ear.

"I want my own money. Didn't you tell me that I should rely only on myself?"

"Whoa! Slow down!" he says, and finally puts his paper aside.

"What kind of job do you think you can get?"

"I'm thinking about construction."

He rolls his eyes, but now I've got his full attention.

"Construction? You don't know anything about construction! You have no training. You don't belong to a union! And they wouldn't have you anyway."

"I don't need training. I'm strong, and I'll get stronger. I'll just be a laborer."

He stares at me as if I were an exotic lab specimen.

"Am I hearing you correctly? Hard labor?" he says, aghast. "You want to spend your summer in the company of common laborers? Elbow to elbow with a bunch of illiterates? Are you nuts?"

Neither of us speaks.

He sighs. "Why don't I see if I can get you an apprenticeship at the agency?"

"No. I'm not interested in busywork. And I want to be paid. Besides, this isn't something I want you to do for me."

"Then why don't you detail cars with a bunch of the guys, or get with some friends and paint houses?"

"Dad, you don't understand. I want to do something I've never done. Something nobody I know has ever done. I want something hard. I want to see if I can make it on my own, support myself without help."

He shakes his head at the absurdity of it.

"Do you realize what these people are like?" he asks, trying, as usual, to keep it civil. "They're not like us, Harry. You'd stand out like a sore thumb. They'll chew you up and spit you out! I'm serious. You could be in danger with people like that."

"Not likely," I tell him. "But that's part of why I need to do this. I have to do this, Dad."

I don't know why I'm so sure.

He sits back and takes a good look at me.

"Who's going to hire you?" he asks.

"Well, I'll start with Mr. D'Angelo. He won't remember me, but I bet he'll listen. Anyway, it won't hurt to ask."

He gazes into his lap, takes a breath, then looks back up.

"So help me, God. I do not understand you, son. But if you want to spend your summer with the dregs of society, you go right ahead."

We stare at each other across a widening tear in the fabric of our relationship.

As the silence deepens, he reaches for his paper.

"All right. Fine," he says, his voice weary. "I guess you'll have to learn the hard way; you always do. Good luck."

THE PITS

A guy the size of a refrigerator walks me to the office trailer beside a huge open pit full of machines and men.

"Wait here," he says, and ducks inside. As I wait, my dad's dismissive comment about "chewing you up and spitting you out" comes to mind.

"Okay, you can go in," the big guy tells me.

The site supervisor, Mr. D'Angelo, is facing me directly as I step into the trailer.

"Good afternoon, sir, my name is Harry Belmont. You may not remember me. I met you with my father six or so years ago. But I remember you, and I want to work for you this summer."

The man reaches out his hand.

"Sit down, Mr. Belmont."

I take a seat, and he settles into a swivel chair behind the small desk.

He never takes his eyes off me.

"Belmont? We've done some work for your family," he says.

"Yes, sir. You built my father's ad agency headquarters."

"Yeah, that's right," he says.

"I was hoping you would remember, sir."

"You say you want a job?" He tilts his head, letting me know he's skeptical.

"Yes, sir."

"You don't look like a construction grunt, Mr. Belmont."

"No, sir."

"How old are you?"

"I'm sixteen—but soon to be seventeen, sir."

"What kind of job are you looking for?"

"Labor. That's all. I'm ready to work hard, push myself."

"You're young for the kind of work you're looking for. How much do you weigh?"

I tell him.

"How much can you lift?"

"I'm pretty strong."

He glances across the narrow room.

"Can you lift up that file cabinet?"

I look over. The cabinet is my height, but I figure not so big that I can't get my arms around it.

I walk to the cabinet, lift it a foot off the floor, and hold it there.

"That's good," he says, not hiding his surprise. "You can put it down."

"How much does it weigh?" I ask.

"About two hundred pounds," he says, still sizing me up. "That's good, kid. You can handle the heavy lifting. But I'll be honest with you. I'm not sure you're cut out for this kind of work, given your background. The people we got here on this job, all the laborers, good workers. But you're different. Blacks especially, they're not used to people like you. It's a rough crowd. Guys might think you're a pretty boy, overbred, maybe. Call you Hollywood—or worse. They're likely to give you grief, Mr. Belmont. Test you beyond your gentlemanly expectations."

I hear the sarcasm.

"I think I can handle what they dish out, Mr. D'Angelo. But I'll never know unless I try, will I? I'll even work the first week for nothing, no risk to you. So you can see for yourself. All I ask is that you give me a chance."

He gives me a thoughtful, assessing look.

After a moment, he says, "Okay. Be here at seven thirty tomorrow morning, and I'll put you to work. If you can make it through the day, you've got a job."

The next day I spend eight hours loading sixteen tons of site debris and rubble into a Dumpster. Mr. D'Angelo shows up at the end of the day and gives me another long look, this one straight into my eyes.

"All right," he says, resigned, but not without some surprised admiration. "You're hired."

Score one for the pretty boys.

T-BONE

I wind up the youngest and lowest-ranking grunt on a team of la-borers. They give me all the jobs the other grunts can't or won't do. Some days I'm left alone with construction trash in somebody's driveway, loading trucks that roll in and out all day, hauling debris to the dump. Other days I find myself down in the pits at commer-cial building sites, digging all day long with a shovel, and usually the one who gets to dig under exposed sewer lines, which tend to drip all over me. This, need I say, is not conducive to dating at the end of the day.

My first week, I'm pushing two-hundred-pound wheelbarrow loads of wet cement up steep wooden planks that shimmy and shake. It's a near miracle I manage to make it to the ramp tops without tipping over and plunging with the deadweights into the pits below.

It's not just the weight but the balance. Sometimes I can hear the chuckles and mocking laughter, but that only makes me try harder.

Every day I get a little stronger.

When the laughter stops and they can see I'm serious, I request to move down to hell.

I want to see if I can cut it down in the pits.

It's in the pits that I meet my new friend, Alonso Green, who goes by the street name T-Bone. T-Bone takes one look at my labor skills and can only shake his head. He's a respected pit boss, been at the game for almost fifteen years, and it pains him to see the level of outright incompetence that I bring to the job.

Nevertheless, I plug ahead with Spartan abandon. I want a hard body and strong character. All I know is a life of comfort. But down here in the pits, I want to see if I know myself. Content with my lot in hard labor at near slave wages, determined to see it through and be better for it, I work hard, never taking my eye off the mental image of the man I want to be. At least for now. But after a few days, T-Bone feels he has to set me straight.

We're down in a big hole, shoveling.

I've been pushing myself, dripping sweat.

"Lookee he-ah!" he calls to me, with a wave. I walk over, shovel in hand, the newbie, and he says, "We gotta to talk, young blood."

I nod respectfully, and I can see he appreciates that.

"Let me explain something to you, blood," he says, very patiently. "You gotta slow down, way down."

Slow down? Why? Why would I want to slow down?

"Is it bad to work fast?" I ask.

He gives me a look that suggests I might be a slow learner.

"It don' look good," he says, shrugging off my stupid question, "when you diggin' so fast…make me look bad. You unnerstan' what I'm sayin' to you?"

Now I get it. My pride deflates. How could I have been so naïve?

"So, what you gotta do?" he asks, hoping I did get it.

"I gotta slow down," I answer decisively.

"Yeah," he says, nodding approval. "You gotta sloooow down. I'm glad you unnersan'. Now I'm gonna' show you how to slow down."

To my surprise, it turns out there's an art to shoveling. T-Bone shows me the ballet of the shovel, how to leverage the weight of the loaded shovel against the thigh, to use leg muscles—not arms and back muscles—to do most of the heavy lifting, how to rotate into the lifting movement to protect back muscles, even when to breathe—and when not to breathe—during the lift. When he demonstrates these moves together in proper sequence, it's a thing of beauty—and it takes a few tries to get it right. But when I get the hang of it, T-Bone gives me the thumbs-up.

I thank him for the instruction.

"Now you go all day," he says. "You never get tired—an' we both lookin' good!"

To celebrate, he offers me a cigarette. I'm not much of a smoker, but sure, I'll have one, and he extends the Menthol Kools pack. I can see the pack has been opened at the wrong end. But when I flip the lid and try to pull out a cigarette from the filter end, he grabs the pack back.

"No, blood!" he cries. "Don't be doin' that!"

What am I doing wrong?

"Don't never let *nobody* touch the filters," he scolds, amazed at my lack of street etiquette. "You never know where them fingers has been...think about that. Think 'bout all them fingers in all them nasty places! You don' want that shit on yo' lips, unnersan'?"

Yes, I do, most definitely, but I admit that the thought had never crossed my mind.

"No niggah dumb enough to touch another niggah's filter," he explains. I'm surprised to hear him use the *N* word. "On the street, the brothers take the cigarette from the bottom of the pack. Get yo' ass kicked if you don'."

I ask him about the *N* word.

"Black man can call another black man niggah," he says. "But ain't no whitey can't never call a black man niggah. I can talk about niggahs to you, but you can't talk about no niggahs to me."

I take the cigarette from the bottom of the pack on my second try, and we have our smoke.

From that day forward, I work hard and well but never wear myself out in the pits, never get tired. T-Bone keeps an eye on me and watches out for me. He calls me "niggah" every day, which I correctly take as a compliment, letting me know I've passed the test and am now one of his boys.

Later, one of our shovel gang walks over.

"Yo, bro!" he says. "They call me Jeremiah."

I offer my hand.

"No white man ever shake my hand," he says, cocking his head. "No white man ever wanna shake my hand."

"I'm shaking your hand, Jeremiah."

"Yeeaaah." He smiles, slow and easy, his grip firm.

"Tha's what T-Bone say. Say you a brother. We got you back, bro," he says, giving me a light slap on my shoulder.

"I appreciate that. I hope I won't need it."

"Yeah. I know."

After a week working side by side, T-Bone stops to light a Kool. He takes a drag, blowing blue smoke out through his nostrils.

"You a racist, young blood?"

Question right out of nowhere.

A racist? Of course I'm a racist. I live in a racist world, surrounded by racism. Don't know any black people, so I have no way to judge. I just accept the lies, always have. Accepted them as truth because I never knew any better.

"I never really thought about it," I say.

It's the truth. I never had to.

"Maybe? I don't know…"

"Don't know?" T-Bone says, putting an edge on it, very smooth.

16

What is this?

"Ever' white boy hate niggahs, young blood."

What did I do? Should I be scared?

Scared? I'm terrified. Maybe all the lies are true.

"You hate niggahs, young blood?"

T-Bone's eyes are lidded, his gaze curious, like he's studying some species of insect.

"I don't know any colored people except you, T-Bone, and I don't hate you."

That's the God's own truth. Can't he see I'm telling the truth?

He nods, grinning.

"Yeah." He chuckles. "I be the only niggah you ever met. 'Cept my boys here."

He takes another drag. "No niggah woman in yo house?"

"No." I shake my head.

It's true. All our women are Irish.

"How 'bout yo white-boy friends? They call you niggah-lover?"

"They don't know you, so they don't ask."

"Yeah, but the I-talians, the boys on the job here. They call you niggah-lover?"

"T-Bone, I don't want to talk about this."

"Shee-it," he says, head lowered, eyes raised. "I-talians. They badass."

I'm thinking of Sal Salantino, brooding hulk and feared foreman on the bucket team, mixing and hauling cement, calling out to me, "Yo, Squire! Don't get your fingernails dirty down there in the pit with the jigaboos!"

Big Sally, who on the first day saw I was an outlander, he pegged me as Squire, and now everybody calls me that. Sal, with his arms like tree trunks and a tattoo of "Mom" in a red heart on his right bicep and a flag of Italy on his left. On the second day as I climb out of the pit, he mutters under his breath, "Hey, Squire, remember what I told you? Don't get too cozy with the coloreds!"

By the third day, it's, "What did I tell you about socializing with the niggers, Squire?" On the fourth day, he calls, "Hey! Nigger lover!" loud enough so T-Bone and the blacks in the pit can hear clearly, and the punk Italians in the work gang topside get a good laugh.

T-Bone takes a toothpick from behind his ear and sticks it in his mouth.

"That big mothafucker," T-Bone says, gesturing topside. "He want me to pay him five dollah a day for protection so the I-talians don't beat the shit out of me and my boys down here in the pit. No fuckin' way. I tol' him go fuck hisself.

"Tha's why I ax, you a racist, young blood. 'Cause I gotta know you okay. I gotta know, can I trust you?"

Then slick as a snake, he clicks a stiletto switchblade out of his pocket and holds it so I can see it.

"This be my protection. Don' need no mothafuckin' I-talians." Then, relaxed, he says, "Jus' so you unnerstan' me, blood, I done kill't two men. They got what they deserved, and I done my time. I-talians fuck with me, I kill them too. You unnerstan'?"

I take a good look at the knife.

"I don't have any fight with you, T-Bone. In fact, I'd rather be down here with you than up there with those assholes."

T- Bone gives me an appraising look.

"Ooooh-weeee!" he breathes. "You one crazy-ass honky mothafucker!"

Two days later, three guys from the Italian bucket team, with a little time on their hands and nothing better to do, climb down into the dig looking for trouble.

"Hey, Squire," one of them calls, "What's it like livin' down here in the dirt with the niggers?"

T-Bone looks at the visitors but says nothing.

"Shit," another guy says. "Is it just me, Jimmy, or does it smell like shit down here?"

The third guy says, "Yeah, that's what niggers smell like. Buncha fuckin' animals!"

Before I see it coming, T-Bone's shovel lands with a resounding metallic *thwang*, full in the face of the Italian guy, who goes over like a fallen tree. Before he even hits the floor of the pit, the shovel whacks the second guy—*thwang*—and on the same arc, hits the third guy in the head. It happens to fast, I hardly have time to blink before T Bone is standing over them with the shovel raised high, looking for an excuse to swing again. It's a full two minutes before the first one staggers to his feet, groaning and dazed, and heads with difficulty up the ladder. He leaves a trail of blood from his nose and mouth in the mud. It takes almost ten minutes for the next two to extricate themselves. T-Bone kicks them in the ass to hasten them on their way.

"You a dead nigger," the last one growls as he nears the top of the ladder. His ear is a mess of drying blood. "You too, nigger lover," he adds, looking over his shoulder at me.

T-Bone grabs him by the belt and hurls him back to the dirt, the point of the switch blade already halfway up the man's nose.

He's got a knee on the punk's chest.

"You a slow learner, mothafucker. So T-Bone gonna give you somethin' to think about." A flick of the knife splits the punk's nostril in half, sending a spray of crimson across his face.

The Italian squeals in pain and struggles to escape.

"Lookee he-ah," T-Bone says. "Ain' no dead niggahs here. You tell yo' boys topside T-Bone a stone killah, an' they ain't gonna be no dead niggahs. You got that?"

The punk nods vigorously, and T-Bone lets him scramble to his feet and up the ladder.

Not ten minutes go by before a man in a suit tells T-Bone to come up out of the pit.

"Now you gonna see what the white man can do to a niggah," T-Bone mutters to me as he heads for the ladder. "That man be a Mafia mothafucker."

I have images of T- Bone, shot in the head and thrown into one of the giant foundation cement mixers. Or cut into pieces and sealed into a fifty-five-gallon steel drum and dropped in the river.

T-Bone climbs out of the pit, leaving me with the glowering shovel boys.

But my concerns for T-Bone are displaced by a chilling fear for my own life.

What awaits me topside? Will the bucket boys wreak their vengeance on the nigger lover? Have I misjudged, got myself into the kind of trouble that could get me killed. Should I have listened to my father?

I feel unnerved, alone, as vulnerable as I've ever felt in my life. T-Bone's gone. Nobody's smiling. Nobody's saying anything.

I'm thinking about heading to the ladder when Jeremiah walks over.

"Yo, niggah!" he says. "Yeah, you!"

I take his offered hand.

"Now I got your back. We all got your back," he says, gesturing toward the boys behind him. They nod assent, but nobody's smiling. This is serious business.

Jeremiah with his sly, watchful eyes. Jeremiah knows nobody's got his back. He knows the Italians are protected by the "Mafia mothafucker." But the shovel crew is on its own. If it ever came down to it, he fully understands that half the shovel crew could disappear tomorrow, and nobody would know and nobody would care.

"We keep an eye out fo' you, young blood. Jus' like T-Bone say, you be safe down here in the pit."

I climb out of the hole at the end of the day, looking in every direction, only to discover that nobody seems very interested in me at all. There's not a bucket boy in sight, and no goons at the gate.

But the next day T-Bone doesn't show up in the pits. Mr. D'Angelo comes down to have a word. This puts me on high alert. I'm scared for T-Bone and for myself.

"Can you describe what you saw here yesterday in the altercation between Mr. Green and the boys on bucket crew?" he asks.

Describe what I saw? I saw T-Bone almost kill three men.

"Some of the bucket guys came down looking for a fight, and T-Bone had to defend himself," I tell him.

"And how exactly did he defend himself?"

"With his shovel."

"Yes, I know. But precisely what happened, please?"

"Mr. D'Angelo, it happened so fast, I don't really know," I lie. "It was just a blur."

The project foreman takes a good look at me.

"I see," he says. After a moment, he looks down. Is he thinking, maybe let this dog lie, not force me to rat out T-Bone?

With a hint of a grin, he says, "T-Bone scored a hat trick in the pits, did he?"

Now I'm thinking maybe T-Bone isn't okay after all.

"So where is T-Bone today?" I ask.

"He's the best shovel crew boss we've got," Mr. D'Angelo confides. "We wouldn't want to lose him over a little school-yard rumble."

"Yes, and he's a good teacher too," I venture.

We both nod, smiling coconspirators.

"Yo, young blood!" a voice calls out a little later. I turn and see T-Bone coming down the ladder. "Young blood!"

I walk over, grinning with relief and pleasure.

"It be cool, blood," T-Bone says.

He gives me a little fist pump to his chest, T-Bone's version of a thumbs-up. My man T-Bone, master shovel guru, teacher, pit boss, and model of manhood and self-reliance.

WINDEMERE

Rolling north into the dark heart of New England with my father, I gaze out the car window, counting trees, cows, birds. We pass a leaning farmhouse with a caving roof, peeling paint, the whole place falling apart, sinking back into the earth. Maybe some old people inside, maybe already dead and nobody knows. It's a depressing scene but an accurate reflection of my state of mind.

Our destination is Windemere, my father's school and his father's and grandfather's before him.

I've been dreading this day almost as long as I can remember.

The tension in the car is palpable.

"Cat got your tongue?" my father asks, finally breaking a long silence.

I don't want to feel this vague anger, this resentment. But I can't help myself. It won't go away.

"No. Just thinking…" I imagine a crazy riot of cats and reeking cat shit in the collapsing house.

"About what?"

I look over.

"Just wondering why I'm in this car. Asking myself, what am I doing going off to what amounts to a four-year lockup?"

"What kind of crazy question is that?"

I drop it.

But he won't let it go.

"You're going to one of the finest boarding schools in the country, Harry. That's what you're doing."

I just peer out the window at uninterrupted grayness and empty distances.

"Do you remember what boarding school was like?" I ask after a while. "You've told me all about Windermere yourself. It's a monastery. Not a girl for twenty miles. Kids forced to wear gray suits all day and blue suits every night. Remember? Food so bad sometimes just the smell of it made you feel sick. Oh, and let's not forget Saturday classes and chapel twice a day."

What a hypocrite, I'm thinking.

Hoping he's remembering all that I'm about to face, I add:

"Why is any of that superior, or even good?"

His hand strikes the steering wheel.

There can be no honest resolution to this confrontation, and he knows it.

"Stop this nonsense!" he barks, clearly in no mood to debate the merits of the inevitable. This deal was sealed way before I was even born.

"That's how it is at all the best boarding schools—and you know it! Why do you always have to make everything so difficult? Get used to it! You get a great education. You work hard. You make friends. You play sports and keep out of trouble. Why is that a bad thing? And why is that so hard for you to understand?"

I know he's struggling to put a good face on it. But I won't let up until he gives me a straight answer.

"Tell me honestly, Dad, how did you really feel about boarding school?"

"Is this a quiz?"

"Yes."

He glances over, clearly annoyed.

"Okay—I got used to it!"

"Got used to it?"

"What do you want me to say?"

"I want you to tell the truth. I think the truth is that you hated it. You hated it, and you know I'll hate it. But telling me all my life, 'It's tradition; it's what one does' is no good reason to do anything.

"In fact," I add, "It's bullshit."

He gives me a pass on the language.

"I did what I had to do. I don't know what else to tell you," he says dismissively. "We do what we have to do—and so must you!"

It's beginning to rain. Cows in a pasture lower their heads.

"And just because you may not like it," he adds, "doesn't mean that it's not good for you."

Four years? Really? Four years?

"Want to know the real reason you were sent away to boarding school, Dad?" I ask him.

I let it hover, watching him study the road until he looks at me.

"Okay, smart guy. What's the real reason?"

"To get rid of you."

He shoots me a look.

"Get rid of me? Why would you say that?"

"It's the same reason your friends send their children to boarding school. So Mom and Dad can play and let somebody else worry about raising the kids. Most of the kids I know want to get rid of their parents as much as their parents want to get rid of them. It's all right, Dad. It's the same down the generations. It happened to you. And now it's happening to me. So, it's okay. But I'm not totally stupid."

"Do you really believe that?"

"Sure, I do, and you know it's true."

"You really believe that your mother and I want to get rid of you?"

"Of course, you do—and your parents wanted to get rid of you. There's a word for that. It's called *tradition*."

Rain comes harder now, and the wipers flap back and forth. I see an imperfect reflection of myself in the cold glass.

"It's a privilege, you know," he says, changing tactics, cooling it down. "Not everyone can afford to send their kids to boarding school. It costs a fortune, and I'd like to believe we're getting our money's worth. I went to Windemere, and I'm better for it. My dad went to Windemere, and he would tell you the same thing. You'll be better for it too. And someday so will your sons, my grandsons... There's nothing wrong with that."

"Really? Don't count on me to keep this Windemere thing going."

I can imagine his frustration. He means well. But if he thinks he's telling the truth, he no longer recognizes the truth.

"Do you understand that you need a good education to compete successfully in the world?"

"I'm not worried."

"Maybe you should be."

"The only person I plan to compete with is myself."

"Well, well, genius," he says after a moment, his voice dripping with spleen. "Obviously, Windemere will have nothing to teach you because you already know everything."

MIKE

My lack of enthusiasm for boarding school in general, and Windermere in particular, remains unabated until a few weeks later when I meet Mike Cunningham by accident. Literally. He's rounding a corner, and I'm late for class. I run right into him. The next thing I know, I'm flat on my back.

I look up, and here's this big lug extending a hand.

"Jesus, Mary, and Joseph! Are you hurt, boyo?"

I grip his hand, and he pulls me up.

"Did you say, Jesus, Mary, and Joseph?"

"I did."

"Well, just Harry will do," I tell him.

"Ah! Well, then, Harry it is! I didn't mean to knock you down, Harry. My name is Mike. Mike Cunningham."

"Thanks for the hand, Mike. Are you Irish? You sound Irish."

"I'm not. It's a long story, Harry."

The next time we run into each other, we're on the football field in the first scrimmage of the season. Mike lays me flat on my back as I try to cut up the middle.

Once again, he's pulling me to my feet.

"You okay?" he says.

"Mike! You nailed me good."

"I love to hit, Harry. But I'll never hit you so hard you can't get up."

"That's nice to know. Kind of like my life is in your hands?"

"Tis, Harry," he says, moving me along with a pat on the back. "Tis. But I'm not so nice when we play against other teams."

And so it is.

After that first freshman practice and punishing scrimmage, Mike and I are in the student lounge sitting together over coffee.

"I hate to think what would happen if you didn't treat me with kid gloves," I tell him.

Mike chuckles.

"Somebody's got to score the touchdowns, Harry. We'll save the rough stuff for the real games."

He's smiling, but I can see the cold steel of competition in his eyes.

"So how come you aren't Irish?" I ask.

"I was born in an Irish Catholic family in Boston, eleven brothers and sisters."

I wince. "That's a lot of kids."

"Yes, it is. A baby a year most years. And I was number six. You don't want to hear the whole tragic saga."

"Yes, I do."

"Well…okay. My father wanted to be a cop, like his father and grandfather. But he drank too much and wound up riding shotgun on a city garbage truck. One day he showed up drunk, fell into the compactor, and got squashed down to the size of a suitcase. I remember my mother crying and chain smoking in the kitchen for three weeks. Then, one day she just fell on the floor. Heart attack."

"Oh my God."

"Yeah. Me too. Anyway, the four oldest were sent to foster care. They were sixteen to twelve. The youngest seven, we all got sent to orphanages. No two of us together. I wound up in one run by the nuns. I was eight. I lived there for two years."

"Nuns? Well, that's good."

"Harry, have you ever met a nun?"

I think about it. I can picture the Flying Nun.

"No, I don't think I have," I admit.

"Every single nun in this orphanage was born Irish. From Ireland. And if you've never met an Irish nun, Harry, count yourself lucky."

I take a sip of coffee, waiting.

"An Irish nun is mean as a snake, Harry."

"A snake? All of them?"

"Every last one."

"How can a nun be so bad?"

Mike laughs out loud.

"I had this one nun who had it in for me the moment I walked in the door," he says. "I was a big kid, and she called me Mr. Big Breeches. I didn't even know what breeches were. The first thing she does is give me a smack on the top of my head. Every time I see her after that she gives me another slap. To this day, I don't know why. When I finally asked her, she said, 'I'll beat the devil out of ye yet!'

"Devil? Me? The devil isn't in me!"

She catches me a good one right across the side of the head.

"'Talk back to me? I'll show you the devil!' she's screaming. She walks away but comes right back with a stick and starts flailing at me. I can feel blood going into my eye, and I'm seeing stars.

"The next thing I know, I'm wrenching the stick out of her hands, roaring like a fucking lion, right in her face, and I just keep on roaring until she runs away.

"After that, she didn't bother me. But then one day she just disappeared. We heard she hit another kid so hard he had to be rushed to the hospital. To this day, every time I see a nun, I think of her."

"Is that what you were thinking about when you laid me flat again today?"

He laughs.

"No. I save the nuns for the games."

We both have a good laugh.

"Do you know any Irish people, Harry?"

"Yes, sure I do."

"Really? I didn't expect that."

"Why not?"

"Wasps aren't known for their love of the Irish. Who are these Irish people you know?"

"Maeve and Teresa. They work in my house."

"Maids?"

"That's right. I even had a bit of a brogue when I was little. Until I was four, I wasn't sure who my real mother was."

"You're kidding."

"No. I loved them. Still do. Not like your nuns. Teresa took me to Catholic mass with her. Two hours. People wandering around swinging incense, mumbling in Latin. I had no idea what was going on. She said I'd go to hell if I didn't attend mass, and she'd make me stick it out for the full two hours every time. What she did was guarantee I'd never set foot in church ever again."

Mike's nodding in affirmation.

"Amen to that!"

We're both smiling, sharing heresies.

"So, how did you escape the orphanage?"

He gets serious.

"One day a couple comes in. They'd lost their only son in a car accident, and they were looking to adopt a ten-year-old boy. I liked them, and I guess they liked me. They took me home, and now they're like my real parents."

"Where was this?"

"Lynn, Mass. My dad's in the plumbing business. Commercial and residential."

"How about your mother?" I ask.

"My mom teaches school. She was my teacher in eighth grade."

"She give you all A's?"

"No. But I told her I thought I deserved A's. I think she was a tougher on me than the other kids because she didn't want anybody to think I was her favorite. I still made honor roll…"

He pauses.

"The funny thing is, my folks are not even Catholic. I gotta believe after my troubles with the nuns, the orphanage made sure I never wound up in a Catholic home!"

"Sounds like you turned out okay, even without the Hail Marys. How did you wind up at Windemere?"

"Football scholarship."

"Well, that's an honor. They don't take many."

"Without the football, we could never afford a place like this. How about you?"

"My father went here. And my grandfather."

He nods.

"You come from a rich family, huh?"

"Well, I guess you could say that. Almost everybody here does."

"Yeah, I know. Remember, I'm a scholarship kid. They don't let me forget that."

By sophomore season, the word is out. Several boys are carried off the field after colliding with big Mike. Teams change their play books to circumvent the hulk in the middle of the Windemere defense. By the time he's on the varsity starting lineup, Mike is known throughout the entire league as Stone Wall.

To have a tag line all your own is a level of respect not often bestowed in our league.

Teams compete with each other for bragging rights as to who is the top dog. Stone Wall is lead contender.

Mike and I became best buddies. It was a friendship that lasted for the four years of Windemere and on into college, when Mike died late in our freshman year.

THE STRANGE CASE
OF DR. ARMFIELD

Toward the end of term, our Latin teacher, Dr. Armfield, walks into class, and we can all see something's wrong. For one thing, he's late. He's never late. And he looks bad. He starts coughing almost immediately, hacking so fitfully into his handkerchief we think he might pass out. Or vomit. Or both.

I give Mike a look, and he shakes his head.

When Armfield regains his composure, he seats himself without a word and mops his jowls and lips, a familiar but dreaded behavior that's inspired generations of students to develop a repertoire of artful dodges to avoid shaking his fish hand. Strategies range from averting eye contact to feigning injury of the right arm. One year, such a strange plague of hand, arm, and elbow injures sweeps the Latin students that the headmaster fears a kind of hysteria of self-abuse might have gripped the campus.

Outwardly, Armfield is an old-school, striped-tie sort of fellow. A soft-spoken academic, gentleman scholar with a friendly, accessible smile. The kind of unprepossessing, ineffectual bachelor figure you might expect to find at almost any good school. So mild-mannered and forgettable, he'd make a good spy.

But every boy knows that inside, he's a tempest of repressed passions and dashed hopes. We've caught glimpses of a broken man who self-medicates to make it through what we believed was an endless monotony of identical days and the crushing loneliness of long nights. So, his boozing is an open secret. Yet the quality of his work remains unblemished. He manages to hide his addiction with such brilliant daily demonstrations of intellect and discipline that he wins the grudging admiration of even the most cynical among us. Granted, on infrequent occasions he's been rescued from snowdrifts or dragged from under bushes. But in the main, he's managed to sustain this courtly charade with astonishing aplomb.

Today, however, is clearly not just another hangover.

Armfield is blinking rapidly, something we've never seen him do, as if he's been dazed by an explosion in his head. Before he can speak, he levitates out of his seat, then pitches forward with a coughing spasm so violent the boys in the front row throw open their desktops and hide behind them.

It's an alarming, malevolent attack. We are all spellbound—and frightened.

Then, just when we think the worst is over, the hand gripping the handkerchief begins to shake. Armfield looks worried. He puts his other hand on the desk for support. He loosens his tie, unbuttons his shirt at the neck and struggles to catch his breath. We sense that the delicate fabric of all he holds dear is starting to unravel.

Finally, he says, "I can't seem to remember what I'm doing here." He looks up. "Why am I here?"

"Class, sir," someone says. "Latin class."

"Latin?" he repeats. "Well, then," he says, brightening. "Latin it will be."

His voice is treacled with phlegm. I want to tell him to cough it up, be done with it.

A tongue of cold air licks through the casement. Outside a sigh of wind, ominous but oddly normal, rattles the lead windows. I'm heartened to imagine myself soaring above this sad, sunless dungeon and its woeful ills.

Is our teacher dying? Right here in his own classroom?

Should we do something?

"Ah, yes. I know why I am here," Armfield says, with some effort. "I have something I want to share with you. But first you must open your books."

"Which page, sir?"

"Page...sixteen."

The flurry of pages turning sounds like startled birds flapping in the silence of a deep wood.

Armfield looks out the window, and his face softens. We follow his eyes to the window but see nothing.

"Sir?" Mike asks. "Page sixteen...?"

"I know now what it is I want to say to you," he announces, still staring out the window, his voice distant.

"I have killed a man," he says, thoughtful and deliberate.

He turns to watch us, his eyes probing through the silence and across our faces. Incapable of returning the bold stare, I glance away, seized by the crushing sense of shock that fills the room and locks us all in frozen silence.

"What did you say, sir?" someone asks finally.

Armfield pulls out the handkerchief and wipes it in a long, slow move across his brow.

"Are you translating, sir?" I ask. "Is this part of the lesson?"

"No. I am confessing," he says. "I have killed a man." He falls silent. "You have no idea what a relief it is to say those words..."

"Sir, are you all right?" a boy asks.

"No, I am not all right," he says, stronger. "In fact, I am not well. Not well at all. Actually, I am on my way out..."

"What are you talking about, sir?" someone asks, frightened. "You know what you're saying?"

His eyes drift back to the window. We can see what looks like the beginning of a smile. "Oh, I know exactly what I am saying... and I have a great deal to tell you."

"Did you really kill someone, sir?"

Armfield looks down at us.

"It is a shameful thing," he says, shaking his head. "Shameful."

"But I mean, what was it like? What was it like when you actually...did it...sir?"

"Sir, go on—tell us what happened."

Armfield looks in the direction of the questioners.

"You want to know...what happened..." he says, as if hearing his own voice for the first time.

"I was...frightened..."

"Yes? Tell us everything."

We're on the edge of our chairs, wired with anticipation, fighting to keep a civil lid on our morbid, juvenile excitement.

For a dreadful moment, he appears to sink into a private meditation, even sleep.

When his eyes open, he seems a different man.

"I was frightened, but nothing has pleased me more in my life, *nothing*!" he snarls, striking the desktop as if he were stabbing a mortal enemy. At this sudden flare-up, he stuffs the famed handkerchief into his mouth. We all have the same thought: Will he succumb and tip over before he can finish his story?

Presently he collects himself, returns the handkerchief to his pocket, and looks around the room.

"It was long ago," he begins. "But I can remember it better than what happened yesterday."

"How did you kill this man, sir?"

"I shot him."

Dr. Armfield? Armfield shooting anyone, or committing any act of violence is unimaginable.

"Why, sir?" a boy asks, incredulous.

"Because…he was hurting my mother…"

Even now we can see his sorrow and pain.

"He was not a man unknown to me." Then he says, "He was my father."

We all gasp, and the class falls into a suspended silence, each of us with our own thoughts.

"Your father, sir? Your real father?

I'm electrified by the revelation and deeply uncomfortable.

Armfield sighs.

"I have never been so terrified in my life. I did not think myself capable of such a thing. But I could not bear to watch him beat her," he goes on. "I was crying, actually crying…How strange it is to talk about this now."

He looks toward the ceiling, as if appealing to the divine.

"The gun was so heavy, I could hardly hold it in my hands… I warned him to stop. But then he turned on me in a drunken rage, and I shot him…in the heart. The blast almost knocked me down…"

We wait while he seems to brace himself and gather his thoughts.

"This is my confession," he says quietly. "This is the first time I have ever spoken of this terrible thing."

"Why didn't you tell anyone, sir?"

"Because…because my mother took the blame," he says, struggling to contain his tears. "She cleaned the grip of the gun, held it in her hand, and then prepared a story for the police."

He takes a breath and forges on.

"She was acquitted at her trial. But she swore me to secrecy, and I have never told another soul until this day."

"Why today, sir?"

"And why us…?"

He sags in resignation.

"I am confessing this crime now because I must," he answers. "I can no longer keep this terrible burden to myself. It is like a poison, and I believe it is killing me."

His voice catches.

"I am confessing to you because I want you boys to be my jury. I want you to judge me, not for the crime itself—although it is a monstrous thing—but because I was happy to see my father dead."

The words hit us like a slap in the face.

"Yes, I don't wonder that you are surprised," he adds, seeing the looks on our faces. "I have asked myself a thousand times, nay a thousand, thousand times, 'What kind of man murders his father and can say he has no remorse—in fact, is happier for it? What kind of man is that?'

"Ask yourselves that question, and tell me what you think. Tell me honestly what you think."

Mike and I look at one another and wonder what we're supposed to do.

"Well, come on," Armfield says. "Come on. Someone speak up. I need to know what you think."

Has this man no redemption but schoolboys in a classroom?

A voice from the front of the class says quietly, "Sir, we don't know what to tell you."

He seems surprised.

"Of course you do," he responds. "Of course you do. The question is very simple. Which is the greater sin? To kill your own father? Or to kill your father and be happy for it?"

Someone says, "That is not simple, sir. That is a complicated question. Nobody can answer that but you!"

"Very good," Armfield says. "Anybody else? Am I the only person who can answer that question?"

"You did it, sir. You killed your father," someone says.

"Whether you felt guilty about it or not, sir, you killed your father." A second opinion.

"Yes, I did," Armfield says, warming to the subject. "But am I really guilty? You heard my story. Am I really guilty?"

"If you did it, sir, you are guilty, aren't you?"

Armfield shoots back: "Yes—under extenuating circumstances that would certainly have exonerated a terrified young boy. I speak now in self-defense, though in my mind I am already convicted and condemned."

Then, slowly: "I am asking you, boys, as members of my only jury, is it worse than murder to kill your own father and actually be happy about it? That is the question that is killing me."

"I don't know, sir," I hear myself say, "but watching someone beat my mother, I think I might have felt the same and done the same."

Armfield gives me a long look of appreciation. For what, I am not certain.

"Did you hear that?" he asks the class. "What do you think of that? Would you have done the same?"

No one moves. "Anyone?"

"If you would have done the same, raise your hand."

There is another very long pause before one hand tentatively inches into the air. In a moment, another hand goes up. Then, slowly, silently, all hands rise like telltale flags.

"I am gratified," Armfield says, just loudly enough to be heard, "that you have answered my question in this way...you are unanimous. It is really quite unexpected."

As we lower our hands, I think I can see tears in his eyes.

"Not exactly, sir," a small voice speaks.

The shiest boy in the class, Havens, is slowly raising his hand.

"Not unanimous, sir."

Armfield blinks and turns to Havens.

"Say again?'

"Not unanimous sir." Havens is forcing himself to say the words.

"Not unanimous?" Armfield echoes, distraught. "Not unanimous…?"

"No, sir."

Havens looks up, but he still hesitates.

"We will wait until you are ready," Armfield says softly. "We are content to sit here and await your opinion."

"Tell us, Havens," someone says.

Havens looks around the room, and for a moment, he is on the brink of tears. Then his face hardens.

"Sir. 'Thou shalt not kill.' The Bible tells us so. There are no exceptions, sir."

Armfield stares at Havens as the words sink in, his expression blank. "Quite so, Havens," he says finally. "Quite so…then I must plead guilty to murder?"

"Yes, sir. I think so."

"Thank you. I accept your verdict."

The fingers of his right hand begin to tremble.

"And on the matter of killing and having no remorse, Havens. What do you think about that?"

"Only you can be the judge of that, sir," Havens replies quietly.

"In that case, Havens, I must be guilty twice over."

With that, Armfield looks again at the pale light coming in the windows, and with a wave of his hand, he dismisses the class.

We file out without a word.

That very evening Armfield goes missing. A search of his home and the surrounding woods turns up not a clue, leaving the school in a state of paranoia and high anxiety. And we students don't know what happened.

Two weeks later that mystery is solved when a sport fisherman turns up a body, bloated and pale as a dead fish, clad in bow tie and tweeds, wedged under a sunken tree in the Avon River, downstream of the old Manawauk Bridge.

No one ever says it, but we all know it is suicide.

Suicide. A mortifying embarrassment and sensitive subject in a private school. Armfield's demise is acknowledged with no more than a brief chapel announcement and an even briefer prayer. Nobody cares. Not a single tribute. Gone and forgotten in a single day, as if nothing had happened. In a few more days, his position is quietly filled.

It's been a week since the whole terrible thing blew over. Those of us who knew Armfield are still trying to make sense of what happened.

"I'm having a problem with the fact that somebody can kill his own father and get away with it," Mike says. "Now we're looking at a capital crime. That's serious stuff."

I'm shaking my head.

"No, that's not what this is about," I argue. "It's not the legal issue. It's about his choices, and how his life ended."

"Really?"

"Sure. Look. Here's a person who gives his life, sacrifices everything, for hundreds of people who maybe don't even remember him, and for a school—his home and his work for forty years—and in the end they all betray him, dismiss him. I don't think he ever had a family. The school was his family, really, and when he died, his family deserted him, disowned him."

"Yeah, in a way I can relate to that," Mike says.

Mike, the orphan, deserted by one family, rescued by another.

"Yes. In a way, I can relate to that too," I say. "I can't *stop* thinking about it. Because I don't want to wind up like that."

"You don't mean *kill* yourself?"

"No, no, no. I mean have a job where you spend your whole life devoted to something that you realize too late was maybe a big mistake. Too late to change and get out, or start again."

"Well," Mike says, "what are you most worried about? The fact that he killed himself and nobody seemed to care? Or that he chose a life that didn't fulfill him, and people didn't properly appreciate?"

Good question. I give it a moment.

"It's both, really. In the big picture, for him it was a bad decision that led to a bad end. The miracle is he went so long with his terrible secret and nobody knew. Maybe because he made what he thought was the right choice but found out too late it wasn't right for him. Either way, I think it was *not confessing* the murder that finally caught up with him and did him in. He died with a ton of personal baggage and unresolved issues."

Mike nods.

"Well, any Catholic knows a good confession when he hears one, and we saw a doozy," he says. "Must have felt good finally to get it off his chest. But for old Armfield I'm afraid it was way too late."

I can see Armfield at the blackboard, patiently parsing Latin passages with four infinitives at the end of each ten-line sentence, structures so complex the predicate nominative couldn't find the verb—or verbs—with radar.

I can picture him at the head of the class translating from Cicero, quoting Ovid, and bringing the ancient Roman Empire to life with readings from *Histories* by Tacitus.

All of that.

"Sure, he was a good teacher. But it seemed like the passion had gone out of him," Mike says.

We both nod in confirmation.

I tell Mike, "The way I see it, his entire life—and death— amounted to nothing more than the hole you leave when you pull your fingers out of a glass of water. A life essentially wasted. Definitely not how I want to end up."

But, exactly how *do* I want to end up?

COACH

"Squire Belmont," the coach says, working the ace bandage around my ankle. Squire. Just like Big Sally in the bucket crew. "Have you been smoking cigarettes?"

Busted.

The mints are worthless.

He calls us all Squire. Behind his back, we call him Chief. Coach Cochran, full-blooded Algonquin Indian, weathered face like Geronimo, and a son on scholarship at Yale, captain of the football team. Our team uniforms are not Windemere colors but blue, white, and gold. Yale colors.

We all know the Chief's story: Born in a tribal village in Quebec, he contracted polio as a child and overcame his handicap by hauling logs up hills with chains. He was a lacrosse semipro superstar in Canada, eventually ended up a legendary football and lacrosse coach in New England boarding schools.

We are fortunate to have him.

"Just one, Coach."

"Well, Mr. Belmont, that's one too many. You know my rules. Report to me on the field."

Ten minutes later we line up on the fifty-yard line.

New England autumn is painting rolling hills red and gold. Cotton clouds drift across a soft-blue sky. A fresh breeze out of the northwest puts a sharp nip in the air.

I wish I could relive the last hours.

Favoring his bad leg, Chief moves out to the middle of the field.

"Squire Belmont, step forward and face your teammates," Chief growls.

I position myself and look into the faces of the entire varsity Windemere football team.

In matters of school sports, Chief is the undisputed god of field combat, feared and revered by students, athletes, and faculty alike. Just one hard look from those unsmiling, coal-black eyes is enough to shut us up and shut us down.

"Mr. Belmont, tell your teammates why I have asked you to stand and face them."

"I smoked a cigarette before practice today, Coach."

"That is correct. Gentlemen, did you hear that? Squire Belmont smoked a cigarette today. Tell the team the penalty for smoking."

"The penalty for smoking is automatic suspension from the team, two missed games, and two weeks' hard time in the mudhole and on the sled, Coach."

"That is correct, Mr. Belmont. Now, you fine young gentlemen understand that Squire Belmont is also subject to possible expulsion from the team. Is that correct?"

Nobody says a word.

"I can't hear you!" Coach bellows.

"*Yes, Coach!*" the team roars back, in a single voice.

"Now I want every one of you boys who has also smoked to step forward with Mr. Belmont."

Clearly, no one saw that coming.

Everyone is frozen in excruciating silence.

"Gentlemen, I will wait until sundown if I have to," Chief says. "I want all of you who have broken my rule for smoking to step forward."

After an awkward eternity in which no one dares lower his eyes, lest he appear guilty, Mike, my best buddy since the first day of school over a year ago, 240 pounds of legendary ferocity on the field, leaves the line.

He stands alone.

I can't help but smile.

I can always count on Mike. Big Mike. Undisputed king of locker-room jokes, Giants fan and beer enthusiast, Mike is about to take a bullet for me. And Mike doesn't even smoke.

I can see other teammates glancing right and left.

Suddenly, Tom Petris, running back, takes one step forward, followed immediately by Bob Hacker, defensive end, then two more. In the next thirty seconds, the entire team has stepped forward.

There's a long pause as the coach surveys the line.

"I am disappointed, gentlemen," he says. "But not surprised. There is no way I will ever know if all you gentlemen did break training, or whether you have come forward to show your support for Squire Belmont. Either way, you know the penalty. If one man breaks the rules, then every man must endure the consequences. However, because you have stepped forward as a team, I'll give any man who can beat me from centerfield to the goal line the rest of the day off."

When the whistle blows, we all explode toward the end zone. But Chief breaks from the herd in just seconds and like a racehorse gallops out ahead of the whole team, bad leg and all. He leaves even the running backs like me in his wake. By the time we cross the goal line, he's already in the touchdown zone, waiting for us to catch up.

Most of us are heaving, gasping for air.

He's not even breathing hard.

The rest of the day, we hit the sleds, two players crashing into the pads as many times as it takes to force the seven-hundred-pound sleds back ten yards with a dozen teammates riding on them. After an hour, we can hardly stand. But the afternoon has just begun. Next, we stand in "the hole," a grassless patch of field in which we must halt the repeated charges of teammates whose objective is to run us over. The running lane is only three feet wide, so there's no escape. Like two trains rushing at each other on a single track, you collide head on with your opponent. If you stand your ground with a hammerhead tackle, you may send a friend pinwheeling into the air. After three hours of this unrelenting assault, Chief herds us double time, bloodied and bruised, back up the hill in a crazy scramble to the gym, where we collapse in the locker room.

I'm hunched over on a bench, holding my head in my hands, fatigue and humiliation my only thoughts.

"Squire…"

I look up.

"Chief…"

Standing over me, he nods. Then he puts his hand on my shoulder.

"*Onishishin*," he says.

Later I learn it means "good" in Algonquin.

I realize too late he's letting me know it's all right.

It's the only time I ever see him smile.

MAFIA KID

Not a month into my freshman year, it becomes abundantly clear that it's better to be a dorm monitor than just another campus drone. Monitors have bigger rooms, get to stay up later, and boss other kids around. The thought of being in better circumstances, if only slightly better circumstances, is enough for me to sit down with Dean Pruitt and apply for the job.

"Well, it's interesting that you are here, Mr. Belmont," the Dean says, "because just this week we were discussing freshman candidates, and your name came up. You're the kind of boy we like having here at Windermere. I'm sure you will provide the kind of student leadership we want. Like your father and your grandfather before you. I am fairly confident that you will be appointed. You'll be notified shortly. Now, if we have no further business, I bid you good day."

Legacy talks. Nothing to it.

"Thank you, sir," I say, shaking his hand.

The first challenge in my new assignment is a lesson in life, Conflict Management 101.

An hour after lights out, a routine head check reveals that one of the dorm's students, Cosimo Frisco, is missing. Of all the students in all four dorms, the student you don't want to go missing is Cosimo. His father, Enrico "Richy Thumbs" Frisco, is a New Jersey Mafia boss straight out of central casting. "Thumbs" because it's said he has a fondness for gouging out his adversaries' eyes. Mr. Frisco's own famously heavy-lidded eyes behind yellow sunglasses never smile. They don't have to. He is a man of few words and has a majority interest in a professional soccer team, an estate in Princeton, and a restaurant with a boccie pit in Hoboken. He also has an olive oil import/export business that's under constant surveillance by half a dozen federal, state, and local agencies. So far, they've turned up nothing, but he's been in and out of the Newark federal building so many times he's become a newspaper celebrity. Pictures show him waving like the pope as he steps into his black Caddy limo.

Don Frisco has visited the campus twice, both times with a "driver." The shadow is never more than four feet away. Coincidently, last year, the school officially opened the new Windermere gym, the Frisco Sports Center. He has ambitious plans for Cosimo.

Tonight, the only thing on my mind is finding the son.

We have no illusions about what fate might await if we fail to find Cosimo and get him back to his room before his absence becomes generally known. We can only hope he hasn't run away. Or worse, that nobody's kidnapped him right out from under our noses. After all, blackmailing a Mafia don could result in significant unforeseen collateral damage.

"I'll take care of this dorm," I say to a posse of monitors assembled to track him down.

"You guys search the other dorms."

After a flashlight sweep of the dorm floor turns up nothing, I make my way quietly downstairs and move through recreation rooms, a few classrooms, and utility rooms. In the dark, I listen for voices and sniff the air for cigarette smoke.

I'm about to step outside when a faint squeaking sound catches my ear. Coming from somewhere behind me, I hear muffled voices. I retrace my steps to a door under the stairs that I had overlooked.

Without a sound, I open the door. In the flashlight beam, a pair of buttocks is poised in midthrust between two upstretched legs.

Over his shoulder Cosimo mumbles, "The fugg?"

"Cosimo, you've got to go back to your room."

Whoever the girl is, she's in no hurry to move. The legs are down but the knees are still up.

"Can't you see I'm busy here? For Christ's sake, give me a fuggin' minute."

I give him a pass for sheer outrageous balls.

"Make it fast, Cos," I say, and shut the door.

The squeaking accelerates immediately, accompanied by rapid grunting and a female cry.

This girl has obviously got no compunctions—and next to no inhibitions.

Two minutes later Cosimo steps out, tucking in his shirt, followed by—good God!—Wendy Pruitt, the dean's daughter. Surly, pouting, perpetually sullen Wendy, with the angry eyes and "attitude." She's staring at me defiantly.

"You gonna rat me out?"

"It doesn't bother you that you were caught fucking?"

She says nothing, locking eyes, challenging me to a staring contest.

"Go home," I tell her. "But if I catch you again, I'll make sure your father knows all about it."

"Like he doesn't know," she says, brushing past me and flipping me the finger. "He was the first."

I'm too stunned to speak to Cosimo.

Mild-mannered Harvard man Dean Pruitt. Smiling, affable, harmless Dean Pruitt with the tweed suit, wire specs, and briar pipe. Could it possibly be? Or is this skanky bitch of a daughter just evil enough to tell sick lies about her own father? I'd never want to see that girl with a gun in her hand.

I sit Cosimo down upstairs.

"That was stupid, buddy."

"Whatever—you just don't have a proper appreciation of pussy, Harry. If you did, you'd be fucking her too."

I let it go.

"You don't have a proper appreciation of the fact that one word from me, asshole, and you're toast. How do you think your father's going to feel if you get kicked out?"

"No different from how he feels when I get kicked out of any school. He says he wants me to get an education, but he never even *went* to school. When I get kicked out, he just buys me into the next place. That's how I got in here."

"You don't care?"

"I don't give a shit."

"You don't give shit about much, do you, Cos? If you don't give a shit, why should I?"

He looks away, bored.

"If you gave a shit, you might try to make something out of your fucked-up life."

He gives me an eye roll.

"So, go ahead, turn me in. Then go beat yourself up in the Frisco Sports Center. You don't get it, do you? None of you fuckin' preppies do. My father's got Windermere by the balls. Windermere! What kind of a fuggin' name is that anyway? Sounds like a fuggin' girls' school! In case you don't know, Mr. Big Fuck Monitor, money talks, bullshit walks! If I got thrown out, he'd burn the gym down. It's his way of saying you broke an agreement. In our business, you don't break agreements. And if he knew it was you who ratted me out, he could break your knees. Are we done here?"

"I'll tell you my decision in the morning."

As I turn to the door, I say, "The refrigerator truck? You told me you want to drive a refrigerator truck. Were you serious?"

"No."

"So, what *do* you want to do?"

"I'll work for my father."

Back in my own room, Cos's words keep coming back. "Money talks, bullshit walks."

I think about the "understanding" and about Dean Pruitt. What if Wendy was telling the truth?

Cosimo will always be an unlikable punk. But at least he's an honest punk. He doesn't have much time for the elite class his father wants so much for him to be a part of.

No wonder he doesn't give a shit.

AMBUSH

In our junior year, Coach has Mike do double duty, playing him both as defensive anchor and offensive running back. Double-threat Stone Wall leaves a debris trail of bodies with almost every run. He scores so many touchdowns, Windemere ends the season undefeated. Mike is named all-state in both offensive and defensive positions.

Perfect setup for our senior year.

Before school starts in the fall, Mike and I agree to meet in New York for a last blast before the tough months ahead. He knows an Irish pub where they don't ask for IDs if you look even remotely Gaelic. Mike's got the reddish hair and freckles, so we walk straight to the bar and start drinking Guinness on tap.

I can tell he's feeling right at home. He likes his suds, and I've seen him overdo it more than once. The beers come in big glasses, and he tosses back his first until his mouth is frothed in foam.

"Ah, now that's a fine draft!" he declares, wiping his lips with the back of his hand. "None finer in the land."

I try to duplicate his move, but I have to stop after one big gulp.

"So, boyo, how was the summer?"

"I worked construction. My dad thought I wouldn't be able to do it. But I surprised myself. They made me dig under leaking sewer pipes. What a shitty job."

"Oh, that's lame, boyo. But I get it. You know my dad's in the plumbing business. He let me tag along other summers. But this summer I was in charge of toilet repair. You need a toilet fixed, I'm your man."

"That's good to know."

"What's the chance two guys, best friends, and both had shitty summer jobs?"

We laugh and slap a high five.

"Only problem with this place," he says, looking around, "is there are too many guys and not enough girls."

I'm nodding. Just like Windemere.

The pub is full of men drinking pints.

"Mike," I say, glancing at him, "this is going to be a hard year. Do you have a plan for what's after school?"

"A plan?"

"Yeah. I mean a plan for life, for the future."

"I'm not even plannin' what I'm gonna eat for breakfast tomorrow, boyo."

For a moment, we sit in silence nursing our beers, and I'm afraid I've made a mistake getting serious.

"Well, to tell you the truth," he says finally, "I *have* thought about it."

He drains his glass and signals the bartender.

"And...?"

"I haven't even told my parents. Have you heard of the Navy SEALs?"

"Sure! Toughest guys in the service."

"Well, I've been thinking about the SEALs."

"You mean after we graduate?"

"No, I'm thinking after college."

"I like how you think, Mike. But the SEALs. Very tough to qualify. You think you can make the cut?"

He gives me a long and patient look.

"Harry, if I decide to do it, believe me, I will. Nothing will stop me."

"Oh, I believe it." I see the wreckage of failed tackles, bodies sprawled on the field all the way to the goal line.

"What about you, boyo?"

"Actually, I've thought about being a fighter pilot. Even took flying lessons. But I decided I'm not cut out to be in the military."

Mike takes another long chug.

"If I went for a military career, fighter pilot would be my second choice. But I'm too big. You couldn't squeeze me into the cockpit. And if you did, I'd burn up all my fuel just trying to get to the target."

"Yeah. Maybe you should stick with the SEALs," I say, raising my glass to his. "You know what else I've been thinking about?"

"What?"

"I've been thinking about taking a year off."

"A year off from what?"

"Just a year off. I don't know."

"To do what?"

"Travel. See the world. See what's out there. I've already got a plan."

"I like it," Mike says, nodding. "What made you think of that?"

"Armfield, partly."

"Armfield?"

"Yeah."

"Poor bastard. Yeah, I know what you mean. Makes you wonder, doesn't it?"

"Yes, it does make you wonder what you want out of life."

"Armfield didn't figure it out, did he? Then like a ghost, he just disappears, and nobody gives a shit."

"That's it, exactly. So much to do, so little time."

"Year off...I like it!" Mike says.

At that moment, two unaccompanied females approach the bar. Mike immediately gets off his stool, effectively cutting off any interference from potential rivals, and ushers the ladies toward our spot.

The pretty one and I lock eyes right away. But I'm way out of my element in this place, so I let Mike take the lead. He chats them right up to the bar, and I provide two empty stools. We seat the girls, and Mike and I stand.

"May we offer you two lovely ladies something to drink?" Mike says. The pretty one shoots me a smile.

"Are you boys Irish?" the other one asks.

"I was born Irish," Mike says, giving her a complicit smile. "Are you Irish?"

They giggle, not able to decide who should answer. "I'm Maureen," the other one says, "and this is Bridgett. We're both working as au pairs with New York families. This is our day off."

"What's it like, two looooovely ladies of Erin working all alone in the big, bad city?" Mike asks.

"Well, the truth is, we don't get much time off, if you must know," Bridgett says.

Mike gives me a conspiratorial wink.

"Well then, this must be our lucky night, all of us!" he says. "There's no better place to meet new friends than in an Irish pub! My granddaddy once told me, ya know..."

He's full of Irish charm, captivating the girls with stories. I can only watch with admiration as he rolls out his skills as a raconteur. The deeper he gets into the beer and the blarney, the more Irish his accent becomes.

He tosses back half a pint of stout in one gulp and tells a joke about a priest and a rabbi. The girls laugh until their eyes tear up.

The joke isn't that funny, I'm thinking. Maybe you need to be Irish.

"Are *you* Irish, Harry?" Bridgett asks.

"No, but I am tonight."

"Ah, go on!" she says, giving me a friendly push. "If yer not Irish, then what are ye?"

"Just a plain old American boy. Mike here…he's trying to turn me into an Irishman."

"Well, what do you think of that, Maureen?" Bridgett exclaims, turning to her friend. "Do ye think this fine American boy would make a good Irishman?"

Mike's nodding.

I look at him. He's swaying gently like a big oak in a gale, his signature grin spreading from one ear to the other. But his eyes are a little unfocused.

"Whoa!" he says, steadying himself.

I know the signs.

"Okay, buddy. It's time to go."

Mike looks disappointed.

"Ah, so that's it?" he says, surprisingly sheepish. Maybe he's more far gone than I know. "I thought we were having such a fine time…"

He starts to tilt but catches himself.

How did he drink so much so fast?

"We were. We are. But it's late, and it's starting to rain. If we wait, we'll never get a cab, and it's a long walk back to the hotel."

Mike nods. I'm relieved he's not resisting. In fact, he looks relaxed, even sleepy.

"Well, then, ladies, I regret that I must bid ya farewell," he says, with a courtly bow.

I look over my shoulder on the way out. The girls look genuinely disappointed. I can only imagine what might have been.

What a shame.

"Ah...you feel that air, boyo?" Mike says as we step outside. He takes a deep breath, turns his face up to the raindrops, and sticks out his tongue. "This reminds me of when I was five years old."

"Catching raindrops," I say.

We start walking. The bracing air is doing him good. The grin is gone. He's on the march, shaking off the woozies, his face a mask of determination. It's the same hard look I've seen behind the face guard of his helmet in the split second before he sends me flying into the air.

"You okay?" I ask.

"I'm okay. This cold air is good. I'm fine."

Just then, a hooded figure steps out of the darkness right in front of me. I'm staring down the barrel of a gun.

"Gimme your fuckin' money!"

I freeze, my mind racing, unable to move or react. Before I can utter a sound, the cold steel is on my forehead.

"Gimme your fuckin' money, asshole!"

Mike streaks across my line of sight with the roar of a wild beast. He slams into the assailant, sending him airborne through a plate-glass window. An explosion of shattered crystal sends shrapnel flying into the falling rain. The gun clatters to the pavement and skitters away. Shards of glass plunge on the gunman like guillotine blades.

We run for our lives and don't look back.

It's not until we are safely in the hotel that we stop, catch our breaths, and think about what just happened.

I sit on the edge of my bed, still in shock, letting the enormity of the whole thing sink in.

"You saved my life, Mike," I say finally. "You saved both our lives."

Mike sits on his bed with his head in his hands.

"Did you hear what I said?" I ask him. "You're a hero, a fucking hero."

He holds his hands in front of his face.

"Look at that. Heroes' hands don't tremble. I don't even remember what happened. When I saw the gun, something snapped. After that, it's just a blur."

"Maybe it's all that beer that makes your fingers tremble."

"Right now, I'm sober as a judge," he says. "Do you think I killed him?"

"I don't know. I don't think so. But I do know he could have killed you, both of us. Probably on drugs. We must have looked like sitting ducks. Two guys coming out of a bar, feeling no pain. But you took him out. As far as I'm concerned, you saved my life. I owe you."

"What you owe me is a case of beer," Mike says.

Minutes later he's sound asleep.

THE BIG BASH

For anyone needing a reminder that excess is much to be admired and a very good thing indeed, there's nothing like an old-fashioned debutante party to set things right and put priorities back on track.

Debutante parties are a hallowed rite of passage, even for the most mournfully unattractive girls. They exist solely to ensure that the gene pool stays in the social loop, along with the money. Which both do. Each summer "season" sees a debutante party under a vast tent almost every night. In winter, the extravaganzas are held in upscale hotel ballrooms. You congregate with the same people all night, every night, sometimes to the break of day. The same potential brides and the same eligible bachelors, every night, in ball gowns and black ties.

That's why, at some point, even excess fails to excite. After a while, we all suffer from grinding déjà vu, oppressive ennui, and a pervasive spiritual numbness that puts a pall on everything. So, we drink more and party harder to make it go away.

By the end of the season, if we weren't so young, we'd all be dead.

Mike would never be comfortable in these shamelessly extravagant pageants of overindulgence, nor approve. He'd take a quick look around and say he'd never seen so many phonies in his life. But for me it's all part of the high life, my life, another perfect day of pomp and pretense in paradise.

I may be smug and judgmental, even self-righteous, but not so smug and judgmental—nor hypocritical—that I'm about to turn my back on the benefits that accrue from nothing more than simple heritage.

On a hot June night, a caravan of expensive cars pulls up to the entrance of a grand country house on an estate outside Philadelphia. A receiving line of black ties and gowns awaits glittering guests, who proceed through illuminated halls and galleries to a torch-lit path leading to a tent the size of a hangar.

Under the tent, a New York set designer has created a giant Garden of Eden, festooned with fifty thousand white roses. Scattered about the perimeter is an artificial forest of live orange, lemon, and palm trees trucked in from Florida. Nearby tents offer tables groaning under piles of caviar, French cheeses, smoked wild Scottish salmon, exotic canapés by the thousands. Famous chefs man food stations offering lavish delicacies you might expect to find only in the finest restaurants.

Another tent has three crowded bars with dozens of bartenders and waiters dispensing endless cases of the world's best champagnes, fine wines, and spirits.

A forty-piece band in black ties and tails dominates the stage at the far end of the main tent.

The center of attention of all this spectacular excess is Daphne, a bold, dark-eyed feline with the eye-catching body of a ballerina smoldering with contained energy begging for release. People have come from great distances, and her mom and dad spare no expense for their only daughter's coming-out party.

The crowd is, of course, the same cast of players you partied with just a few days earlier in New York or Boston: the überelite—preposterously rich, elegant, well connected, and Hollywood beautiful.

Every deb has her beau. On this night, since we happen to be dating seriously at the time, I have the honor of being the beau.

Champagne is flowing, and the night's still young. Outside, stars are so bright you might think the gods are smiling on the whole dazzling affair. Silver clouds scud under a rising moon. The tent is lit up like a cruise ship sailing magically through darkened, slumbering countryside, and night breezes carry smells of the earth up from the valley below.

The stage is set for a night to remember.

Just then, Caleb, an ingratiating poseur from New York, grabs my elbow. He's a nasty little anathema with good will toward none and plenty of ill will toward almost everybody. I'm certainly no exception. He must know I don't like him.

"Harry!" he says, leaning in, speaking just loudly enough to be heard over the music.

"Didn't you used to date Alexa Fullerton?"

"Still do, occasionally."

He nods knowingly.

I'm waiting. But then he says, "Man, I wish I had your looks, buddy! All the girls you get, and now here you are, the man of the hour! Mr. Hollywood in the spotlight!"

He gives me a big fake grin.

"So, what about Alexa?"

He looks me right in the eyes, and I can see satisfaction there.

"She's down on the lawn right now, shitfaced out of her mind and gangbanging a bunch of guys."

I want to swat the smug look right off his face.

"You sure it's her? I don't think she was invited."

"It's her all right."

"She crashed the party?" I ask, incredulous.

It takes me a moment to replay what he's just said.

"Yep. Sorry, pal."

"Did you do her?"

"Nope."

"Why not?" I ask, feeling suddenly uncharitable toward my part-time girlfriend in the grass and the spiteful peckerhead standing next to me. "Sounds like she wouldn't know the difference."

"Came up to tell you," he explains. "Don't shoot the messenger. Just thought you might want to know."

"How many guys?"

"Three or four, last I looked," he says. "A couple of other guys standing around watching."

Walking into the darkness with the music and lights fading behind us, Caleb says, "Down there."

I move to stand with five other young men watching Alexa, snow-white ball gown hiked up to her chest and knees pulled almost up to her ears, pleasuring a guy I've never met. He's still wearing his tuxedo, making fast work of it, propping himself up on his arms to try to avoid grass stains. Alexa has taken no such precautions. Even in the faint light from the tent, I can see her elegant and very expensive dress is ruined. And the boy straddling her is pumping himself into her with a vengeance.

Another horndog, unzipped and tool in hand, stands ready to jump right in.

The pelvic thruster jumps up, sated, to make room for the next player.

"More! More!" Alexa shouts. I can hear the alcohol in her voice. Her legs are open as wide as they can go.

"Somebody fuck me!"

"I'd be delighted!" announces...number unknown, glancing with a broad smile over at his appreciative audience and more than happy to oblige.

Our eyes meet.

"Harry?" he says, halting his forward motion, self-conscious as a kid caught with his hand in the cookie jar.

"You want to go next?"

Before I can answer, Alexa spots me.

"Harry Belmont! You prick!" her ugly, drunken snarl accuses me. I'm embarrassed to be recognized, called out in front of these familiar people.

"Harry, you can go fuck yourself!"

I try to salvage some dignity and cool.

"Well, that's not going to happen."

With that I shoot a quick thumbs up to the guy still standing with his dick in his hand.

"Cocksucker!" she screams.

It's the last thing I hear as I return to the party.

On cue from the conductor, the band strikes up a robust Viennese waltz, and the dance floor clears while proud dad whisks Daphne—glowing like a fairy princess in her sequined white silk designer ball gown—out onto the varnished boards.

They swoop in arcing circles as the music swells around them, pressed on by a thousand smiles and waves of enthusiastic applause as the entire assembly signals its hearty approval.

As her escort, I'm next.

In a fluid, seamless motion, the dad and I are supposed to exchange places. It's a tricky move, and I feel like a running back getting a handoff from the quarterback. I can't fumble this one. I like my date, and need to play my role without a hitch.

The daughter and I glide off to the center of the floor. Just the two of us filling the ballroom. She looks beautiful. I'm proud to be with her.

But no sooner do we pause to acknowledge our guests than we sense something's wrong. The waltz is still going strong, but the applause is fading. A buzz of alarm rises, and the assembled glitterati are fixed on a disturbance at the edge of the crowd.

A girl bursts out, lurching alone across the floor in our direction.

Time stands still while she heads right at us.

The music dies.

"Jesus!" Daphne mutters to me. "What's that bitch doing here?"

Here comes Alexa in full feral fury, banned from the guest list by the girl currently in my arms. Alexa, a nightmare of unleashed female spite, anger, and hurt, her ripped dress stained with grass and dirt. She strides drunkenly, hair wild, face streaked with mascara, hurling threats at both of us.

At the front of the crowd, both parents freeze, mouths agape. They've been preparing eighteen years for this golden moment— only to witness a breach so shocking it violates every code they know.

But the guests love it. They're titillated by the break in the routine. It's as if they they've got front seats at a cockfight.

"Who the *fuck* is that?" Someone breaks the spell.

Alexa's clawed hands are raised to strike her adversary.

"You fucking *cunt!*" she shrieks.

"Stop!" I shout.

I manage to catch her upraised arm. She counters with her other arm, but not before Daphne, the lady of hour, scores a lucky punch with a surprisingly fast fist to the face.

It's a fine punch, delivered with remarkable precision.

The intruder stops dead in her tracks. Blood spouts from her nose. Her eyes roll up into her head. She sinks to her knees, then collapses on the floor.

Two waiters promptly scoop her up and take her away.

The crowd breaks the silence with what sounds like a collective orgasm. Then hundreds of conversations pick up where they left off. The music strikes up again. Halftime entertainment is over, and the game is back on. No more waltz. Now it's rock 'n' roll. The old guard shuffles off, but the young crowd is loosening up, ready to party, stoked by champagne and unexpected violence.

I look at my debutante with new admiration.

"How did you do that?"

"My brother taught me how to box," she says.

A TOAST TO ELLEN

At a summer deb season bachelor party, and before our friend Tom's wedding, one of the ushers gets up to toast the groom. He's Barron Beaseley, a smart guy just out of Harvard, irreverent to a fault, and we know we can count on him for a devastating round of cruel fun.

A drunken chorus of appreciation rises as Barron gets to his feet. Same guys in the crowd as always. We all know each other, probably too well.

He surveys the room, shaking his head in mock disapproval.

"You guys look like shit!" he says.

A huge cheer.

Barron nods and grins, soaking up the boisterous feedback.

"The bad news is that Tom's heading down the long, lonely road of domesticity," he begins. "But the good news is that as far as I know, Ellen's got no extra fingers or toes. Which is amazing, considering the gene pool we are all descended from. You know, we all talk about lucky sperm. But lucky sperm counts for nothing if the genes get messed up. Look to your right. Now, look to your left. Both those people are related to you. The same is true for every girl you know! You don't have to be a Nobel-Prize-winning genealogist to know that can't be good for your DNA. So you'd better be careful about whom you fuck!"

A burst of guilty chuckles, nods of affirmation.

"The gene pool issue really hit home with me the other night when I was out with a girl we all know," Barron continues. "A girl who has successfully fended off the advances of almost every guy in this room. I can't tell you *how*, but I finally got to the bottom of *why* she's been so preoccupied for so long about protecting her virtue...and I mean the bottom."

He pauses a moment, looking carefully around the room.

We're all waiting.

"It turns out," he says, "that it has nothing to do with her virtue, but everything to do with the fact that she was born without a vagina!"

"*Bullshit!*" someone shouts, amid a roar of rowdy hoots and laughs. "You don't know that! We don't know that, so how can you know that?"

"Trust me," he says, dismissing all objections with a wave. "And I'm wondering," he continues, ignoring a few lingering wolf howls, "could this be nature's way of telling us enough is enough? Nature saying, hey, isn't it time we stop fucking our cousins?"

Everybody's cheering.

But Tom's not so sure.

"Now, Tom is safe," Barron assures us, with a glance to Tom. "Because Ellen is Tom's fourth cousin, and fourth cousins don't count!"

He pauses again.

"And we all know that Ellen's *definitely* got a vagina!"

Thunderous cheers, more wild affirmation.

I look at Tom, a sober-minded law student typically not given to frivolity of any kind, relieved and delighted to see that he's loving it, holding his champagne glass high and whooping it up right along with the rest of us.

"To Ellen!" he roars.

Everybody grabs a glass, and now all glasses are in the air, champagne flying everywhere.

"To Ellen!" we all thunder.

"And to Ellen's vagina!" somebody shouts.

We're laughing so hard it's all we can do to keep from choking to death.

Not surprisingly, Tom, not exactly a pauper himself, is marrying into big money. But I'm one of the eligible bachelors short on cash, because for whatever reason, no one ever set up a trust fund for me, and there are no handouts in my family. In fact, the old money is pretty much gone. So, I face no existential traumas or tough decisions, because the comfortable options available to my buddies aren't there for me.

Maybe that's one of the reasons I feel I need to be a tougher and stronger than some of these other guys. Why I have to keep proving myself. And maybe that's why I have a lot of respect for people my own age who already are. People not like me or the people I grew up with.

DOM

Right under our noses, on the other side of town in the blue-collar neighborhoods of Philadelphia, people who actually work for a living are enjoying themselves too. We who live the highlife are largely unaware that this parallel world exists. The two worlds, though close, don't connect. So, I'm surprised one day when Dominic Bonfiglio, a coworker from my construction days with T-Bone, invites me to his neighborhood in South Philly. It's the oldest Italian-American part of the city. We take seats at the bar and order a Pabst on tap.

Waiting for the Phillies game to start, Dominic leans into the polished wood and asks, "So, Harry, what's it like?"

"What's what like?

"What's it like being rich?"

"I'm not rich."

"Ah c'mon."

"What makes you think I'm rich?"

"Just 'cause I'm from South Philly don't make me stupid. You got rich written all over you."

"Really? I thought I looked kind of...normal."

"Yeah, you look normal rich. We used to drive out to the burbs and kick the shit out of guys like you," he says, grinning. "We call people like you *pezzonavante*."

"What does it mean?"

"It means somebody that don't matter."

"How come these guys aren't kicking the shit out of me right now?"

"'Cause I got your back. You ain't with me, you don't even make it to the bar before one of these guys throws you out. I got a coupla uncles, made men. If I like you, they like you. These here guys respect that."

"Well, I take that as an honor, Dom. So how come you got my back?"

"Why? I have no fuggin' idea why. I didn't like you when I first saw you. But I found out I can talk to you. And you got no problem talking to people like me."

I look around. These guys are tough. Some of them are big. A few of them are looking at me. A lot of dark, unfriendly eyes. I'm the only guy in the whole bar who isn't Italian-American.

"You see those guys at the round table in the corner?"

I look over.

"The guy in the black shirt? That's my uncle Vin. They call him Vinny the Pick because he always makes his point with an ice pick. Ice pick? Get it?"

"I get it."

"The fat guy with the fedora and the stick in his mouth? That's my uncle Tony. The call him Tony Pops 'cause he's always suckin' on popsicle sticks."

"What are they doing here?"

"This is like a social club. It's where they spend their time. The wives, they don't want 'em around the house. So they come here. Any woman comes in, she's automatically a hooker. Goes straight to the back room."

"Who's in the back room?"

"That's the boss."

"Who's the boss?"

"Hey, you gotta know every fuggin' thing?"

"Just curious."

"You never heard of Johnny the Mooch?"

"Maybe…but I can't place the name."

He leans in.

"You live in Philadelphia? You don't know Johnny the Mooch? Johnny Carmelucci?"

I shake my head.

His voice sinks to a whisper.

"Only the biggest boss in Philadelphia and South Jersey."

"Mafia boss?"

"Yo! Harry! No such thing as the Mafia! You hear me? You understand me?"

"I understand you."

"Don't even say that word in here," he says. "We say 'Cosa Nostra.' Means 'Our Thing.' And you don't mention that neither. You're a smart guy. You're with me. If somebody talks to you, be polite, but don't say too much. The whole place is probably wired."

"Now are you going to have to kill me because you told me?"

"Nah," he says. "But if you repeat any of this and I find out about it, I'll make sure you have a very bad day."

"I won't say a thing."

"That's good. If you are my friend, you'll keep everything you hear—but maybe shouldn't know—just between us."

"Done. You can relax. I am your friend."

He raises his beer glass.

"Salut!"

"Salut."

Dom motions for another draft.

There's a poke on my back.

"Yo! Look who's here! Slummin' in the neighborhood!"

Big Sally Salantino from the bucket crew looks even bigger than I remembered, standing right next to me.

"Mr. Salantino!"

I wonder if he's going to pick me up and throw me out. But he reaches for my hand.

"You gave as good as you got down there in the pits with T-Bone and his crew. Where I come from, that counts for somethin'."

He's still shaking my hand. "You didn't quit."

"Thank you, Sal."

"Hey, Dom," Sally says. "Am I right? He ain't like them other rich fucks. He ain't afraid to work."

"My advice? I was you?" Dom turns back to me. "I wouldn't believe any bullshit from this guy. What the fuck does he know?"

"Fuck you!" Sal says, laughing. "Bustin' my balls!"

"You ain't got no balls to bust!"

"Get outta here!"

Both men are loving the banter.

Big Sally fist bumps Dom, then pats my shoulder.

"See you in the movies, kid," he says, and walks away.

Dom doesn't look at me.

"You live in a big house, Harry?"

"I guess you could say so."

"Swimming pool? I hear some of them big houses even have tennis courts?"

"Some do."

"You got maids?"

"Two."

"They good lookin'?"

"No."

"You fuck the maids?"

"Not a good idea, Dom. Besides, they're too old."

"Oh, that's too bad. I guarantee you, I ever had a maid, she'd be too busy takin' care of me to clean the house. "

"So how come you say you ain't rich?"

"It's my grandmother who has the money, Dom."

"Oh. So, she pays for everything?"

"Pretty much."

"Pays for you to go to one of them fancy private schools, right?"

"Yep."

"You got girls in your private school?"

"Nope. No girls, that's a real problem."

"Yeah, I can imagine," he says. "Guys like me, we can get laid anytime we want."

"That must be nice."

"So, where is your house?" he asks.

"If I tell you, is Uncle Tony going to want to have a sit-down with my grandmother?"

He looks at me.

"You tryin' to be wise?"

"No. I was trying to be funny."

"I'd appreciate a little respect. No. Uncle Tony ain't goin' nowhere near your grandmother. Okay? Where does she live?"

I tell him the address.

"Oh yeah," he says. "The mayor lives there. He's one of ours. Everybody in that neighborhood can sleep like a baby, including your grandmother. It's the safest neighborhood in Philadelphia."

I'm thinking back to Carl, the local street punk from the other side of the tracks who tried to steal my bike.

"So, your grandmother...she a good cook?"

I almost choke on my beer.

"She can't even find the kitchen, Dom. She once told me she didn't know how to boil water."

He gives me a doubting look.

"Seriously? Your grandmother don't cook? You gotta be kidding!"

"No."

"So…your mother cooks?"

"No."

"Then who the fugg cooks?"

"The cook cooks."

"What, like a chef? You got a fuggin' chef in the house?"

"Yeah, my grandmother does. Kind of like a live-in chef."

"Well, I got a live-in chef too," Dom says. "That would be *my* grandmother, Angelica Fiametta Calibreze. Old country. Born in Calabria. She don't speak English. No need for it, and no desire to learn it. You should see her! You try to talk English, she waves you away. She says Italian is like beautiful music. But English…she says English sounds like ducks quacking."

"You speak Italian?" I ask him.

"No. I speak American. But I can sometimes understand my grandmother. I just can't talk to her."

"And your grandmother lives in your house?"

"Yeah. And my parents, four brothers, two sisters, and a great aunt in a wheelchair."

"How big is the house?"

"It's a brick row house. The whole thing prob'ly fit in your garage."

"What's it like, everybody living in the same house?"

"What's it like? You live in the same house with your family too, right?"

"No. My grandmother lives about a mile away."

"You and your parents live in a different big house?"

"Yes."

He says nothing.

"I'll bet your grandmother is a great cook," I say.

His face animates.

"You walk into my house, the first thing you smell is oregano and basil. You go to the kitchen, she pulls a hot loaf of Italian bread outta the oven, puts it on the table. She chops up fresh garlic, puts it in a bowl with this green Sicilian olive oil she pours out of a big can, throws in a little sea salt. You pull off a nice warm chunk with the steam coming out and dip it in…"

I'm hungry, imagining the fresh bread dripping with green olive oil. I reach for a pretzel on the bar.

"You get that every day?"

"Every day, sure."

"I want to live in your house."

"You can move in with my great-aunt," he says.

"I'd do it just for the bread."

"It gets better. Everything my grandmother cooks, it's like a religious thing. We call her *Strega*, means sorceress. She's got this recipe book from the old country, was her mother's. She can't even read one word. She keeps it on a shelf next to a wooden cross under picture of Jesus. She touches it all the time, speaking Italian. I don't know what the fuck she's saying, but it sounds like little prayers."

"What kind of things does she cook?"

"You name it. Something new every day. Spaghetti with meat sauce. Ravioli. Linguini with clam sauce. Lasagna. It's like the spaghetti sauce oozes right out of the magic book. The smells! Man, it drives me crazy. Every time I go in the kitchen, she gives me a little plate. You'll never taste better Italian, and I know every Italian restaurant in South Philly. When we all sit down at the table, it's so good, nobody says nothin'. We eat everything on the plate, every meal. Never any leftovers."

"Sounds pretty good," I say, reaching for another pretzel. "I'm surprised you don't weigh three hundred pounds."

He laughs. "Give it time," he says, patting his stomach.

"You eat Italian food?" Dom asks me.

"Hoagies."

"That's it?"

"Are cheese hoagies Italian?"

"Sure. Best cheese steaks and pizza hoagies in Philly are just a coupla blocks over."

"When I'm home I eat a hoagie every chance I get. Cheese steak with pizza sauce."

"You sure you ain't Italian?" Dom laughs, and I do too.

"So who's the chef in your grandmother's house?"

"Juliette. She's French."

"Ooooooooooh. French!" he jibes, wiggling his hand for emphasis. "What? Like snails? Whadyacallem?"

"Escargots."

"You eat…that?"

"Sometimes. But she's cooking for my grandmother, and my grandmother likes it simple. Basic stuff—meat, potatoes, green beans. But she can't taste anymore, so she's got this little silver boat on the table full of salt. She takes a spoon and covers everything until it's all white on top. Looks like snow."

"I don't understand you people," he says, shaking his head. "The chef cooks a nice meal. But your grandmother can't taste it. The chef could give her dog food, she wouldn't know."

"One day Juliette opens a pot to let me see what what's she's cooking. I'm looking at a huge tongue."

"A tongue?" he says.

"Disgusting. You could see the *roots*. I thought I'd be sick."

"Who eats tongue?"

"My grandmother does. I tried it. With currant sauce. I actually liked it."

"I'll stick with pasta."

"You can't go wrong with that."

"So…you got other people runnin' around, takin' care of your grandmother? She can't boil water, what the fugg *can* she do? No disrespect."

"Not much. She's got a couple of maids and a butler."

"A butler?"

"Juliette's husband, Paul. He's old now, but once he was on the French national soccer team."

"No shit!" Dom looks at me, nodding appreciatively.

I remember how my grandmother created a miniature French country village near her faux Loire Philadelphia chateau to attract Paul and Juliette.

Somebody once had to work hard to make that kind of money. I know my grandfather's father dropped dead of a heart attack, pitching into a bowl of mock turtle soup in the management dining room of the family brokerage. His younger brother worked himself to death at forty-three, building the family's coal-mining operations. But I'm sure none of this ever crossed my grandmother's mind.

"Anybody else takin' care of your grandmother?"

"Yes. Paul takes care of the inside. But there's another guy, Red, who takes care of the outside. They call him Red because of his red hair. His real name is Anthony, like your uncle Tony. Red Anthony Costello. Came over from Ireland."

"Ireland? With a name like that?"

"Black Irish. He's descended from survivors of a ship wrecked off the coast of Ireland when the Spanish were trying to invade England."

"So how come his hair ain't black?"

"It happened a long time ago. In the meantime, my grand-mother's sister has a guy called Green."

"Green?" He chuckles. "You people...very colorful. Red and Green. You got any pets?"

"Just a dog. We call him Awful."

"That's his name?"

"A terrible dog. He barks and bites. The other day, I caught him trying to kill a puppy. I kicked him eight feet, but he came right back and tore a hole in my pants."

Dom almost spits out a mouthful of beer. "I was you, I'd shoot the dog!"

DEATH ON WHEELS

Mike and I wound up roommates in college in our freshman year. It was supposed to be one of the best years ever, the start of a whole new adventure. But it ended up being the saddest year of my life.

Mike saved my life that awful night of shattered glass in New York. But I will always live with the knowledge that I am responsible for his death.

I'm still racked by terrible, wrenching guilt—because if it hadn't been for me, if I hadn't let him down, he'd still be alive.

Mike, my loyal buddy, my best friend. Big Mike, who came to the fraternity party in *my* car, lying there soaking wet in two inches of beer on the basement floor. Laughing to himself, too drunk to talk, just a huge baby flopping around and happy as a mud guppy in a swamp.

"Mike!" I'm shouting. "Mike! Get up! Get up! I'm leaving! It's two a.m.! I'm *leaving! You gotta get up!*"

Mike, shaking his head, giving me the stupid grin, refusing to budge. I try to pull him off the floor, but he's too big, too heavy, too drunk. Somebody else tries to help, but it's no use.

"Okay, I'm leaving," I shout, way out of patience. "I'm leaving now. You're on your own!"

Next morning a voice is shaking me and hollering, "Wake up! Wake up!" and I open my eyes. It's another friend. His eyes are red and swollen. Something is terribly wrong.

"Mike..." he says, "Mike..." But he can't finish the words.

I jump out of the bed, heart in freefall because I know, I know, and I'm on my feet, shouting, "What? Tell me. What is it?" But now he's starting to break down and cry.

"Is Mike...oh no! Oh *no!*" My voice is breaking into pieces. I don't recognize it.

He can't look at me, and I feel my knees go weak.

Mike, who always had my back. My closest friend, and now... he's dead. *Because I didn't have his back.* I'm sick with grief and stabbing remorse, and I puke even before I get to the bathroom.

The details, I learn, are even more horrible than I could have imagined. Just before dawn, somehow Mike drags himself off the floor and gets the only ride available, on the back of a mutual friend's motorcycle. They crash at high speed into a row of parked cars. Mike is hurled through the air like a mannequin. Witnesses say bones are sticking out of his arms and legs, right through his clothes. But he's so strong and still so drunk, he manages to achieve the impossible in his last moments on earth, pulling himself almost to a standing position before his body finally fails and he collapses into a pool of blood.

I'll never get over his death and the bitter knowledge that I could have prevented it. Against all odds, and in a most unexpected way, the unthinkable actually happened. To my best friend. And now I know it could happen to me.

BREAKAWAY

The fall semester after Mike's death, I have a talk with my father. "What did you say?" he asks, looking up from his paperwork and lowering his specs. "Run that by me again?"

"I said I've decided to quit college."

He gives me a long look.

This isn't going to go well.

"Just like that? You want to drop everything and quit college? Do you know what you're saying?"

"I need to get away, Dad. I need to know what else is out there. This is not my life…I don't think it'll ever be my life."

He stares at me.

"Sit down," he says. "We need to talk."

He studies my face, trying to get a good read.

I'd rather stand, but I ease myself into one of his big leather armchairs.

"Now," he says, his eyes dark with disapproval but struggling to keep it civil, "since this is the first I've heard of this, maybe we should start at the beginning?"

"I've been thinking about this for a long time, since before college."

"Thinking about what?"

I don't want to talk about Mike. I don't think he'd understand the depth of my guilt and sense of loss. But I do want to live life. I want to get out before it's too late.

"Thinking about my life here, thinking about Philadelphia. Thinking about what I want to do with my life."

"And...?"

"I feel like I'm suffocating. The only thing that anybody here is interested in is Philadelphia. Which is the last thing that interests me—"

He interrupts.

"You actually think quitting college at one of the most important moments in your life is going to make everything better or change Philadelphia? You realize how childish, how immature that sounds? Nothing could be so bad that you have to quit your education."

"My *formal* education," I correct him. "And it's just an interruption."

"Interruption? I don't care what you call it. You can wait until you finish college and then take a year off, like everybody else!"

"We're talking about three more years, Dad. By then my brain will turn to mush. I'll be just another stiff, thinking about cocktails and bridge, chased by a golf game. Can't you understand that?"

"Why would you expect me to understand that? You come in here raving about how you can't stand your life and you need to quit. You can't really expect me to understand that."

He stares at me for a moment. "What are you going to do to pay your bills? How will you live?"

"I'll support myself."

"Oh, really? How?"

"I have a plan. I'll be fine."

He glowers, contempt unmistakable.

"You have a good life here. Your family is here. Your friends are here. You're smart, a good athlete. You want for nothing. You live the good life.

"Your Mother and I have worked hard and planned carefully so you would have these things. Why in the world is that not good enough for you?"

"It's a question I've asked myself. And the answer is part of the reason I need to go. I don't want to live surrounded by the kind of people who live here. Marrying my second or third cousin and having a kid with a dick coming straight out of the side of his head."

I'm letting it all out.

"I don't want to dedicate my entire life to making money and socializing. I don't want to live in some kind of a delusional day-dream that I'm better than ninety-nine percent of the world—even though I've got absolutely nothing to show for it, except maybe privilege and wealth that I never earned for myself."

He's watching, listening, trying to take it in.

For a moment, he seems at a loss for words.

"Maybe you've noticed that almost everybody you know is an alcoholic?" I say.

He shifts in his chair.

"Maybe you've also noticed that your whole life revolves around clubs, parties, and games? Most of your friends don't work," I press on. "If that's what they call the good life, then maybe the good life is not for me."

Could that be a flicker of recognition I see? Did something click? But I also see anger building, or maybe frustration. Whatever it is, I wonder how much further I can go before he blows.

I don't have to wait long.

"Cut the crap! Where did all this foolishness come from? What do you know about life?"

He has no idea how to deal with this.

"That's the whole point, Dad. I don't know much, but I want to know everything—and if I stay here, I won't ever know anything!"

"Enough! What gives you the right to make these uninformed, juvenile judgments? I forbid you to quit school!"

Sudden heat flushes my face. I choke it down, force myself to keep cool. But I'm screaming inside.

I go straight at him. "You wasted your life. You sold out. You think I don't know? You could have been somebody, but you're still just a hack copywriter. Admit it! You missed your shot—well, I'm not going to miss mine!"

There, I've played my trump card.

I know I should put a lid on it, but I can't stop.

"Who with any balls or ambition can stand this place?" I almost scream. "How can *you* freaking stand it?

Dead silence.

"Oh, how sharper than a serpent's tooth it is to have an ungrateful child!"

Then..."Do you know your Lear?"

A single fly, buzzing between us in the heavy air, is the only sound.

He's a learned man. I can never take that away from him. He deserves to be admired, and he is. But in this precise moment, something essential has changed between us, maybe forever.

I know I've trespassed into taboo territory. Too late now to worry if maybe I should have held my tongue. I've finally done it, and now I can only wait for the verdict.

Here it comes.

"Get out!" he commands, pointing to the door. "*Get out!*"

Exit ungrateful child.

MRS. SYMONETTE'S

E ven before the screen door closes, I have a frightening sense
I'm not alone in the dark. I crack open the refrigerator door
enough to let cold neon light spill into the kitchen, and when I
look over my shoulder, I see the room is actually full of people.
They sit silent in straight-back chairs against the walls, motionless
and apparently awake. An older woman, wearing only a bra, stares
at me with vacant, uncomprehending eyes. The guy next to her is
catching flies out of the air, or maybe conducting a symphony in
his mind. A slack-mouthed mulatto lady in ratty dreads scratches
her knees. Her lips move silently as if she were in the middle of an
intensely private conversation with herself. A man in the corner is
nodding back and forth like a rabbi in prayer. Every time he comes
upright, a rivulet of drool slides out of the corner of his mouth.

It's just another airless tropical night at Mrs. Symonette's rooming house, a swayback, island frame cottage with floors that tip
off at odd angles, making nighttime navigation sometimes precari-
ous. Air conditioning is not on the list of amenities. Choking heat
is everywhere, a suffocating blanket over darkened streets.

In Mrs. Symonette's kitchen at midnight, the zombies, dripping sweat, have gathered to await the dawn. I'm soon to discover that my good landlady has opened her home to inbred relatives from the outer islands who need help. The original Symonettes were Loyalists who fled America during the Revolution. The diaspora did not go well. Today, most of the family line has been reduced to mutants and morons. It's so bad that the issue has assumed critical mass, demanding urgent intervention. So, Mrs. Symonette, a hard-bitten, weathered island woman who nevertheless appears fit and altogether within her faculties, has stepped up to the plate. And now some of the worst cases reside right here in her kitchen because no guest beds are available anywhere in the house.

Even with the zombies, for thirty bucks a week, Mrs. Symonette's is exactly what I'm looking for.

Gordo, an old friend from my early school days, is with me. He's no Mike, but he's okay. To put a roof over our heads, I draw pictures in cafés and rum dives. Maybe someday I'll be a real artist. But the only skill I need now is the ability to cadge tourists and sketch plain pencil portraits in less than ten minutes.

Since my arrival a month ago, I've made arrangements with some of the hottest local nightclubs, including the Junkanoo, the Black Cat, and the tonier Confidential Club, which is not far from the old casino. They provide free working space and booze at the bar. In return, I kick back some of the picture profits. Not much, but it's not a bad deal.

Gordo's job is to help drum up business—mostly from single female American tourists well into their rum punches—while I stay busy sipping rum and Cokes deep into the night, drawing one picture after another, at ten bucks a pop. Happily, the Calypso music is loud, the rum abundant and inexpensive, and the light not so good, so nobody seems to notice that as the evening goes on, the quality of the drawings goes down.

Sometimes, I pretend to be a local island white, accent and all. Some ladies seem to find the "Conky Joe" island-guy persona intriguing. Which of course leads to some very late nights.

It's not until almost dawn after a long night at the Junkanoo that I stagger back to Mrs. Symonette's and discover the zombies in the kitchen.

Near collapse, in want of sleep, I grope my way up to my room to find my bed.

I'm about to throw myself on the sheets when something stirs in the near darkness.

"Who dat? Who dat?" a startled voice breaks the silence. I jump back.

"Who are *you?*" I reply. "You are in my bed. This is *my* room."

"My name is Captain Adderley," the man says, sitting up. "An' what you doin' on my boat?"

"This is not a boat, Mr. Adderley," I say. "This is Mrs. Symonette's rooming house."

"You talkin' crazy, mon," Mr. Adderley admonishes. "I be de captain o' dis boat, mon. I know ma' own boat, mon, and you be *trespassin'!*"

Which makes me think it might be time to move.

At that moment Gordo steps into the room.

"We gotta get outta of this dump, man," he says. "Somebody took a crap in my dresser drawer."

85

HOUSE OF LOVE

Our new residence is way, way over the hill in a part of town I would not want to call home for long. But space is at a premium for the budget prices we are willing to pay. So we take rooms in the best we can find—a pink house that looks nice enough on a sandy lane with some flowers out front. Never mind that a few of the windows are broken.

My room has just enough space for a single bed. There's a shared bathroom down the hall. It's been a long night and a hard day, so I turn in early, lock the door, and I'm out like a light.

The next thing I know, there's a loud crash. I wake to find that somebody just punched a hole right through my bedroom door. People are shouting in the hall. Footsteps are running up and down the corridor, doors opening and closing, giggles, shouts, and laughs, the voices of many women.

Then I hear heavy breathing. When I finally get up the nerve to open the door and see what's going on, it's chaos in the hall. Pretty black women are coming in and out of the rooms and one of them clasps her hand between my legs, pushes me back, closes the door, and asks me if I want to party.

"This whole house is a party," I say. And suddenly it dawns on me that this whole house is a whorehouse.

She shows me her breasts.

"I be talkin' private party, baby mon," she says. "You like what you see?"

I do like what I see, but I know enough not to jump into the sack with this lady.

She's waiting for an answer.

"Oh, yeah," I say, then quickly add, "but what happened to my door? Why was somebody trying to break into my room?"

"Dat mon tink his girlfriend in here wid another mon," she says. "But she be down de hall wid his son."

"His son?" I say.

"Mmmm hmmmm," she purrs. "Now dey both be in the room wid dat same girl."

"Both?" I say, genuinely incredulous. "How does that work?"

She's not interested, doesn't care, and she has no time to educate me.

"How much money you got, baby mon?" she says.

"Not enough for a party," I lie.

In the room next door, the bedstead is banging against the wall, and there's a lot of grunting.

"How much you want to spend?" she asks.

The place is hopping. Time is precious, and she's losing patience.

"I gotta get some sleep," I say lamely.

She can see she's wasting her time, gives me a look, then disappears, closing the door behind her, leaving me staring through the gaping fist hole.

Even with my head buried under the pillow, it's another long night. The bedstead in the room next door never stops banging on the wall.

Sometime around dawn Gordo shouts through the gap in the door that he's had enough and we're going to Princess House.

JUNKANOO

Princess House is Gordo's family's island getaway. Our refuge of last resort, a place to fall back on if all else fails. It sits just below Government House on a hill overlooking the town, baby pink, stately, and historic, a grand old tropical mansion from the days of colonial rule. Reminds me of an island version of my parents' house in Philadelphia.

The night after our move, we show up for work at the Junkanoo to find the place is packed with tourists who've come to see the weekly limbo extravaganza, complete with drums, torches, wild Calypso music, and plenty of dark local rum. The limbo lady, Jama, star of the show, invites people in the audience to try their hand (and feet) at limboing under the bar.

To demonstrate how it's done, several extremely fit black guys with zero body fat in tight-fitting red Speedos slither like lizards under the bar, just eight inches off the floor. Jama narrates their progress, noting how the toes help inch the body slowly under the bar and how the legs and stomach muscles help get you back up off the ground after you've cleared the bar.

The audience is cheeseburger-fed and paunchy and in no way resembles the zero-fat professional island dancers. But that's no obstacle because the rum is flowing freely, and some of these ladies and gents feel so good, they fall into in a loose conga line and follow each other under the limbo bar. It starts at five feet off the ground.

No problem.

At three feet, the pork chops are throwing in the towel and getting back to serious drinking. Some island folks from the bar are now taking up the challenge, and a few young local men make it all the way down to two feet. One of them slips under the one-foot mark, and now the bar is down to ten inches. The whole place is hooting and shouting.

And it is *hot.*

One guy takes off his shirt and pants, and wearing only skivvies to give him flexibility, shimmies under the ten-inch mark.

Applause. Whistles, jeers, and a lot of *ya, mon.*

Then Jama, with whom I have a friendly relationship, embarrasses me on a live mic.

"Who wants to try to top that?" she asks the crowd.

Jama, with the voodoo eyes, mahogany skin, the firehouse-red lipstick, tight dancer's body, and a pelvic thrust in the drum dance that would knock a monkey out of a tree. Jama, with her sly looks and occasional little pats on my ass.

Jama points her finger directly at me and calls me out.

"The Great White Hope!" she declares, playing with me, making me part of the show. "Come to me, baby. Show this black boy he ain' got nothin'!"

It's a sandbag.

The crowd starts clapping, and I know I can't just walk away.

I strip down to jockey shorts and try to remember the black guy's moves. Then the drums pick up, and torches are spinning. Now I'm flat on my back with my knees splayed like a frog, raising my upper body off the floor, trying to waggle my feet and toes to drag me ever so slowly under the impossibly low ten-inch bar.

Just when I think I'm not going to make it, pride kicks in. I somehow manage to wiggle through to the other side. When my head finally clears the bar, the muscles of my legs are screaming. I'm covered with sweat, and I need a little help getting up.

Jama grabs my hand and thrusts it over my head.

"The champ!" she declares. "The one and only white limbo champ!"

Then she puts her hand over the mic and whispers, like she's telling me a big secret, "There's a prize...a *nice* prize, you know..."

I happily accept accolades from the cheering, rum-soaked crowd before making my way back to my table near the real bar, where new customers are already lining up to have their sketches done.

Later, Gordo and I are the last ones to leave.

Jama's locking the gate behind us.

"Hey, baby," she says, turning and touching my arm. "I wan' talk some bidness wid you."

"Business?"

"Ya, mon. We got some bidness to discuss."

Gordo gives me a little salute. "See you back at the ranch," he says, and disappears into the darkness.

Jama steers me to her purple dune buggy. When we pull up to an empty beach, the full moon hangs silver over a sea of sparkling platinum. Palm fronds rustle in the breeze. I'm riveted by the magic of the night, marveling at the romantic beauty of it all.

We stand barefoot together in the sand.

"Nice place for a business meeting," I say, expecting Jama might jump me without delay. But I'm also thinking maybe I'll put the moves on her. She's alive with some kind of primal energy that's wrapping itself around me, pulling me to her like a tractor beam.

"Ever' time da moon be big, mon, I tink about it. And dat make me tink about bidness. You ever tink about da moon, Harry?"

The moon is mesmerizing, seductive.

The longer I stare, the bigger it seems to get. I can smell vanilla. It must be Jama. Even in the sultry air, I can feel her body heat.

I turn to look at her. There's humor in those eyes. But there's also hunger. I am stirring.

"You ever wonder what the moon made of, Harry?" she asks, her voice low, playful.

"The moon is made of dust and rocks."

She gives me a long, baffled look.

"Who tol' you dat?" she says, seemingly aghast at my ignorance.

"Nobody told me that. Everybody knows that."

"Harry, da moon be made of cheese."

I laugh out loud.

"Cheese, Jama? The moon is made of cheese? Only kids believe that. You're jerking me around."

She looks a little hurt.

"I be serious, Harry."

Okay, I'll play along and wait for her to stop clowning, but she just keeps looking at me.

"What kind of cheese?" I ask, hoping to set up her punch line.

"Swiss cheese!"

"Why Swiss cheese?"

She shakes her head. "Because you can see the holes! Harry, you a dumbass white boy. Only white boys don't know da moon made of cheese."

And now I can see it, the eyes laughing. Jama enjoying her little moment of fun before the main event.

Dumbass white boy.

"Okay, Jama," I say, cracking a grin. "You got me. We're here to argue about the moon and build sand castles, aren't we?"

"No, mon," she says, all bright eyes and perfect teeth. "Da bidness we need to talk about be monkey bidness."

I'm nodding in appreciation.

"You da white champ, Harry. And da champ win da prize. I'm da prize! You ever fuck an islan' girl, Harry?"

"Yes, I have. But not like you, Jama. You're going to be something special."

She smiles.

The full length of her steps closer, into my space, into my arms.

"Baby mon," she whispers, sweet breath on my lips, "you got no idea. I got something between my legs make a dead man come."

I'm hard as a chrome pipe.

"*Now* we talkin' badness! Ya, mon! We be talkin'..." she breathes, teasing, her voice thick with anticipation. "Harry, I tink you got something between *your* legs gonna make Jama come..."

She throws a blanket on the sand. We strip and collide in a passionate animal embrace that sends us sinking together to the sand. This *is* different. No phony protesting. No false words. Entwined in direct concert, we're humping into delirious abandon.

I'm astonished by her joyful enthusiasm. She wraps her legs around my pelvis and pulls her body up with each thrust. She locks on my intense gaze, her eyes alive with wild pleasure. It's way, way beyond the diffident debs back home, with their icy, unyielding bodies, worrying themselves sick about what might become of their reputations.

Too fast, we explode together in a jerking, groaning, altogether primitive orgasm unlike any I'd ever experienced.

Gasping, I roll on my back, slippery with our sweat, and stare in open-mouthed amazement at the moon.

Jama's not even breathing hard.

"Baby mon," she purrs, rolling up on her elbow, looking me straight in the eye. "You done restin'? Jama's ready to go again! Before we done, Jama's gonna milk ever' drop out you big bamboo."

CASINO

Our new arrangement on the third floor of Princess House provides perks and access to the good life not available to us when we were trying to rough it "over the hill" on our own.

Gordo's parents are down for the weekend. That's how we find ourselves socializing in the bar at the casino, where rich Wasps in black tie have come to gamble and chase women. I immediately recognize one of them, a particularly licentious fat cat, Thaddeus Whitlock, sole heir to a steel fortune. His son and I were high-school classmates. But the boozy dad has no idea who I am.

Gordo's parents, our sponsors in this cushy private club, have a quick martini, then head off for some serious gambling.

Gordo and I are too young to engage actively in all the fun—these people are more than twice our age—but we're are still having a pretty good time ourselves, drinking beer and checking out some of the fine-looking, apparently unaffiliated thirtyish women. Through a cloud of curling blue smoke, Mr. Whitlock is saying something to the stunner at his side.

His wife is nowhere to be seen, probably not even on the island.

The lady sucks on what looks like a pink candy cigarette in a long holder. She notices us, and I watch her lean in and whisper in his ear. He doesn't recognize me, but he turns and hands me a hundred-dollar chip, and another to Gordo.

"Why don't you boys go try your luck?"

When we come back about forty minutes later, we are seven hundred dollars richer in casino chips.

I hand them to Mr. Whitlock.

"Well now...what have we here?" He shakes the chips appreciatively in his cupped hands, then drops them into his jacket pocket.

"Well done, well done," he mumbles, and turns back to the woman. After a moment, he looks up. "What is it, boys?"

Finally, he says, "Ahhh, Of course, of course! Almost forgot!"

He reaches into a different pocket, pulls out a thick wad of cash, strips off a ten spot, and gives us five bucks each. In appreciation of our remarkable gambling skills.

He'll cash in the other $690 and pocket it.

Later, when he goes off to relieve himself, the stunner is staring at me. I'm tempted to try to get some purchase with this lovely lady while the fat cat's away. But before I can even make a move, she's leaning in, blowing smoke in my face and purring, "How would you boys like to have a ménage a trois?"

I'm about to respond with a resounding *yes!* when tightwad Whitlock returns. The pretty lady shoots me a "it would have been nice" glance and promptly resumes her attentive posture.

Close, but no cigar.

The next night the Junkanoo is thinning out, and I've set aside my drawing pad. A couple of the torch-dance girls are waving good-bye on their way out the door. Augustus, a local hustler, is chatting up a pretty blond American girl at the far end of the bar.

"So, did you make it with Jama?" Gordo says, pulling up a chair to my little table near the bar.

I'd been wondering when he'd ask.

"We had a nice time at the beach."

"What's that supposed to mean, 'We had a nice time at the beach'? Did you fuck her?"

"Gordo, Jama's a friend of mine. A friend of yours too. It's no big deal. And it's none of your business."

"Oh, I see, you righteous prick. If it's no big deal, why can't you tell me?"

"Because some things are private, and you're just curious about Jama."

He throws his hands up, exasperated.

"You never made it home last night," I say, hoping to change the subject. "So, you must have had a nice time yourself."

His face lights up.

"You wouldn't believe it."

"And…"

"Un-fucking-believable!" he hoots. "The girls on this island fuck like rabbits, Harry! Three of them last night. *Three!*"

I take a long look at Gordo.

"Sounds like you're the rabbit."

"I don't remember their names, and I don't give a shit if I ever see any of them again. But, man, can they fuck! It's like stealing candy from a baby."

"You don't have to steal, Gordo; they're happy to give. The girls you're talking about don't give a shit about you either. They do it because they like it and it feels good. Not like the girls we're used to back home. I guarantee you they don't give a flying fuck whether they ever see you again either."

"How old were you when you first got laid?" Gordo asks.

"Fourteen. How about you?"

"Thirteen. My father set it up. She was an older woman, a hooker."

95

"Really?" I say. "In Philadelphia?"

"No. He took me with him on a business trip. Maybe just to get me laid. Afterward, they took me to a bar and gave me a beer." He chuckles, remembering.

"I always thought your father was a typical, buttoned-down Philadelphia stiff, no disrespect. A no-surprises kind of guy."

"My father's full of surprises. Like the porn collection he keeps in a box under the bed."

"I wouldn't have guessed. Does your mother know?"

"She does now. When she confronted him with it, he gave her a smack."

"You don't like your father much, do you?"

He shakes his head. "No. And I don't think he likes women very much."

"Really? Maybe that's why you treat women like shit."

"Like shit?" he says, indignant. "I don't treat 'em like shit. I find 'em, feel 'em, fuck 'em, and forget 'em!"

"You make my case," I say. "You ever been in love?"

"Love? What the fuck does love have to do with it?"

"There's a difference between fucking and making love. It's a totally different thing. But you don't have to be *in love* to *make love*."

"Here we go again with the self-righteous bullshit. What do you know about it, Harry? You sound like some little old man."

I have to laugh.

"You're two months older than I am, don't forget!"

He gives me a pained look.

"Making love, as opposed to fucking," he mocks. "Why does it have to be so complicated?"

"It's not complicated, Gordo. It's simple. But if I have to explain it to you, there's no point."

Gordo is turning out to be a hopeless bonehead. But I'll play along.

"So...what was it like, being with a hooker the first time?" I ask.

"Pretty good. But I was so excited, I came before I could even get it in!"

I laugh lightly, remembering my own first experience.

It's not something I would ever tell Gordo. But I recall every detail of the night Mike and I hung out in my room swapping stories of our first grown-up sex.

THE DAY OF THE HUNTER

"I'll just drop you off," my mother says. "I don't want to speak to that man."

I nod and step out of the car.

"You be careful with that gun. Don't load it until you are out of the house, and keep the safety on until you use it."

I give her a long look.

"Mom," I say, and close the car door.

Uncle Bertie appears in the grand portico, drink in hand, grinning broadly. The car kicks up a little too much gravel on the way out, but Bertie seems not to notice. He's smiling like the Cheshire Cat.

"Come in, come in, my boy," he says, with an expansive wave of his arm, and ushers me inside. "Rabbits are everywhere," he says. "Can't grow a thing."

He removes a Remington .22 from the gun rack on the wall, locks and unlocks the breach, peers into the firing chamber, then hands me the rifle and a handful of long rounds from his jacket pocket.

"Little devils thick as thieves. Bruiser kills a couple every day, leaves them at the door for me, but they just multiply like—well, like rabbits!" He laughs a hucking sound, eyes wide, as if he had just seen a shooting star. "Rabbits!" he roars. "Get it?"

No wonder my mom doesn't much like him. When I don't respond, he frowns and asks, "Ever hear of Leporidae?" I shake my head. "That's the Latin name for rabbit. Also known as Lagomorpha. Domesticated in the New World from the Old World species *Orctolagus cuniculus.*"

He stares at me, grinning crazily, awaiting a reply. When none is forthcoming, he takes a slug of his Southern Comfort.

"Cuniculus! Get it? Sounds like a vagina to me!" he says, saluting the air with his glass.

I hear movement and turn to see his wife, Mrs. Hunter, standing in the doorway, wrapped in a gossamer kimono of some sort, taking a delicate sip from a glass filled with clear liquid. Vodka? Is everybody in this house on the sauce before lunchtime?

I can see outlines of her legs though the fabric. Breasts threaten to burst through deep cleavage. A dangerously exhilarating hot flush flares through my entire body, and I glance down at the rug.

"Rabbits and vaginas?" she says, and now I look up.

"They do seem to have something in common, don't they?" she adds, looking directly at me. Then, to her husband: "Uncle Bertie doesn't know much. But he does know about rabbits and vaginas. And little pussy cats too. Isn't that right, Berton?"

Uncle Bertie is very quiet, the big grin melting away, replaced by a tight, thin-lipped frown, the look of a man forced to hold his hand to the flame. I feel a tingle of electricity crawl up my legs straight out of the floor.

"I think I'll go down—" he blurts, but Mrs. Hunter interrupts.

"Do you know, Harry," she says, cocking her head toward me, "what a vagina is?"

My face is on fire.

Uncle Bertie tenses.

My heart is banging, and I wonder if they can hear it.

"I believe 'vagina' is also a Latin word, Berton. Is that not so?"

"Virginia, this boy is too young even for you," Uncle Bertie hisses, his voice almost unrecognizable.

"Yes, I know what a…vagina is," I say, turning to answer the question, staring right into her eyes, surprised at my own audacity. "I know about vaginas."

She eyes me with an assessing curiosity, as if I might suddenly erupt in flames.

"How old are you?" Mrs. Hunter asks after a long look, playful now, eyes filled with amusement.

"Fifteen," I lie.

"Ha!" she laughs. "Dear boy, I know how old you are. Your mother and I have been fast friends since we were little, and I've been watching you grow every year. You're only fourteen, but you look sixteen. You're very big for your age. Do you know that? Isn't that what all the girls tell you, that…you're big?" she teases, winking shamelessly.

"Virginia!" Uncle Bertie cuts in, his voice hoarse now, almost a growl. With the grin and the goofy chuckle evaporated, Uncle Bertie seems to have disappeared too.

The man's eyes are dark, menacing.

"Come with me," he commands.

As I follow him out of the house, glass in his hand, rifle cradled under his arm, Mrs. Hunter calls after us: "Be careful, Berton! Don't let that boy hurt himself!" And then, softly, to herself, as she sips from her glass and watches as we cross the terrace, "He's such a beautiful boy."

The Hunter garden, under an early-summer sky, is an exploding orgy of poppies, black-eyed Susans, baby's breath, roses, English daisies, lilies, delphiniums, and butterfly bushes, a riot of color the size of a football field.

Heady perfumes fill the air. I've never seen so many butterflies, nor heard so many furiously industrious bees. A blue jay scolds from a tree branch. A cardinal flits by, a streak of red. I close my eyes and breathe it all in. My heart slows, and now I'm as still as a pond inside, surrendering to an overwhelming sense of well-being, as if somehow I belong here.

Now I understand why I've come back to this house.

Or do I?

I tell myself I've come to bask once again in all this splendor and natural abundance.

But haven't I really come back for something else?

"You know the drill," says Uncle Bertie, grinning, back to his old self. "After you kill them, bring them up to the house, and I'll give them to the cook. I'll pay you a dollar for every one you bag."

I'm already calculating. Last year it was five dollars.

"I'm going into the city to see a lawyer, and I won't be back until the end of the day," Uncle Bertie adds. "If you are not here, I'll give the money to Mrs. Hunter, and she can give it to your mother."

"Yes, sir."

"Look sharp," Uncle Bert says. "And don't shoot any vaginas!"

He guffaws too loudly, slaps me too hard on the back, then strides back toward the house.

As I watch him walk away, I ask myself: Didn't I really come back for Mrs. Hunter?

Why did he say how long he would be gone?

I'm embraced by a supernatural quality of light that seems to radiate all around me. But in my mind, I'm drawn into the infinitely seductive, ever-so-languid eyes of Mrs. Hunter.

My meditation is shattered by sudden commotion.

A raptor suddenly swoops down out of the sky, plunging into a bed of flowers not twenty feet away. Unseen violence erupts, scalding the stillness. I listen to the sound of wings thrashing and a tiny voice, almost human, screeching in bottomless terror. I believe I can sense the frantic beating of this creature's anxious little heart.

Now in a single majestic motion, the great hawk rises on powerful thrusts of wings, wide like the wings of a dark angel. Talons clamp on the rabbit, which still kicks, no longer able to gain purchase with the ground. The hawk soars to the sky. The rabbit, silent now, looks to the earth, acceptance and resignation his only options. I wonder if he's marveling at the miracle of flight and the wonderful things he can see in the moments before he's torn to pieces.

Then, I'm aware of another disturbance. An olfactory ripple in the air. A sweet musk.

She is very near.

What is this strange ache? Is it hunger? Is it fear?

Am I predator or prey?

She is directly behind me now, just inches away.

"Now there's a real killer," she purrs. "But you don't look like a killer, Harry."

I turn, gaze with new boldness directly into her lidded eyes, black with knowing.

"You've been down here quite a while," she says. "I've been watching you from up there, the terrace."

I step back, feeling off balance, light-headed.

Mrs. Hunter is my mother's friend…and she is…old. She must be thirty-five years old. Lustful longing screams in every cell of my body. Still, I'm conflicted, confused.

"Are you afraid of me?" she asks.

Oh God. Yes, I am, I'm thinking. *I'm afraid of you, and this thing that you are doing to me.*

But I want it.

"No, I'm not afraid," I lie, unable now to hold her gaze, ashamed of myself for lowering my eyes.

She's stolen my power.

How did she do that?

"Look at me," she says, in a steady voice.

I hesitate, then force myself to meet her gaze and hold it. For a moment that seems never to end. I'm lost in the eyes, eyes like Little Egypt, the forbidden photo of the dancing girl I hide in my room.

"I don't bite," she says.

I feel the stirring and wonder if she can see it.

Now her hand lifts to my shoulder.

"Look at me," she says again, this time, very softly.

The garden is alive and watching.

"You know what I am doing, don't you?" she says.

I nod.

"What do you think? I can walk away now, and we can pretend I never came down to the garden and we never had this conversation," she says.

I feel almost naked with unbridled arousal.

But right now it doesn't seem to matter.

"I didn't know we were having a conversation," I tell her.

She smiles.

Sexual tension is so strong, I know there's no point in trying to conceal it or to stifle the outlaw passion that threatens to overrule reason and discretion.

Now she stares shamelessly at the painful evidence, unspoken signal of my desire. It's a long, appreciative look, a bold look that lingers behind her delicate smile.

"I'm going to go back up to the house now," she says after a moment. "Would you like to join me?"

There's no mistaking her meaning.

It's the voice of an angel calling me to glory, and I can't believe my good fortune.

Yes, yes, I would, of course I would, I'm thinking, trying desperately not to reveal the rush of colliding thoughts and childlike excitement boiling inside.

"I'm here for the rabbits," I manage finally, not sure if I hate myself more for clumsy uncertainty or because I have disappointed myself by betraying it.

For a black instant, I feel a sudden, sickening weakness.

"And what about Mr. Hunter?" I hear myself say.

"Mr. Hunter," she says, with quiet patience, "is in town hunting his own game. He's got a little pussy cat in an apartment. Do you get my meaning?"

"I understand," I say, too softly. But in fact, I am surprised by her candor.

"Do you mind if I speak directly?" Mrs. Hunter says, her tone more serious now.

I am on full alert, tense like the rabbits hiding in the garden.

"You are very young. But you have the body of a man," she says. "And I believe you think like a man. I am older than you. But I have the body of a girl, and I think like a woman half my age."

She steps closer. "Am I wrong?"

After a pause, I tell her, "You have a beautiful body." The words seem to come from someplace outside of me. I can't believe I'm talking to a friend of my mother.

"I want to be very honest with you, Harry," she says, her gaze steady, her voice almost matter-of-fact. "I rarely sleep with my husband. The sad thing is, we don't seem to like each other very much. I don't expect that we will be married very much longer. And I am lonely. There. Now I've said it."

She gives me a long, emphatic look.

I'm guessing she has done this before, and that makes me want her all the more.

"Follow me in five minutes. Take the stairs at the end of the hall on the left. I'll be at the far end of the house toward the pool, in the last bedroom on the right," she says, and walks away.

"If you change your mind, it's all right," she says over her shoulder, then disappears up the path.

Exactly five minutes later, I'm at the top of the stairs and on my way down the hall.

I open the door and walk in.

Blinds are drawn in the room.

"Mrs. Hunter?"

She steps out from the adjacent private bath. In the half light, I can see her gossamer kimono hanging open. I marvel at her full, so womanly breasts, resplendent in their nakedness, and the exquisite darkness between her legs.

For a moment I'm afraid to move, frozen like a child cradling a wondrous but fragile gift.

"Are you okay?" she asks.

The voice seems remote, almost unworldly, coming from a far place.

"Yes, I'm okay," I assure her, exhaling.

But I'm thinking it's all so fast, so unexpected. And what if Uncle Bert suddenly shows up and finds me here in this room with his wife?

Uncle Bert with all his guns.

"Close the door," I hear her say calmly.

She lets the robe fall to the floor and moves barefoot toward me, stopping by the end of the bed.

"Come here," she says, glancing down at the prominence that defines me. Now she's standing only inches away. I want to grab her, engulf her, hurl her onto the bed. But I wait, uncertain, trying to breathe evenly, curious to understand what comes next.

Her breath is maddeningly fragrant. Or is it her skin? She is a flower. Lavender?

She reminds me of hot winds in the garden.

She unbuttons my shirt.

"I'll do it," I insist, suddenly impatient, yanking the shirt off with a single motion and tossing it.

Now she's unbuckling my belt.

I touch the skin of her shoulders. It's amazingly warm, smooth as a child's.

My pants fall to the floor.

Breath coming faster now, deeper. Almost shaking, near bursting.

Lightning crackles in my groin as she touches me, gripping lightly, fingers familiar with the ways of men.

I feel her breath. Her lips come close, then touch mine with the gentleness of petals opening to the sun. In an instant, the kiss goes intense, hard, tight, and gripping us both in a shared delirious passion, a spontaneous seizure.

Together now sliding, falling forever through a dream in slow motion onto the bed.

She gasps.

"Oh my," she whispers. "You are very anxious."

"Oh…God" is all I can manage.

"Be still," she says, almost breathless. "Be still…be still."

I roll on my back, staring at the ceiling.

"What do you want me to do?" I ask.

"You don't have to do anything."

Her lips run down my chest, past my navel.

I will always remember the next moment as an epiphany like no other—the instant I step out of the sandbox and into the world of men.

Almost impossibly, she seems to consume me whole.

But even before I'm fully aware of what's happening, I'm transported, convulsing, off the bed, and propelled, gasping, straight to the stars.

I imagine I'm dying, maybe already dead.

Consumed in unbearable light, I'm sure I can see the face of God. I hear a terrible groan, a jarring cry of pain and ecstasy, shocked to realize the sounds are mine.

She grasps the beast in her fist as if to strangle it, incredulous as the spume of hot life pulses pearls over her lovely hair and face.

"My…" she says. "Aren't you something!"

"I was afraid that might happen," she says, wiping her eyes but smiling.

""Premature…such a terrible waste."

VOODOO

If Mrs. Hunter was goddess, teacher, seducer, and corruptor, handily snatching my virginity at an early age, Jama was sorceress and sexual mentor, an otherworldly sylph who patrolled the indistinct borders between earthly delights and the mysteries of the great beyond.

One night as we watch the celebrated torch dance, an orgy of blazing pyrotechnics erupting in whirling wheels of flame, she leans in above the urgent rhythm of the drums and tells me how important fire is in island life.

And death.

And voodoo.

"Voodoo?" I ask, surprised.

"You know about voodoo, Harry?"

"No."

"I'll tell you a little secret," she says, moving closer, "sumtin you don' know, baby mon. My gra'mama and mama, dey both be voodoo priestesses, dey both mambo, maman. And I am too."

"You're a voodoo priestess?"

She nods.

Jama, a voodoo priestess?

With a sing-song voice, I ask her, "Voodoo girl, tell me true, what do a voodoo priestess do?"

Instead of laughing, her eyes narrow, and she stares directly into me.

I feel a strange sense of unease.

"Don't be jokin', Harry!" she says, slowly, an edge in her voice. "Voodoo be our religion."

I have no doubt she's dead serious.

"So…why are you telling me this?"

Her eyes soften.

"Because I like you, Harry," she says, touching my arm.

I'm taken aback by this profoundly personal show of trust.

"You a different kinda white mon. I wanna show you my worl'," she says. "I wanna show you tings you never see in de white mon worl'. Wonderful tings. Magic an' miracles."

"Miracles? Like zombies?"

"Ya, mon."

I feel like I'm looking at a different person.

"This is kind of unexpected, Jama," I say after a moment. "And it sounds kind of scary. I never met a voodoo priestess before…"

She laughs.

"You got nuttin' to fear, baby mon. Nobody gonna put a hex on Harry."

She looks at me playfully, patting my arm again reassuringly.

"Tink about it. Let me know," she says, turning away.

"I've already thought about it," I say, grabbing her hand. "I want to know your world."

Skeletal fingers of desiccated scrub scrape the purple dune buggy as we bang our way down a rutted island road. Headlights probe ahead into darkness until the trail narrows and sand grabs at the wheels. Finally, the bush swallows us whole, and we jar to a stop.

"Where the hell are we?" says Gordo from the cramped seat behind me. He's nursing yet another beer, disoriented by the bumpy ride.

"Dis be d'end," Jama says, jerking back on the parking brake. "We walk now."

Jama's flashlight leads us along a winding footpath. Thorns rake at our clothes and scratch our bare skin.

"Fuck!" Gordo says. "That hurts. How far is it to this shithole?"

Jama turns on him, practically knocking me over, and jams the flashlight into Gordo's face, blinding him.

"Fuck!" he screams.

"*Shut* you mouth, dumbass! You in *my* worl'. You show some *respec'!*"

We fall into line again, Gordo in the rear.

I knew it was a bad idea to bring him.

"You stupid asshole!" I mutter over my shoulder. "You almost screwed up the whole thing. Just watch and listen."

Even before we spot the distant glow, we smell the sweet tang of burning pine wood. It's a big fire, because we see sparks spiraling into the night sky. Soon we hear ominous sounds like distant artillery, pounding nonstop. After a moment, we realize we're hearing drums. Big drums, little drums, beating faster and faster, building to a frenzy. Wild rhythms assaulting us in the dark.

Gordo freezes.

"What the fuck is that?" he whispers, as if the darkness in this place has ears.

Beneath our feet the earth vibrates. In my mind, I see a dark beast of a thousand legs, a giant millipede dancing, jerking, rolling, leaping around a towering bonfire. We're deep in the bush, far from the nearest village. I'm frightened, torn between my rational mind and the frisson of black magic in the laden air around us.

"What is this crazy shit?" Gordo blurts.

Full in his face, I grab his shoulders.

"Look," I say through my teeth, "we're guests here, not tourists. For Jama, this place is sacred."

He says nothing.

"You can stay or go back. But, if you stay, keep your mouth shut."

"Or Jama will put some bad mojo on my dick and make it fall off, right, Jama?" he says, too loud, making sure she hears him. "Hey, isn't that right, Jama?"

"No, Gordo," she says, turning, her voice measured and full of menace. "I might cast a vodun spell on you, and you will die."

Gordo mocks her, waggling his fingers in the air, like a child pretending to be a ghost. But I can tell it's all bravado. He's nervous as a rat in a snake pit.

"Oooooooo! I'm *sooooooo* scared!" he coos.

"Booga wooga cowabunga!"

The drumbeat seems to have picked up.

Jama's eyes, hypnotic, immobilize Gordo in a malevolent glare. Behind her, flames are flaring and drums are pounding. He goes limp but remains standing, with the vacant look of a man who's just been shot through the heart.

He sinks to his knees.

I look at Jama. "What...?"

But she brushes right past us and marches back down the trail without a word.

It takes a couple of minutes for Gordo to come to his senses.

"What the *fuck* was that?" he mutters, standing and staggering like a drunk.

"Now you've done it, buddy." I turn him around and steer him back down the trail.

I'm surprised to find Jama waiting for us. I pour Gordo into the back of the dune buggy and get in beside her.

"Dat de only voodoo you gonna see tonight, baby mon," she says. "But I ain' done wid dat jackass in de back seat."

⊨ ⊨

A week later, Gordo steps out of his morning shower, cradling his crotch.

"Harry, look at this!" he shouts. "What's happening to me?"

Looking down, I am not sure what he's talking about.

"My dick, Harry. My dick is getting *smaller!*"

"No, Gordo. It is not."

He's really scared.

"I'm telling you, it is."

Could it be?

"I thought it was," he says. "With that Canadian girl I've been dating."

"Did she tell you it was getting smaller?"

"She played with it, and then she gave it a name."

"Well, that doesn't mean it was smaller. Could have been just a term of endearment. What did she call it?"

"She called it Gherkin."

But that isn't the end of it. By the following week, the mystery of Gordo's shrinking dick deepens into a full-blown crisis, and he's panicking.

"Harry, this is really serious."

One look, and I can see he's got a point. In fact, there's not much left to talk about.

"Harry, did Jama put a hex on me?"

"No. Of course not. There's got to be a natural explanation. You don't believe that crap, do you?"

"You can say that, but it isn't your dick that's disappearing!"

Thank goodness.

"Well," he says, thinking back to that bizarre night, "she was seriously pissed."

"Can you blame her? You insulted her. You were a total douchebag, Gordo—and you know it! Can you blame her for trying to give you your comeuppance?"

"Hell, yes, I can blame her!"

"Okay fine," I say, "but what do you want to do?"

"There's only one thing to do. Somebody's got to talk to her."

"So, talk to her. This isn't my problem."

"I can't talk to her!" Gordo screams in my face.

"You expect me to take care of it?"

"Harry, I'm telling you I can't talk to her. She hates me. You've gotta talk to her. Please!"

"Jesus, Gordo, I don't know if she'll even talk to *me!*"

Gordo looks devastated. His eyes are pleading.

"Okay, Gordo, I'll try."

SALVATION

After the last show and the place has emptied out, I invite Jama to join me at my table by the bar.

"You wanna talk to me 'bout sumtin', baby mon?"

"Yes. It's about Gordo."

"What about Gordo?" She gives me an innocent stare. Jama isn't going to make this easy.

"Jama, did you put a hex on Gordo?"

"Why would I do that?"

"Come on! He was a shithead when you tried to show us voodoo."

"You know, Harry, voodoo be serious. Voodoo no joke."

"Yes, I can see that."

After a pause, she says, "So, how is he?"

"He's panicky. His dick looks like a shriveled mushroom. He's really scared."

"What do you want me to do?"

"Is it permanent? Can you fix it?""

"I don't know…that depends."

"Look, I know he can be an asshole. I'm mad at him too—"

"So?"

"But you can't make his dick disappear, Jama!"

"What you want me to do, Harry?"

"Jama, even the worst asshole in the world doesn't deserve to lose his dick. I think he's learned his lesson. I think maybe you should give him his dick back before it disappears entirely."

"You tink so?" she says. "I be doin' de whole worl' a favor, Harry, keepin' Gordo outa da gene pool."

"Jama, you don't mean that."

She looks at her purple nails.

"Jama, are you serious?"

She continues to study her nails.

"Jama…listen to me…you would never do such a thing. Would you?"

"Dot mon insult me, a mambo. An' my religion."

She's got her back to the bar, so maybe she doesn't notice Gordo, poking his head up.

"Gordo hidin' behind the bar, isn't he?" Jama asks, not turning around.

"How did you know?"

"Black magic, Harry."

"No, seriously. How did you know?"

"I can read your eyes, Harry."

"You can?"

"Your eyes tell me more than you know. When I look into your eyes, I can see your soul. When I look into Gordo's eyes, dey ain' nuttin' dere."

"Go away, Gordo," I say, dropping all pretense. "We're still talking."

Jama doesn't look at him.

"Jama!" he cries, flipping the gate on the bar and running over.

"Look at me! Jama, I'm sorry. I'll do anything! Please!"

Finally, she shifts her gaze and looks squarely at him.

"Gordo," she says, her voice calm, "you put de mal mo on me. You mock a mambo. An' you a white man! Lucky you still alive!"

She turns away.

"No, no, no, no, Jama, you don't understand…I'm sorry, I was wrong; I know that. I'll do anything. Please!" he begs, his voice cracking.

She gives me a sideways glance. I can see a hint of laughter in her eyes.

"Gordo…" Turning back, she gives him a fierce look. "Better to be alive wid no dick than dead wid a big one!"

"No. It's *not!*" he cries. "I'd rather be dead! I want my dick back! Give me my fucking dick back!"

"No mo' fuckin', Gordo," she says, keeping it cool. "You kin forget 'bout dat."

He sinks to his knees, eyes tearing.

"I beg you, Jama. Look at me! You're ruining my life!"

Jama takes another appreciative look at her purple nails.

"Harry, you seen dis disappearin' dick?"

"Yes. I've seen what's left."

"You know, sometime, even a mambo can' take back a hex," she says, her voice a little louder, making sure Gordo can hear every word but looking at me.

"What do you mean, 'can't take it back'?" Gordo practically chokes. "You *got to* take it back!"

Jama gives me a wink.

"Maybe…maybe dey *is* one ting I kin do," she says, speaking again directly to me, excluding Gordo from the conversation. "Maybe I call de girls…"

"Girls? What girls?" Gordo pipes up instantly. "I don't want any girls to see me like this!"

"Shut you flappy mouth, dumbass!" Jama snaps. "One mo' word an' you got an extra dick comin' out you haid!"

Gordo has never found himself under the thumb of any woman—much less a voodoo priestess—so I know this isn't easy for him. He sits down, uncharacteristically submissive, and stares straight ahead, accepting whatever ignominious black magic he has to endure.

He'll do whatever it takes to get his dick back.

When La Belle and Daquille, the top-billed flame dancers, show up moments later, I'm thrilled. Maybe now I'll get a peek behind the scenes to witness how Jama's voodoo, which hath taken away, can now restore to a penitent Gordo his most treasured asset.

But no dice.

"Harry, you can' be part o' dis," she says. "Dis jus' fo' de girls an' me."

"But, Jama…"

"No men, Harry. Sorry."

Gordo gives me a worried look.

"Don't worry, buddy. It sounds pretty good to me."

"But I can't *do* anything!"

"You ain' doin' nuttin', dumbass," Jama says. "We doin' sumptin' to *you*."

The girls are giggling, Jama flashing a sly smile.

"What are you going to do?" Gordo asks nervously.

"You keep talkin', I *never* gonna help you," Jama says, waving her finger in his face. Then pointing to his groin, she says, "Jama gonna feed dat baby mushroom to de fish."

Gordo stiffens.

"La Belle, take Mr. Dumbass out back," Jama says, pointing to the door. "You got the chicken?"

I think about following them into the night like a spy. Instead, heeding Jama's request, I pour myself a beer and sit alone at the bar, waiting.

Soon I hear a woman's voice shouting something that sounds like, "Jamboo jamoon jalala jambaya!"

The sounds of women laughing.

"Fuck!"

I recognize Gordo's voice. More laughter.

"Oh, no!"

Gordo again.

What could they be doing?

"Goombay mamoona jambaya nagana chulo!"

"Whoa! Whoa!" Gordo again. "Get that fuckin' chicken outta my face!"

Then silence.

Five minutes later, Gordo walks back in the door, ashen. The women, including Jama, have disappeared.

"What happened? What happened?" I say, putting down my beer and sliding off the stool.

But Gordo walks right by as if he doesn't even see me and heads for the front door.

"I can't talk about it," he mumbles, marching on.

"Why not?" I demand to know.

"Don't ask." He turns to face me. "She warned me that if I ever tell anyone, the curse will come back, and after that there's nothing I can do. She told me, once it's gone, it's gone. I could even wind up with a vagina! And let me tell you, after all this shit, I believe it."

"Okay—but do you think it worked?"

"Two days. She said I'll know in two days."

"You can't tell me anything—anything at all?"

"No. But I can tell you this much. Whatever it was happened out there tonight scared the living shit out of me."

Two days later, I wake up to the sound of exuberant whooping, followed by Gordo bursting into my room swinging his fully resuscitated pecker back and forth like a machine gun.

"Rat tat tat tat tat tat tat tat tat, motherfucker!" he hollers. "I'm back in business!"

POOL HALL

We come close to serious trouble one night after work when we stop by a nearby billiards bar with peeling green walls, two green felt-top tables, and a flickering neon light. A couple dozen local guys are drinking beer and shooting pool. The moment we walk in, the conversation ceases, which gives us pause, but doesn't prevent us from going to the bar to have a beer ourselves. It doesn't escape our attention that we're the only two white guys in the place. Nobody's saying a word. Not a smile in the room. The whites of the eyes of a few of the guys are blood red. They've been smoking the potent local ganja, or maybe worse.

We are not welcome.

And then commences a strange humming noise, like the sound you might expect from a swarm of killer bees.

Orchestrated from deep within the men's throats, it resonates around the room, rising into an ominous, ululating rhythm. Lips start to move. At first the words are incomprehensible, but then we can begin to make them out:

"Here…we…go…loop-de-loo…Here we go loop-de-lay…
Here we go loop-de-lie…All on a Saturday night."

Then again, louder: "Here we go loop-de-loo…Here we go…loop-de-lay…Here we go loop-de-lie…all on a Saturday…"

It's a familiar children's chant. I have no idea what it means. But in this place, it is not good. I assume it's code for *let's mess up these people*. Some of these guys are holding cue sticks across the palms of their hands like billy clubs.

I glance at Gordo. We sprint for the exit as the whole place explodes. Flying out the door like running backs, we take a couple of whacks as we plunge into the street.

We hear footfalls gaining on us. I'm surprised how fast you can run when you think somebody might be trying to kill you.

When we dare to slow down to look back, we're alone and alive in the light of a single street lamp, marveling at our cluelessness.

THE CONCH

On the way home, still shaken, we stop by another island bar, The Conch, slide into a booth, and order a pitcher of island brew. When it arrives with two glasses, Gordo downs his with one long chug. He puts the glass down and looks at me.

"What the *fuck* are we doing here?" As if the question had been on his mind since we set foot on the island and he finally got to say it out loud.

"I thought you knew why we are here," I say, taking a sip.

"Okay, so I must have forgotten. Tell me again?"

"We're here because we don't want to be in Philadelphia."

I finish my glass and reload.

"And don't forget—it was your idea to come here because you thought it would be cheap and your parents are here and we'd have something to fall back on. Like the fancy house on Government Hill, remember? But that's not why I'm here…"

He gives me a long look. "It's not? You don't like the nice warm weather? You don't like the island girls? You don't like all the free booze?"

I nod yes, yes, and yes. "I like that and all the rest. But the reason I'm here is I had to get out from the bullshit before it buried me alive. I felt like I was drowning in Philadelphia. This was the quickest way out. But it's just the beginning. I have to figure out what I want to do and how I want my life to be."

He frowns and finishes off his third glass. Adrenalin starts to slow down.

"You know," he says, "I thought we were here just to have fun and get laid—until we almost got our asses handed to us tonight. Where did those guys come from? I didn't know they had guys like that here."

"I guess they do."

"And you're comfortable with that? You're okay with the idea that a lot of people here obviously hate us?"

It's a good question. Am I?

I roll the whole tropical dropout thing over in my mind.

"Well, yeah, maybe this is turning out to be a little thin. But the main thing is we're not in Philadelphia."

"What's so bad about Philadelphia? Philadelphia has been good to us. What's not to like?"

I finish my glass and pour another.

"I think the question is, what *is* to like? Most of the people you know don't even bother to work for a living. But if you do work, then you'll probably wind up being a lawyer all your life, like your dad, or a banker like your grandfather. If you don't mind being bored for the rest of your life or dealing with parents who drink too much to try to forget they blew it—and that includes almost everybody you know—then Philly's for you. But I want to make something of my life. That's why I want to get out. Can't you see it?"

Gordo looks like he's seeing it but not sure he likes what he hears. Maybe he's seeing me for the first time.

"Wow! I had no idea you were so pissed off. That's some heavy shit…" He nods, slowly, letting it sink in. "How come you never told me any of this?"

"Why would I? It's not your problem, probably won't ever be. I'm as ready to have a good time as you are. But that doesn't mean I can't have a different reason for being here."

"So, you're not going back to Philadelphia?" he asks.

"Sure. I'll go back—to finish college. After that, I don't know. But I do know what I *don't* want. I don't want Philly. And I'm pretty sure I don't want this island life. I thought I'd work it out here, but this isn't the answer either. After here, I don't know, maybe Europe.

"Europe? Why Europe?"

"What kind of a stupid question is that?"

"I'm serious! Why would you want to leave Philly for Europe? You don't know anybody in Europe."

"That's the whole point, fuck head!"

"I don't get it. You don't know any girls in Europe. You stay in Philadelphia, you can get laid almost every night all summer long!"

He takes another long chug and puts the glass down with authority, as if to drive home the point.

"Do you know how dumb you sound, Gordo? After some of the local talent we've met here? The deb ladies just can't hack it against these girls. And look at Europe! Europe is *full* of great-looking women. You never heard of French girls? Swedish girls? Listen. It's beautiful. The food is fantastic. The history is amazing. It's where we all come from. I can't understand why you don't get it, why you don't seem to give a shit."

He points a finger at me.

"I don't understand why you *do* give a shit. Most of those people over there wipe their asses with newspapers! Most of them don't even speak English! And they hate Americans!"

I'm shaking my head.

"You are so fucked up. You sound like an ignorant douchebag."

"I don't care," he shoots back. "I know I'm right. I'm going to be sitting in Philadelphia surrounded by beautiful girls with trust funds, and you're going to be wiping your ass with a newspaper."

"Okay," I say, very patiently. "You can think like a Neanderthal and spend the rest of your life in Philadelphia, which is definitely likely. But on your deathbed, you're going to realize you made a big mistake."

There's a pause.

"And you think you've got it all figured out, huh, Harry? When you get bored hanging around all those foreign countries where you don't know anybody, then what?"

"After college? Maybe New York."

"New York?" he says, with sarcasm. "You think you can cut it in New York?"

"I won't know until I try. But I'll get a job."

"What makes you think so?"

"That's the difference between you and me, Gordo. I know I can, and I know you never will. Aren't you even curious? Don't you think it's great we're pretty much making it on our own down here? Don't you ever question anything about your life?"

Gordo frowns, his face twisted in distain.

"What the fuck is that supposed to mean?" he says. "What is there to question? I'm not worried about any of this shit—and you shouldn't be either! You think I was actually going to hang around and put up with all this island hokey-pokey? Not my style, buddy. I'm set for life. I'll never have to work."

"That's exactly what I'm talking about. But even if you did have to work, or someday decide to work, you'd never leave Philly. You'd get a job so dull you'd hate to go to the office. Two years of that and you'd be such a stiff you'd have to drink a bottle of booze every day just to get by. The bottom line, Gordo, is the only way out—is out."

Gordo empties his glass and stares at me.

"So, how did you get so smart?"

"Just thinking, Gordo, just thinking..."

Gordo raises his glass.

"Good luck with that, asshole," he says. "I salute you. But don't blame me if you wind up in jail or in the poorhouse."

STILLBORN

B ack at Princess House, Gordo, blissfully secure in his world
and untroubled, sleeps like a baby. But I'm wide awake, preoccupied with doubts and questions.

Where did our little adventure go wrong?

I've got my journal pad out and my flashlight on, but I don't
know what to write.

Then it comes to me.

It's more than the near miss tonight. The truth is that for all
its pleasures, the tropical island life just doesn't satisfy. Palm trees,
happy music, sunshine, sand, and warm turquoise seas are all welcome diversions, a tasty slice of life, but that can't be the answer to
what ails me.

What ails me is a thirst for a life of meaning, a life of purpose,
escape from ennui. I can't see myself hustling tourists forever. As
far as I'm concerned, this is a dead end, a nonstarter.

After I've logged that, I'm visited by a dark and unwelcome rec-
ollection of another stillborn event from long ago, a moment that
often comes back to remind me that nothing is certain.

The scene unfolds in my head, and I keep writing.

My father leads me to the stables to witness the birth of a foal.

It all comes back in a vivid rush: the sweet stink of fresh blood, the cloying reek of horse urine and wet hay. How the fluttering wick from the kerosene lantern casts a honeyed, earthy, almost biblical glow about the nesting stall. How the great laden mare gazes at the visitors with enormous moist mahogany eyes, sad, suspicious, but mostly skittish and uncomfortable, perhaps even in great pain, whinnying and swishing her head up and down in the hay, as if imploring the creature inside to come out and have done with it.

Most of all, I remember the mucous froth that bubbles around her lips and teeth, which flies off with every anxious snap of her head, sending the stuff into the darkness. Some of it collects like sea foam on the sinews of her fine amber neck. Sweat on her trembling flanks rises like steam into the lamplight.

The vet walks over and murmurs in low tones to my father. Try as I may, I can neither hear nor understand what they're saying. I can't take my eyes off the mare, who seems to have locked eyes with me. I imagine her imploring, desperate look is trying to tell me something.

I want to help her. But my father picks me up. I can see the foal, half out, slathered in glistening afterbirth slick as hot oil on a spoon, sliding laboriously and reluctantly into the hay, her ears too large for her head. Blood is everywhere, black as hot pitch, pooling out like a dark tide toward my father's boots.

Outside in the damp night, I can smell the dank leathery musk of mushrooms and wet moss. My father walks with me.

"Is the mare going to die?" I ask, alert to the dangers of the night. Somehow, I know.

"Yes."

"Why?"

"She has lost a lot of blood."

"Can't you save her?"

"I don't think so...Bunk is going to put her down."

Put her down? I don't know what that means. "Put her down where?" I ask.

"Bunk has to put her to sleep."

"When will she wake up?"

"She won't wake up."

Won't wake up? "Why?"

"She is dying. That's why Bunk is going to put her to sleep..."

I can sense my father is weary.

"But what about the baby?"

"Baby was born dead..."

We are halfway back to the house when the shot splits the night.

Even now, I feel my gut sink.

Dead at the starting line. Never even made it out of the barn.

GORDO

I look over. Gordo's snoring.

I'm beginning to see a side of him that worries me. And I'm wondering if our friendship may be finished. In the journal, I write about the night recently when Gordo tells me he can't make it to the Junkanoo. He says he's got a meeting, and I'm happy for him, because "meeting" is code for *hot date*.

But when he shows up later and pulls up a chair without a date, he seems strangely elated.

"No hot date?"

"Nope."

"So, why do you look so happy?"

"It's even better," he says, leaning closer.

"What's this, a secret?" I say, barely able to hear my own voice above the din in this corner of the bar. "What's better than a hot date?"

"Are you ready for this?" he says, looking around, in full James Bond mode.

"I'm waiting…"

"You're going to love this…"

"So, tell me, for Christ's sake!"

He's antsy, wired, loving whatever sense of intrigue is making him almost giddy.

"Okay, okay," he says, leaning in closer. "I met a guy who says he can make us a lot of money."

I lean back.

"Well, asshole, don't you want to hear about it?"

"Sure. I know this is going to be good."

"Yes, it is," Gordo says, rushing right back in. "And the best part is we don't have to do anything except carry a bag!"

"We?"

I don't even want to hear about it.

I already know it's just another wacky Gordo birdbath scheme.

Like when he had the brilliant idea of pimping for two of Jama's youngest and cutest dancers. Turns out they had a little side business of their own, mostly with horny American tourists, and were doing just fine without any help from us. Jama was skimming a little of the action for herself and would be none too happy to discover that her two off-island business associates were horning in. Happily, that caper never saw the light of day—nor the dark of night.

Or the time when Gordo bought a rusted-out Ford Falcon and tried to go into business as a tour guide. Never mind that he knew next to nothing about this island or any of the others and couldn't find his way around with radar. He put the car into an irrigation ditch with his first and only client, a young female teacher from Dayton, Ohio. The mishap broke the heap's undercarriage and the woman's nose, and that was the end of the tour-guide business.

Or my all-time favorite: when he tried to set himself up as a wholesale purveyor of ganja to the tourist trade and got busted in his first clandestine meeting by an undercover cop, who also happened to be in the business himself. Gordo would have wound up in jail—if only to take him out of the competition—had Jama not interceded with a blowjob so artfully administered the happy cop couldn't remember his own name.

"This is a new low—even for you," I say, shaking my head.

"New low? What are you talking about? This is a gift from God!"

"Gordo, listen to me. Sometimes I think you really are as dumb as you look."

"Oh, listen to this! Coming from the big genius!"

"Gordo, look at me," I say. "Haven't you learned anything in the last couple of months?"

He stares at me.

"May I ask you a question?" I continue. "Did you ask what was in the bag?"

"Why would I give a fuck?"

I take a slow breath.

"Well, for one thing, the guy wants to pay you to carry the bag, which means he's not willing to risk carrying the bag himself. Does that suggest anything to you?"

He looks like he's about to answer, but I cut him off. "So, has it occurred to you that maybe the contents of the bag in question are illegal drugs?"

"Hey, hey! Just relax!" Gordo interjects, with sudden gusto. "Take it easy! Sure, I understand that. But it's pretty cool, huh? Lots of intrigue? And this is a no-brainer. I get off the plane in Miami, walk straight to the men's room. Put the bag down, take a leak, and somebody picks up the bag and disappears—and that's it!"

He gives me a bright look, as if expecting me to wake up to the promise of great opportunity. Or at least a bit of edgy fun.

"I'm not worried! The guy's a nice guy. He says he's done it *dozens* of times himself! But he's tied up this month, and his other couriers can't do it this month either."

Yes, I'm thinking, because they're probably all in a Miami detention facility, facing trial or extradition.

"So, he's giving me a shot. A chance to score big. And you want to know the best part?" he goes on, almost gleeful. "We are talking serious money! The job pays two grand. *Two. Thousand. Dollars.* To do basically nothing! As I say, man. It's a *no-brainer!*"

"Gordo, you have no idea how right you are."

He doesn't get the irony. I take a long, disconsolate look at him.

"Gordo, listen," I say, trying a different tack. "You are rich. You don't need the money."

"Okay. You're right. I don't need the money. But money makes it real. What I really love is the covert action. I think that's what they call it. Covert? It's like being in a movie, only its real life. Real money. Don't you get that?"

I still can't believe it. But incredibly, he doesn't quit.

"And I don't appreciate your calling me dumb, Harry. You think I don't understand the risk?"

"Even a fifth grader could see that the risk in this crazy-ass idea is way beyond the reward," I stress. "And if you are doing it for some kind of delusional fantasy adventure, you're beyond dumb. I'd say brain-dead. Snap the fuck out of it! I can't believe you're not joking."

"The joke is how easy it is. The guy tells me *nobody* has ever been caught!"

"And you believe this crooked asshole?"

"He's still here, isn't he?"

"Jesus! Gordo! The guy's a fucking crook. He's lying. He *never* did it himself. He's taking you for a fool. And you would put your future in the hands of a dirtbag like that? Just so you can say— what?—that you did it?"

He sits back, assessing.

"You're way overreacting," he says.

"Gee, Gordo," I twist the knife, "I never knew you were the master criminal."

"There you go again, trying to make a big deal out of something routine, happens every day. I know, because I've talked to a couple of guys who did it."

"Friends of your asshole buddy?"

"No, just associates."

"And you believe them?" I ask. "Are you really serious about this shit? You think you may actually do this?"

"Maybe."

"American jails are bad enough. But have you seen an island jail, Gordo?"

"No. Have you?"

"Yes, in the newspapers. Hellholes. No light. No air. No hope. They lock you up and throw away the key. Unless they're paid millions in bribes, you can die in a jail here, Gordo. It makes Alcatraz look like a country club."

I pause, but he just stares at me.

Suddenly, it all adds up.

"Gordo...are you taking drugs? Is that what this is all about?"

He pulls himself up and his gaze narrows.

"That is very insulting," he says, with almost comic dignity.

If it didn't scare me so much, I'd laugh out loud.

"Are you on something now?" I ask.

"Jesus!" he says, looking away. "You are some self-righteous fuck!"

"No!" He turns back. "No! Okay? I'm not on drugs!"

He's practically shouting.

"You should hear yourself."

"Man, you worry too much! What happened to your sense of adventure?"

"My sense of adventure does not include doing jail time for international drug smuggling."

"Fine," he says. "Go ahead. Worry yourself sick over nothing. Your loss. We could have run two bags for a one-grand bonus. Five thousand dollars. Missed opportunity. What a fucking shame."

"Gordo," I say, as if I were talking to a child, "what do I have to do to persuade you that this could easily go very wrong and wind up being the biggest mistake of your life?"

He smirks—as if I'm the one who doesn't get it.

"People do this every day, man. Relax. It's all cool."

The new Gordo: island con man, hip operator. Gordo with the tropical shirt covered with orange parrots and the designer shades, about to star in his own movie.

"I hope I don't see you in jail, buddy."

When I write this, I wonder what will become of Gordo. I wonder too how it came to be that he was for a time a friend. On the threshold of adult life, not yet a man, I can see he's never going to grow up.

BEACH BUM

In pale predawn light, I close the journal. Gordo's still out cold, snorting now like a happy pig. In spite of my misgivings, I have to smile. It looks to be a good morning. Cool air spiced with tangy scents of salt and pinewood smoke from family breakfast fires waft into the room.

A rooster crows.

I get up and walk to the beach, dive into the sea, and surrender myself to a new day. Suffused with a sense of renewal and relief, done with Gordo, I float on my back, eyes closed, and savor the moment.

"Hey!" a voice calls out, interrupting my reverie. "Can you move a bit? You're right where I need to cast my line."

A bearded man with a bucket and tackle stands on the beach where sand meets sea, waving me to one side. He's as tan as a native, dressed only in a pair of well-worn khaki shorts. I make my way out of the water and watch as he casts expertly into shivering ripples that betray the presence of a school of small fish.

"Sorry to bother," he says, studying the movement on the water and deftly working the line. "But that's my breakfast, and I couldn't let opportunity pass me by."

Daybreak clears to the east, and early-morning shadows stripe the beach.

"American?" I ask.

"That's right," he says, reeling the line in and casting again.

"Live here?"

"I do," he says, playing the line with delicate little tugs. "Right here on this beach."

I look around. A hundred yards away, I can see a large beach house, canary yellow in the morning sun and surrounded by stately coconut palms, their crowns of fronds starting to sway gently in the first breaths of day.

"That's some house!" I say, impressed.

He glances over to see where I'm looking.

"The yellow one? Yeah, but that's not me. I live in a little camp right up there, smack on the beach."

I look around but see nothing.

A small grunt hits. He reels it in, puts it in the bucket of seawater, then catches two more in quick succession.

"That should do it. Would you care to come up and join me for breakfast?"

We walk up the beach to a tarp hung between two palm trees with a frond floor. I see a reed mat and blanket for bedding. Mosquito netting has been rolled up to the bottom of the tarp, and a small fire of driftwood is already burning quietly in a ring of coral rock.

"My ever-so-humble abode," the fisherman says, squatting down on the sand and starting to clean the fish. "Not much but all I've got."

"My name is Harry," I say.

We are about to shake hands, but he looks down at the fish slime and scales on his fingers and thinks better of it. He sets an iron skillet on the fire, slicked with half an inch of oil.

"You can call me Stony," he says. "My real name is Anthony, but everybody here calls me Stony."

After he finishes cleaning the grunts, he plunges the filets into the bucket of seawater, turns the pieces in a tin plate of salted cornmeal, and drops them into the hot oil. We watch in silence as the fish fries. A rising bouquet of sea and salt mixed with the frying fish stokes a ferocious appetite. I wonder if he can hear my stomach rumble.

I had no idea I was so hungry.

"Have a seat," he says, popping a piece of fish into his mouth. "I live pretty close to nature here. So, we'll have to eat with our fingers, if you don't mind."

I don't mind at all. In fact, as the first piece of succulent hot fish slides onto my tongue, I'm thinking this is very cool. Live right on the beach for nothing and eat free, fresh fish every day.

Talk about independence.

I could get used to this simple life.

"Amazing," I tell him. "never had fish this good."

For me, it's an epiphany. In just seconds, my new friend has whipped up an implausibly elegant meal that gives new meaning to "fresh."

He nods and smiles.

"One of the advantages of living right on the beach."

I'm tempted to ask about his life, but I resist, afraid to pry, thinking if he wants to tell me, he will.

So we eat in silence. Then he asks, "How long you been down here?

"Not long," I tell him, "and I may not be here much longer."

"Yeah, why is that?"

"Well, I'm between gigs and not sure what I will do next," I explain. "But I don't see much place for me here. I'm sort of conflicted about what to do."

He doesn't question me, but after a few moments, he says, "And I guess you're wondering what I'm doing here?"

"Yes," I nod. "I'd be interested to know."

He thinks for a moment. "Well," he says, "I do have a story to tell. But it's a cautionary tale for a young man like you."

He looks at me, taking my measure.

"I came down here about thirty years ago," he begins. "I thought I might like to be a writer. It was a dream I always had, even before college. Live on a tropical isle and write. Sounded to me like a great life, and it could have been. Maybe."

He pauses and squints at the ocean in the rising light.

"But I was very young, and as it turned out, very gullible," he adds. "Too many women and too much booze. Too many people on vacation and too many nonstop parties. Before I knew it, I was sucked into a life hardly conducive to serious writing."

He chews and swallows another chunk of fish.

"I started promising myself that I'd put all the distractions aside, knuckle down, get to work. Pictured myself as Hemingway, writing at his finca down in Cuba. But I was kidding myself, and it was all just a lie. Pretty soon I was telling myself I was okay, there was always tomorrow. But something always came up—I let it—and tomorrow never came."

He's warming to the story. Maybe he's relieved to be telling it. But I can see the sorrow in his eyes. I'm his only witness in this come-to-Jesus moment of confession and remorse. We both know he's talking to himself as well.

I'll tell his story and its lessons in my journal.

"I wanted to change, to pull out while I had a chance," he continues, "but I couldn't seem to help myself. I became addicted to the soft life down here. After a few years, I realized that nothing was ever going to change, and I resigned myself to a life without ambition, without stimulation, without motivations. Today people think of me as a colorful eccentric, but I know I'm really just a beach bum."

I want to say something, but what is there to say?

I'm thinking of the story of the frog in the cooking pot that never had a clue it was in deep trouble until the water, warming slowly, finally started to boil.

My mind races ahead, picturing myself here in this shelter, a bum on a beach, imperceptibly sinking, inch by inch, fatally succumbing to the easy life, the fresh fish, the freedom, and then one day tragically coming to the numbing awareness that I'd missed my shot.

A frog in boiling water. Just like Stony.

And Dad...?

I thank Stony for breakfast and head back to Princess House. Before I'm even halfway there, I've already planned my escape. I don't want to give my father the satisfaction of knowing my very first baby steps have faltered, so I'll fly back to Philadelphia under the radar and discuss my plans with my mother, who's never wanted for a sense of adventure.

The topical gig may have come to an end, I write in my journal. But that doesn't mean the experience was a waste of time. My father would see failure and probably be glad of it. But I feel mostly success. I learned things I needed to know. After all, I was never looking to live in the islands forever, was I? This life was never more than a stepping stone to see if I could manage on my own. And I passed. I supported myself. And Gordo too. The portraits were getting pretty good. Word was going around, business was good, and if I had a mind to, I could have kept that ball rolling indefinitely.

Maybe for years.

But to what purpose?

Now I'm putting step one behind, leaving on my own terms, looking ahead. I'll buy a motorcycle and safari all over the continent. I'll get money drawing pictures, just as I did in the islands.

I'll keep my journal as I go, see how that feels, with an eye toward maybe someday becoming a writer.

Like my father?

In the end, I'll know whether I'm good enough.

But for now, I'll avoid Dad, have a meeting with Mom. I'm hungry for her affirmation. But can I count on her to give me her blessing? It's been a while since we had a serious talk. The last time we spoke about my plans—it must have been after my sophomore year in Windermere—I was even thinking about a career in the military.

That idea started with Lulu.

LULU

"Oh, Harry!" my mother shouts, banging down the phone. She's already on her way out the door, waving me to follow. "Come on, let's take a ride out to the field. That was my old flying friend, Slim. He's been restoring Lulu, my old Waco biplane. I can't wait to see what she looks like!"

"Can we take the Empress?" I ask, catching up.

"You bet." She motions me to the right-hand driver's seat and throws me the keys to the Rolls.

I steer the ponderous 1950 Phantom, suffused with the scent of ancient leather, out of the garage and down the long drive.

The old girl's fat tires crush hungrily against groomed gravel, a happy sound that from an early age always signaled the start of a new adventure, no matter how small.

"The only thing better than riding a good horse is flying in an open cockpit," my mother announces, breaking the spell. "I used to drop rolls of toilet paper and spiral down, cutting them to pieces as I went."

I look at her.

"You did that?"

"Yes, I did. And barrel rolls and spins and loop-de-loops."

"Sounds dangerous and a little reckless to me."

"I suppose it was," she says, chuckling. "But that's why I did it!"

We laugh.

"It must be exciting," I say. "I'd like to learn to fly myself. In fact, I've been thinking about maybe going into the air force."

"What?" she looks at me closely. "How long have you been thinking about the military?"

"I didn't tell you because I'm only thinking."

"Why the air force?"

"I know a few guys who are talking about signing up. I don't know what else I want to do, so maybe it would be good for me. I'd love to fly jet fighters."

"Well, I can certainly understand that!" she says. "I would too!"

"I like the challenge, the speed, even the danger...I have to admit."

She laughs again.

"Well, you wouldn't be my boy if you didn't! But I thought you were thinking about writing? Or the arts? I don't think you're cut out for the military, Harry. Not as a career."

"It's tempting," I tell her. I can picture myself screaming in low and fast, launching rockets at tanks.

"Slim is an instructor. He can teach you to fly the Waco. Wait'll we see her!"

We turn into the airfield.

"I remember this place," I say. "You brought me here when I was little."

I can see a couple of shacks, a flagpole, and several small planes lined up along the grass strip.

"I'm not sure Dad would have approved."

"He would have forbidden it. There she is! There's Lulu!" She's really excited, pointing. "And there's Slim!"

An older man is waving.

"Slim!" Mom shouts, jumping out of the car. "She looks so beautiful."

The shiny sky-blue biplane crouches on the ground like a dragonfly drying its wings.

"You've done such a wonderful job, Slim," my mother says, giving him a tight embrace. "She looks just like new."

"Thank you."

"Slim, you remember my son, Harry?"

"Yes, I do," Slim says, shaking my hand and smiling. "You've grown up quite a bit."

We walk over to the plane. My mother runs her hand down the leading edge of the wooden propeller.

"I only wish your father had spent more time with me here. But he never had much interest," she says. "Too bad for him! Think of all the fun he missed!"

I touch the plane's glossy skin.

"Canvas."

"That's right," Slim says. "Canvas and wood and wires. But she's tough as a truck. Built for aerial acrobatics and stunt flying."

"My mother tells me you can teach me how to fly."

"Sure, I can."

I look at her.

She nods.

"When can we start?"

I took lessons with Slim all that summer. Plenty of thrills, but no license. It was just enough to show me I didn't want to fly for a living.

RARE BIRD

In my world, debutantes are expected to marry into the circle of social status and wealth and keep their households running conspicuously well. They don't work or seek professional excellence. Nor do they place much value on anything that smacks of the unfamiliar. But not my mother. Fun-loving, risk-taking, kindred spirit, Mom, a different kind of debutante.

In my journal, I describe a bird of a far more colorful plumage. She's just eighteen, sweeping into the institution-sized kitchen of her family's house at four o'clock in the morning, straight from a sparkling ball, bursting with life, her gown flowing behind her. Waltzes, flirtatious conversations, and laughter still echo in her mind. She snatches open the icebox and grabs strips of raw bacon from the larder shelf. She's so eager and impatient she doesn't bother to cook the meat, stuffing ribbons of succulent flesh into her mouth.

She races to the stables, face aglow with anticipation.

In seconds, she's astride her stallion, Gypsy, a flying fantasy of flowing silk-satin and organza on muscled ebony, galloping out of the barn, just as the first salmon streaks of light illuminate the edges of her world.

Alone, she strikes out across open fields, abandoning herself to the wild ride, soaring like the shadow of a cloud over fences, her delirious cries of joy lost in the rolling expanse of glittering emerald hills that seem to go on forever.

Until one day, Gypsy fails to clear a fence.

With health restored and horsemanship temporarily behind her, she turns to tennis. In no time, she's winning club championships. Her male friends don't take it kindly when she whips them consistently on the clay court at the edge of the open meadows beyond the swimming pool.

"There's another one down!" She laughs, throwing her racquet on the sofa in the drawing room. "He wouldn't even stay for iced tea."

I can hear the car roaring away on the gravel drive.

Another, in the midst of a mortifying drubbing, feigns a leg injury and quits before the match is over in a vain attempt to salvage whatever remains of his manly dignity.

"Much too fragile," my mother says. "Can't have that."

One day the club men's singles champ, fed up with all this unseemly nonsense, swaggers into the house and proposes a challenge match on her home court. She offers him an iced tea, and they sit down on the terrace.

"Do you think you can beat me?" my mother asks, bemused by the bravado.

"Of course I can beat you, my dear girl," he says condescendingly. "Why else would I be here? In fact, I am so sure of it. I have fifty dollars that says I'll win. What do you think of that?"

My mother pretends to think about it.

"No, Harold, I won't do it for that kind of money."

"Well, there you are," he says, quite pleased. "That tells me you are simply not up to the challenge."

She regards him patiently.

"What do you say we up the stakes to a hundred dollars?" she counters.

"What…did you say?" Harold sputters, sitting up straight and almost spilling his tea, trying to buy time while he figures out how to dodge this outlandish proposal without embarrassing himself.

"Well, don't you think a hundred dollars is a bit much for a friendly game?" he ventures, hoping for the best.

"No, I don't."

"But I…"

"Oh, shut up, Harold, and put your money where your mouth is," she says, grabbing her racquet and heading for the path. "Put down that glass and meet me out on the court."

After she beats him, she tells him to keep his money.

"Oh dear." She sighs, walking in the door one morning with yet another trophy under her arm. "Whatever am I going to do with all these things?"

When an invitation arrives from the American Wightman Cup Committee for my mother to come to Southern California to be trained for the US tennis team, she's overjoyed.

But her father, my grandfather, won't hear of it.

"I won't have you traipsing about in Southern California with freaks, fairies, degenerate dope fiends, Bohemian movie actors, and God knows what else," he scolds. "You've got to focus on your life here in Philadelphia, on who you are and what is expected of you. You have no business racing off on some wild goose chase when you should be thinking about your coming-out season and finding a suitable husband. Tennis—all sports, for that matter, for a girl your age—are a thoroughly unproductive and frivolous waste of time."

He forbids it.

My father forbade me too, but that didn't stop me. By contrast, my mother consented to her father's wishes. The price was all she held dear for herself. So, I can see how she might look at my new plan the same way her father looked at her, and how her husband looked at me.

In late-afternoon sun, we're standing on the terrace, gazing out over flowing fields undulating to the horizon in green waves. I can smell the horses.

We talk a little about my experiences so far in the islands, and then it's time to broach the new plan.

"Mom, I'm going to Europe."

Her eyes light up, but I can't tell if she's with me.

"Europe?" she says.

"Yes. The islands taught me I can take care of myself, and the next step is Europe. Dad wants me to wait until I'm done with college, but I've thought a lot about this, and I feel the need to go *now.* A really big need."

She looks at me.

"Tell me more."

"Well, I plan to buy a motorcycle in London. I can use my savings for that. Then I'll drive all over Europe and write about everything I see."

"Will you keep a journal?" she asks.

"I've already started one."

"How will you live?"

"I'll make money drawing pictures, like I've been doing."

She nods.

"Well, I like that idea," she says. "But I must say, Harry, it is very hard to do."

"We'll see how it goes."

"Oh, I think that would be a wonderful thing," she says. "I can see you writing. Did you know your father published two best sellers before he bought into the agency?"

Two best sellers? No, I did not know that. How could I grow up in the same house and not know that?

Just then, Orion, grandson of Mom's beloved Gypsy, ambles up to the pasture fence, and we walk out to greet him. My mother holds out her hand and pats his muzzle. Then he comes over to me and extends his neck so I can embrace him and press my head against him, as he knows I like to do.

"He loves you," Mom says.

"I love you too, big guy," I say, and let him go. He breaks into a gallop and charges off across the field toward the other horses.

Her eyes fill with radiant joy.

"Have you ever seen anything so beautiful, so wild and free?"

I watch Orion romping among the distant mares and realize that my mother is sending me a very special message.

Without a word, she steps over and puts her arms around me.

"You know, Mom," I tell her gently, remembering Mike's fate, "I'll be gone a long time, all the time on a motorcycle. If something happens...I mean, I might not...I might not see you again..."

She pulls back and looks me straight in the eye.

"And?"

Does she understand what I'm trying to say?

"Listen," she says, gripping my shoulders, "all of life is a risk. But an adventure without risk...life without risk...is perhaps no life at all."

She pauses, waiting for her words to sink in.

"Do you hear me?"

Yes, I do, my beautiful mom.

LONDON

My mother's blessing manifests as an invitation for me to be a guest for a couple of nights in the official residence of the US ambassador in London. I pick up my new Triumph TR6 on Lambeth Road, across the Thames, and fit myself out in a black surplus British commando field jacket with lots of pockets, leather gloves, boots, shades, and a white helmet. The field jacket is oilskin canvas, tough enough to keep the skin on my body if I go down. The jacket snaps at the neck to keep out the rain.

I don't know how the ambassador and his wife feel about me being there. But in my road gear, I feel like a street urchin at the opera.

Maybe the sooner I hit the road, the better.

But I wake up the first morning with a jackhammer toothache toward the back of my jaw that's sending stabbing pains through my entire skull.

My hostess immediately diagnoses an impacted wisdom tooth.

The family dentist can't be reached, and the pain's so extreme that she hands me an ice pack and sends me down the street to a government medical facility where they can take me immediately.

"All you have to do is walk in and get in line. They've got plenty of dentists. Never mind that many of them are dental students. But they do a ton of procedures. So they've got a lot of experience. And the best part," she says, clasping her hands together, "is that it won't cost a dime."

"Off you go," she says, and whisks me out the door.

Half an hour later, when I step into the great hall, I can't believe my eyes.

A surreal scene right out of the darkest of Dickens—hundreds of people in dental chairs crowding a cavernous, poorly lit chamber.

The air reeks of disinfectant.

Resonating through the gloom, an unearthly noise. Drills whirr into hundreds of teeth. It's a strange sound, a spontaneous chorus of lost souls sharing a miserable fate in medieval medical limbo. The only reason I don't bolt right back down the gloomy Victorian hall is the throbbing pain in my mouth.

My seat assignment is D-18.

When I finally settle in, the first thing I notice is a bent brass injection needle on the dental tray. Apparently it has been used all morning. The young doc wipes away a trace of blood from the needle, and the next thing I know, it's in my mouth. But the numbing does not go well. He tries over and over and I wind up getting stuck a dozen times.

Not what I had in mind for the start of my life-defining adventure.

I am led to a recovery room, where all fifty or sixty of us bleed shamelessly, and copiously, into big wads of gauze the size of diapers. An attendant is moving around with a rolling bucket, mopping fresh blood off the floor.

This is my introduction to England and my first—and only—experience with socialized medicine. The good news—as I keep reminding myself—is that my hostess was right. Everything is free.

I reckon I got what I paid for.

The next morning I'm on my way to France.

NORMANDY

My senses snap to attention even before I step into the Normandy market, an ancient covered chamber so vast it seems to go on forever. Inside, I suck in humid air, laden with competing aromas. Earthy accents of farms, wet hay, and plowed earth mingle with the smell of food, ripe cheeses, even undertones of iced fish on display at the other end of the market.

Living plants and banks of flowers, fresh cut and still damp with morning dew, explode in a rainbow of color. Honey, spice, lemon, lavender, rosemary, and cinnamon mingle in the air.

Never have I seen such a sea of fat lilac hydrangeas or such an abundance of royal lavender, running like purple landing strips the length of the market.

The whole region has awakened from the melting ice of late spring. It a welcome rebirth that draws devout pilgrims to this most venerated of rituals, the weekly market in early June.

Everywhere I look, complete strangers seem to be in a party mood, buzzing in and out of the market stalls, marveling, palpating produce, criticizing. Hands gesticulate, negotiating, arguing, haggling.

Two country women, baskets in hand, discuss the relative merits of a single carrot with the gravity of two diplomats locked in intense debate.

"Texture!" says one. "Feel the texture!"

"No, no, look at the color!" replies the other.

Even with my tentative command of French, I can understand what they are saying.

But I can't tell whether they like the carrot or not.

It hardly seems to matter, because finally they put the carrot back and walk away. The vendor rolls his eyes and shrugs, as only the French shrug, not once, but three times.

A voice to my left interrupts my reverie.

"Monsieur?"

I turn and look into the very bright blue eyes of a man with a weathered face and salt-and-pepper mustache.

"Excuse me," he says in French. "Are you American?"

"Yes. How did you know?"

"Ah, monsieur, everybody can tell an American. Nobody in Europe dresses like an American."

Everything I have on is British surplus, tough gear perfect for my purposes, but certainly not for your average American tourist. So, it must be something else. I'm about to ask him why he wants to know, but I don't have to.

"The Americans liberated this village in the war," he says. "I have always wanted to meet an American so I could say thank you, and today I finally can."

He smiles, holds out his hand, and grips mine.

"And you know," he says, giving me a closer look, "I must tell you that you remind me of my son. He's in the army now."

"Nice to meet you," I say, trying to imagine what it would be like to be in the French army.

"I would like you to be my guest at lunch," he says. "I know a nice place where the food is good."

He looks at me expectantly.

I give it a moment. But I can see he means it.

"All right," I say.

"My name is Henri," he says in English, and we shake hands again.

"I'm Harry."

I get to have lunch in a French restaurant I could probably never otherwise afford, nor find, and practice my French with an authentic local.

"Haree?" he repeats the name. "Sorry, Haree. I do not speak *anglais*."

I nod, not to worry.

"Okay, Haree. Let's go!"

The café is on a back street. We sit at one of two small tables out front.

A thin man in a clean white shirt and slim black tie comes to the table.

"Gilbert!" Henri says. "I want you to meet my new American friend, Monsieur Haree!"

"American?" Gilbert says. He reaches out and grabs my hand, holding it firmly in both of his. He won't let go. "I love Americans! Monsieur Haree. You save my country!"

"Thank you. I am happy for France. I've only read about the war. But I am a great fan of your country too."

He gives my hand one last pump and releases it.

"*Vive Amerique!*" he says, and calls for his wife to come out and meet the distinguished visitor.

An overfed peasant woman with pink cheeks, a bright red nose, and jolly eyes arrives at the table. She gives a tiny curtsy, wipes both hands on a kitchen towel tucked into her apron, and extends one to me.

I stand, though the thin man encourages me to stay seated.

"*Enchante*," I say.

I don't deserve all the attention, and it's making me self-conscious. So I try to keep it brief. With niceties behind us, Gilbert, the proprietor, happily gets down to business. He recommends today's special, the chicken with herbs, so I order that.

Henri orders the horse.

…Horse?

Cheval? Did he say cheval?

"Cheval?" I ask him, certain I had misunderstood.

"Yes, of course," he says. "Would you like to have the cheval?"

He can see I'm puzzled, uncertain.

"You don't like the horse?" he asks.

"No, no. I like the horse. I just don't eat the horse," I try to clarify. "But here, you eat the horse, right?"

"Oh yes," he says. "In France, the horse is a delicacy."

A delicacy?

"No. In America, I never heard of anyone eating a horse. Unless maybe they were starving to death."

He's clearly surprised.

"And my mother is what some people call a horse whisperer," I continue, only adding to his puzzlement.

"Whisper?"

"She has a gift. She talks to horses."

I let it go, adding only that she grew up with horses, and so did I, and it would be impossible for either of us ever to eat a horse.

"That is a shame," he says, obviously disappointed that his special guest is about to miss out on a rare treat. "The horse is really delicious. In France, everybody likes to eat the horse. In fact, this restaurant specializes in horse. I like it even better than the cow."

Gilbert returns with a carafe of purplish-red wine, which he announces is courtesy of the house.

Henri raises his glass, and I reach out to touch mine to his.

It's no doubt a local wine, just a house table wine. But the instant it's in my mouth, I can tell it's good. Considering my age and unsophisticated palate, that might not be saying much. But I've had some pretty nice ones. All those deb parties. Plus the leftovers I used to sneak after formal dinner parties of my well-traveled parents.

"This is excellent," I say. "Where does it come from?"

"Just one hectare over there." Henri gestures over his shoulder.

"Very good, yes? The family owns this restaurant and also the vines," he says. "A wine merchant from Paris wanted to buy the whole hectare. He offered a fortune, but the family was not interested."

Only in France.

The plates arrive with a nicely browned chicken covered with fresh herbs on mine, and on his, a grilled piece of nearly blackened meat that looks almost like a filet mignon.

"Bon appetite," Henri says, and pops the first bite of grilled rare horseflesh into his mouth.

"*Ah, mon Dieu!*" he sighs, closing his eyes in reverent appreciation. "*C'est delicieux!*"

After espresso, we compliment Gilbert and his beaming wife, take our leave, and walk through town.

"Would you like to see the rest of the market?" Henri asks.

Yes, I would, very much.

The morning crowds have thinned, but there's still action everywhere.

In the bustling fish section, fishmongers throw whole fish back and forth or hold them by the tail, like trophies. The most experienced customers survey the show but hold back, feigning disinterest. Then, just minutes before the market closes, they'll jump in to get the best price.

In huge display cases of crushed ice, sea bass, scallops, whole shrimp, crabs, halibut, sole, octopus, and assorted exotic marine creatures are presented as a great galleon sailing on a seaweed sea through islands of stacked clams and mussels.

We move deeper into the market through precincts of fresh green produce from local farms featuring cabbages the size of basketballs, incongruous tomatoes the color of pastel Easter eggs, stacks of kale, green beans, broccoli, celery, watercress, and spinach. Purple potatoes from Peru harvested now in French fields, pink squash the size of pullets, and bundles of carrots that were in the ground only yesterday, if not this very morning.

A mini jungle of impossibly fresh and colorful food.

On we go, past the spice and herb vendors, where the air's thick with intoxicating accents of thyme, basil, oregano, rosemary, sage, dill, coriander, tarragon, and chives, topped with sweeter layers of fenugreek, cinnamon, cloves, allspice, ginger, and cardamom.

Never have I smelled anything to compare to it.

Henri leads me further, past mountains of fine cheeses and farm-fresh eggs, past mouth-watering displays of fresh-baked breads and pastries, all the way back to the sprawling meat section with its galleries of splendid red flesh, enough to satisfy the appetites of ten thousand hearty eaters at a convention of carnivores.

Entire half-steer carcasses hang on the walls. Sausages, rabbits, ducks, geese, and huge hams are on display everywhere, like carnal Christmas bunting. Customers take numbers and wait patiently in line to place their orders. All the white-aproned butchers are busy, furiously slicing, dicing, and grinding, trying to keep up with demand.

It's clearly more meat than this village could devour in a year, so I know that this place must be something special and that food shoppers must be coming from miles around.

Finally, Henri stops at an unobtrusive-looking door at the very back of the meat emporium. The market has no refrigeration. So I am acutely aware of the cloying smell of slaughter that suddenly seems to shroud us as Henri pulls the door open.

"I want to show you something," he says, ushering me inside.

ABATTOIR

At first, I'm aware only of the smell of blood. But then I see the skinned horses' heads hanging on meat hooks suspended from the ceiling. Before I can even grasp the reality, my stomach sinks involuntarily, then rises frighteningly, and for an awful moment, I think I might vomit.

"You see?" Henri says. "This is different from America, no? They kill the horses in an abattoir just behind the market and bring them here for the butchers to prepare."

No words come.

Instead, I find myself spiraling in freefall back to a time and place of dreadful, suppressed memory. I feel utterly helpless. It's the stench that brings it all back.

Was it the stench?

Or was it my outright defiance of my father, who had made me swear never to go near that place? Or was it simply childlike curiosity on an idle summer afternoon when I was nine years old?

"Give me your word!" he had insisted. "Look me in the eye, and promise me you will never go there!"

I had given my solemn pledge.

Whatever the reason, despite the keening objections of my inner voices, I'm hopelessly attracted to this strange place of mystery, like a fly to a carcass.

I remember how gentle the day was. Cotton candy clouds. The delicious warmth of the sun. A chorus of cicadas crying out for love in the summer haze. The startled flight of a single quail in the meadow.

But just ahead, packed in stacks, moldering hides alive with blizzards of black flies fester in a nuclear furnace of sun.

A hot pillow of vile air stops me dead in my tracks.

I retch and retch again.

I want to bolt and run.

Instead, I push open the door and step into a kind of hell. Heat, darkness, bellowing animals, men's voices and laughter, the reek of blood, tobacco, and urine. Streaks of mote-filled light from small, high windows slash through shadowed space to reveal strange shapes moving.

Men are smiling through their amazing chores, whacking and cutting and telling stories. After a moment, I can see the Killer Man moving gracefully across the floor. A cigarette hangs from his loose mouth. One of the men is in the middle of telling a joke. Blood, skin, and fat fly through the gloom. The Killer Man climbs up on the soap box next to the chute where the animals come in, with his .22 rifle and a fine flashing blade like the curved sword of Ali Baba stuck in his leather belt.

Everybody is good natured, relaxed, genial.

"Hell, I wouldn't listen to him," the Killer Man is saying, balancing himself, aiming the rifle at the pig's head. "I wouldn't listen to him 'tall. I believe that man does not know how to tell the truth." The great hog, jammed tight, tries desperately to look around, protesting now with ear-piercing squeals that sound like a child's screams. The Killer Man squeezes off a round, the sound of a whip cracking, and the boar collapses dead as a rock with a bolt of lead administered expertly to the front of the cerebral cortex.

"Shit," the Killer Man mutters. "This animal does kick all right. Git holtun his head!" In a flash, the magnificent curved blade unleashes a shocking fan of blood that bursts from the exposed neck in an awesome splash.

"Whoa!" the Killer Man says. "Holt that hoof. Git aloft, there…" Both ears are sliced off, bloodless, like wedges of vanilla candy, and tossed into a black barrel standing in a tide of offal and entrails.

"Haul that chain there now!" the Killer Man commands.

In the upper chambers of the abattoir, dusty umber light seeps through a skylight, suspending steam and fat rising from rendering vats. Blue cigarette smoke ghosts the strange twilight. The chain, always moving, clatters like the anchor chain on a ship's prow.

"That man took to drinkin' in the morning. He did smell of it," the Killer Man says. "I had a feeling he would kill a man. He did have a wild look."

The great axes are swinging swiftly, chunking into soft flesh with violence as routine as the flies spinning aimlessly in the haze. Knives do even brisker work on the fresh meat, licking and plunging, malicious steel tongues separating carcasses into ever smaller pieces.

In another stall on the far side of the chamber, a steer, locked in the stocks, awaits its fate. In seconds, the steer is upside down hanging from the chain and swinging aloft toward the Killer Man.

I want to flee, but I can't seem to move, can't pull my eyes from the horror.

The Killer Man wipes his knife on his long leather apron, then sharpens it. Steel sings against the whetstone. The knife is sharp and wicked as a shard of razor glass.

Suddenly the Killer Man, shark eyes empty and black as obsidian, spots me. But to my great relief, he just shrugs and turns his attention back to the work at hand, drawing his knife in a tidy sweep across the next steer's neck.

Now the carcass swings high, as the head falls free in slow motion.

"Fellatio was it?" one man asks.

"It was fellatio," the Killer Man says. "Ida kilt him myself. Ida kilt her, too."

"Sure, that's right," one of the black men says.

The rhythm of The Killer Man sharpening his blade is hypnotic.

"Let's see," another man says. "That was Jerome Phail."

"Him and his brother both done her."

"That was him, all right."

In less than a minute, it's all over, and two massive sides of beef ride the high rail into a dark place.

The men are hard at it, comfortable with the work, stepping effortlessly over and under dismembered pieces, expert in their easy grace, moving their own hands and limbs dangerously close to each other's knives, secure in the knowledge that they are all safe.

"Git that water on the floor over here," The Killer Man says. "That'll do it. That's good."

Now the Killer Man is turning back in my direction, ever so slowly. I'm frozen, wishing I were invisible, hoping against hope that it will pass and he will ignore me again.

"Boy!" barks the Killer Man, his face a pocked mask of blood and sweat, shark eyes, now the eyes of a demon, bloodshot and wild. The Killer Man.

The knife, a glint of steel dripping crimson, stabs the gloom.

"Sir?" My voice quavers.

Oh God, don't kill me, please. Please.

"Git!"

Still paralyzed, I choke back a rising flume of panic.

"Git, boy! Git the hell outta here!"

Stumbling backward, heart slamming, I fall out the door, slapped senseless by the white-hot phosphorous glare, blinded for a moment, and never happier to be alive.

But then I'm drowned in shadow, the blazing sun eclipsed by the terrifying shape of a dark stranger who I realize is my father.

"Haree?"

Someone is calling.

"Haree!"

Henri has me by the arm, hustling me out of the nightmarish abattoir and back into the comforting familiarity of the market.

"Are you okay, Haree?"

"Sorry. I was just remembering my family's farm a long time ago."

Later, writing in my journal, I realize that what I've witnessed is no nightmare. At nine I couldn't see it. But it's clear to me now that this village—and the countryside for miles around—depends on what goes on here every day behind the scenes, out of sight and out of mind.

"Thanks for the tour," I say. "This was something I had to see."

He gives me another little French shrug, pretending to understand me, and we make our way back outside into the sunlight.

FRENCH FOX

Early the next day, I'm roaring down a shaded rural road that snakes out of the village through woods that eventually give way to open country. Happy to be back in the saddle, moving on, I feel free as a falcon. But my mind keeps going back to horse heads on meat hooks and the Killer Man.

I pass small farms with cows and horses grazing. I know that most of them will wind up on somebody's plate. Or hanging from the ceiling back at the Normandy Market. Killing for food. I get that. I'm also thinking about blood sports, the kind of killing that's more familiar to me: shooting pheasants out of the sky, hauling Marlin the size of pickup trucks out of the ocean, killing antlered stags in the woods, killing the fox in a hunt.

"Damn!" I remember my father saying, cracking his tooth on a shotgun pellet as he bites down on a mouthful of wild pheasant he'd shot.

"Serves you right!" My mother laughs. She sees neither joy nor virtue in shooting pheasant—even though she's a better shot than my father.

A village filters in and out of the landscape, surrounded by a marching army of golden sunflowers, all turned in exactly the same direction to follow the life-giving path of the sun across a cloudless sky. A few kilometers beyond, I glimpse another small village and turn off the road, pulling up moments later to a small *épicerie*—a grocery store—with pears, apples, pomegranates, and lemons on display out front under a green awning. It's a happy splash of color complementing a spicy taste in the air, like cinnamon, wafting around the produce.

The proprietor, a diminutive man not five feet tall, rises from a folding chair on the sunny sidewalk. He offers a welcoming smile and ushers me inside with a theatrical bow.

I'm probably the first customer of the day.

"Bonjour, monsieur," he says with great dignity. "May I help you?"

"Yes, thank you," I say. "I'm visiting France, and I would like to learn something about French food. I will be camping tonight, and I am hoping you might be able to suggest something typically French that I could grill over a campfire? Anything other than cheval, that is," I add, not ready to go all in, yet.

He nods and shoots me a knowing look, followed by a conspiratorial Gallic wink, clearly delighted to have an opportunity to show his stuff.

"Monsieur, I am more than happy to help you. And I might add, monsieur, that as luck would have it, you are speaking at this moment with an individual—none other than myself—who is rather well regarded hereabouts on matters of the table and the palate."

He pauses to make sure I fully appreciate the import, the solemn gravity of what he has just confided.

Dutifully impressed, I reply, "Monsieur, I am honored."

He clasps his hands together and, tipping his head slightly, calls out, "Lapin!" through the curtain at the back of the shop.

"The rabbit! Very French, monsieur, and an excellent choice, if I may say so myself."

A woman appears through the curtain with a furry brown rabbit in her arms, carrying it like a baby. She strokes it affectionately and whispers something into its ear, and before it fully dawns on me, she picks up a wooden mallet and delivers an expert whack to its head.

The rabbit droops on the woman's forearm, eyes staring sightless, as a tiny driblet of dark blood starts to emerge from the little pink nose.

Now the proprietor and the lady, both very pleased, await my reaction.

I force a smile, and manage to say, as casually as I can, "Ah! What a beautiful rabbit!"

"*Mais oui!*" the proprietor says, arms extended expansively, beaming with pride. "A French rabbit! A *very fresh* French rabbit! No other rabbit in the world can compare, monsieur!"

"One moment, monsieur." Together they duck through the curtain, leaving me to remind myself that it's all about the food chain; it's how things work.

Except the rabbit never had a sporting chance.

By the time they come back with the headless, footless, dressed rabbit, which now looks a little like an oddly shaped chicken, I could care less about the lapin's sacrifice.

In fact, I'm already working up an appetite.

The proprietor wraps my dinner in brown paper, rolls in small packets of salt, pepper, and herbs, then ties the whole package up with string. He coaches me on how properly to impale the rabbit with a green twig and mount the meal on a makeshift rig that allows easy rotation for slow roasting over the fire.

My ride takes me the rest of the day through colorful patchworks of back-country France, marveling at the sharp quality of morning light as it gradually morphs to honey in the heady *chaleur* of late afternoon. All the way, past ancient farmhouses, cows, sheep, and the bark of working dogs, I delight in fragrances rising from the land, a sweet scent of lavender, fresh-cut hay, and sun-warmed earth.

Lunch is brie, half a baguette, and an apple on the banks of a tree-lined brook. Finally, near the end of the day, I wheel the bike off the road and park it under a fat oak.

First, I collect stones and kindling in the woods, then clear a camp space at the edge of an adjacent wheat field. I assemble the makeshift barbeque of green twigs and branches, as the shopkeeper instructed, and light a small fire. Warming quickly to the task, I rub salt, pepper, and herbs on the rabbit, impale it on a sharp stick, and prop it just so over the fire. Then I sit back to wait, moving only to rotate the spit as the meat drips and sizzles into the fire, turning brown and crisp, smoke sending an insanely delicious smell into the air that fires my appetite.

But then there's something entirely new.

At first, it's just the faintest ripple at the back of my consciousness but enough suddenly to make me tense.

I look around, not sure what I'm looking for.

I hear nothing. All is calm.

Not even a cricket.

Not even a cricket?

I remember hearing that crickets often go silent when they sense a threatening presence in their giddy world of music and sex.

Wasn't there a movie where the cowboys were warned about undetected hostile Indians when the crickets stopped singing? Now I'm surrounded by a total absence of sound at the very moment when crickets should be warming up for their nightly party.

It's not frightening, exactly. But it is odd. So, I give the rabbit another turn on the fire and sit perfectly still, waiting, alert.

It's already there before I even have a chance to observe it moving out of the grass and into the edge of the clearing, not twenty feet away.

A red fox appears, silent as a ghost.

One glance tells me: male, bushy, white-tipped tail, healthy.

For an impossibly long moment, the fox's eyes lock directly on mine. We stare at each other. I'm waiting for him to turn and run.

But he stands his ground, undaunted by my steady gaze.

What wild animal doesn't back down from a staring contest with a human?

What wild animal isn't afraid of fire?

Has hunger eclipsed his natural fear of humans?

His nose is twitching. Has he smelled, perhaps from afar, the rabbit roasting on the open fire?

Standing there, is he challenging me for the rabbit?

After a few minutes, I move with extra care to rotate the rabbit. The fox watches this new action with singular interest, turning its full attention to the rabbit, then back again to me.

For ten more minutes, we sit in silence, observing one another, while the rabbit continues to cook.

Finally, I begin to speak to him, softly, as if this fox were a human companion. At first, his ears snap back, and he stiffens. But then he seems to relax.

"I wonder what your name is?" I say. "Would you like to have a French name? How about I call you Pepé? Pepé Le Pew? But you're not a skunk, are you? Or maybe you're a skunk in disguise...I think I'll call you Pepé anyway."

He cocks his head, still staring.

Through time, civilizations have honored, even worshipped, these wily creatures as the cleverest of beasts. And in this moment, in a scene that could have taken place a hundred thousand years ago, I'm sensing the remarkable intelligence behind those wild eyes.

How man met dog.

As I ramble on in my one-sided conversation, the fox continues to probe my eyes with his. Maybe trying to decide if he can trust me.

Maybe we're both trying to decide the same thing.

Gradually, I'm feeling an attachment, even a bond with this particular creature.

As a child, I had a strong feeling of pity and protectiveness for the foxes my mother and her friends hunted on our property. My mother was the only woman master of the hunt in her club in its history.

I remember standing on the ground beside her, watching as she swings herself up into the saddle on her great stallion, Gypsy.

I gaze up at her dressed in full hunting regalia, an imposing horsewoman, as she leans down to take my upreached hand. A battalion of mounted scarlet dragoons assembles around her, and the dogs begin to bark and bay.

"It's a frivolous pursuit, Harry," my mother tells me. "But there is absolutely nothing—nothing—in the world to compare to the thrill of it."

"Are you going to kill the fox, Mother?" I ask.

"No, no, no, Harry. Be assured that as long as I am master of hounds, every fox is safe."

"You promise?"

"Yes, I do," she says, and I can tell by the way she looks down at me she means it. "No animal that can overcome staggering odds and outsmart a small army of tin soldiers like us and live to see another day—which is usually the case, Harry—should ever be rewarded for its superior survival skills by being torn to pieces by dogs!"

By my fire, I'm smiling to myself.

Lucky fox.

"You would like my mother, Pepé..." I say out loud.

Just then, to my astonishment, the fox lowers himself to the ground.

"And she would like you."

For a hungry fox, he seems remarkably patient.

"Now, if you will give me a minute, I'm going to get our dinner ready."

I set the rabbit, now fully roasted, on a flat stone, where pooling in its juices, it will cool.

Pepé stands but does not withdraw, riveted on the food, but giving no sign that he might be planning a snatch and run.

I tear off a hot chunk of roasted rabbit and offer it, arm outreached to the fox.

He's having none of that, as I knew he wouldn't. So, I crawl a few more feet and lay the roasted lapin on the ground, about ten feet from him.

Not surprisingly, he steps back.

I can see he's staying for dinner, retreating just enough to reestablish his zone of comfort.

He's a wild animal, I remind myself, and I can't expect him to just walk up and lick my face.

But then, suddenly the fox dashes in and hightails it with the rabbit chunk in his teeth. And just as suddenly, he stops at the edge of the clearing, turns, and looks once again directly into my eyes.

"So long, Pepé," I say. "Sorry you won't stay."

Later, sleeping under the stars, I'm dreamless. A new sound, a kind of swishing, brings me awake shortly after sunrise, before the heat of the day. I open my eyes, squinting against early-morning needles of sunlight piercing high wheat where I've made my bed. I sit up, wondering if I might again see the fox. Instead, I lock eyes with a farmer poised to swing a scythe right where I lay. He's as shocked as I am, and we both let out a whoop. One swing of the scythe just a second later could have taken off my head. I leap to my feet as he jumps back, eyes popping. We're both shouting at once, jolted by fear and surprise. We make no sense to one another, but I'm rushing to grab my things and get out. Even after I crank up the bike and disappear down the road, he's still shouting.

SPRINGTIME IN PARIS

With the arrival of warming temperatures and a feeling of spring in the air, Paris cafés are full. Young lovers promenade up and down the Champs-Élysées and browse bookstalls along the Seine near Notre-Dame, while in parks all over the city pensioners with small dogs warm themselves in the sun.

I wind up in a tiny hotel on the Left Bank called the Hotel des Deux Continents. The common bathroom is all the way down the hall, so I pee in the bidet, a scandalous act, I later learn, that would shock even the most bohemian Parisian.

There's a small balcony with a rope and pulley attached to a basket. In the morning, when the lady with the fresh bread and flowers comes down the Rue Jacob on her bike and rings her bell, I lower the rope with some francs in the basket and pull up a couple of croissants or a baguette.

I hear a good place to meet girls is a barge converted to a swimming pool on the Seine called the Piscine Deligny. You can spend all day catching rays and talking up the ladies.

I go looking for French girls but wind up talking to Pauline, an eye-popping English dancer who works in the chorus line at the Folies Bergère, the famous nightclub and tourist trap on the Champs-Élysées. When I ask in French if she'd mind if I take the chaise next to her, I think I'm talking to a *parisienne.*

She takes a look at me, shading her eyes against the sun, and decides I'm not French.

"Are you English?" she asks.

"American."

"Have a seat," she says. "And mind you, the only reason I'm saying yes is because I've seen lots of American movies, but I've never actually met an American."

"Thanks," I say, and make myself comfortable.

"What's your name?" When I tell her, she says, "Okay, Harry. What are you doing in Paris?"

I tell her my story. She seems interested, removing her shades to get a better look at me. Her eyes are a startling turquoise. I'm about to comment on those tropical eyes, when she says, "Your eyes are…not blue. Are they green?"

I have to laugh.

"I was about to tell you that *your* eyes are green," I tell her, trying to keep it going.

"No, I'm more aqua," she says. "But it's interesting, isn't it? We seem to have almost the same color eyes."

"I think that's a good sign, don't you?" I say.

"A good sign of what?"

I know she's being coy, playing with me, seeing where I'm going to go with it.

She's just lying there, smiling.

"I think it's a sign that we were supposed to meet."

The words come out feeling self-conscious and clumsy. But I think they may be telling the truth.

"Maybe," she says, giving me a look. "We'll just have to see, won't we?"

Then a moment later, she asks, "How old are you anyway?"

I tell her I'm twenty-one, a necessary lie.

She laughs out loud.

"Twenty-one!" she says. "That's too old for me!"

I'm guessing she's twenty-three, maybe twenty-four. But I don't ask.

Now I'm laughing, going along with it, and beginning to think this might work. She gives me another look, and I lie back, offering myself up to the sun.

The morning rolls on, and the lady orders a lunch of chicken salad and champagne for two under a yellow umbrella.

Champagne? This is the life. Who can afford champagne? I'm already beginning to feel like a kept man. But my pride has no conviction, and I'm more than happy to accept her generous invitation.

Pauline tells me that she's the daughter of a baker in Manchester, where it rains all the time and the air smells like burned rubber. She's working as a fashion model when she meets a musician but finds out too late that he's a drunk and a heroin addict. When he accuses her of seeing someone else and throws the *telly* out the window in a jealous rage, she heads for the door, terrified. But he grabs her and punches her so hard he fractures her jaw. She fights for her life, escapes down the stairs, and staggers home in the rain, dripping blood and tears.

Then comes the shrieking, incoherent phone call in the night, when he threatens to throw acid in her face or maybe cut her up and toss the pieces into the river.

I can't believe what I'm hearing. I'm thinking romance, but she's reliving a nightmare.

I feel awkward, bearing witness to her anguish, but the champagne sheds my discomfort, and the story's not over.

The police bring in the musician for questioning. She hires a lawyer, looking to put him in jail. But one day he rings her up and whispers in a sober, measured voice that if she takes him to court, he will have her killed. "Make no mistake," he hisses, and hangs up.

The next day she's on the Dover ferry to seek a new life. She winds up in Paris, where they like leggy English dancers. Her only friend from home, a fan dancer at the Folies, suggests she try out for the chorus line. She goes to dancing class for a week. When she comes out, her high kick is seven feet.

I look over at all nearly six feet of her stretched out on the chaise next to me. Practically naked in a bikini, soaking up the sun. I can understand why they hired her on the spot.

"That's quite a story, but it sounds like everything has worked out okay."

"I like my job," she says. "And I like Paris. You'll never bloody catch me back in Manchester."

The Folies job must pay well because the waiter's asking if she'd like more champagne.

"Mais oui," she says. *"Peut-être un petit plus, Marcel. Merci."*

Marcel.

"Where did you learn to speak French?" I ask.

"I'm good at languages."

"Sounds like they know you pretty well here."

"I come here a lot." She empties the flute. "Do you want to see where I live?"

Pauline lives with a couple of other English showgirls in a houseboat on the Seine. I motion toward another cabin, where a roommate is doing her nails.

"No worries," she says,

I'd been anticipating a headwind of coy negotiation and endless foreplay. So I can't believe my good luck when the tumble is straightforward. I've been spending too much time on my motorcycle, so when we finally separate, I'm soaked with sweat, lying on my back, gasping for air, wondering what the roommate is thinking, and wondering if maybe Pauline might ask me for money.

To my relief, she says, "Not bad. I think maybe you were right."

"Right about what?" I ask, looking over.

"Maybe we were meant to meet, Mr. Green Eyes," she says, and she gives me a little poke.

She lights up a Gauloises that smells like a horse stable. It's a distinctive smell that reminds me of smoky cafés and cheaper Left Bank bistros.

"I'm thinking of becoming an actress," she says, venting smoke from her nostrils. "What do you think of that?"

I look at her. "You've got the looks. Yeah, I can see you up there."

"I'm being serious, you know," she says. "I'm taking acting classes on Tuesdays and Thursdays."

"In Paris?" I say, a little surprised.

The next day, she takes me with her to the little acting studio on the Rue Napoleon. They're preparing a Shakespeare performance in English. Pauline is the prettiest girl in the class.

We have a light dinner, then I take her on the bike up the Champs-Élysées to the Folies theater. We go in through the stage door past a goon with a gun.

We make our way to a dressing room Pauline shares with half a dozen practically naked dancers. I've never seen so many good-looking girls in one place at one time. They're all very friendly, giving me little smiles and winks, not the least bit inhibited.

"Steady, Green Eyes, steady," Pauline says. "Don't let it go to your head—either one!"

I take a seat on a folding chair and gaze in childlike wonder, trying to appear urbane and casual, struggling not to obsess on any one particular breast or fanny. Just profoundly grateful to be young, male, and free, backstage at the Folies Bergère.

The two-minute call comes for the first show, and the room empties like peacocks stampeding in a fire drill.

When the orchestra strikes up, the audience whistles and cheers. There are so many beautiful women, I can't pick Pauline out of the crowd. It's a real spectacle, straight out of the Gay Nineties, with feathers and boas, flouncy skirts pulled high, and thirty pairs of legs kicking in a rousing *cancan*. I'm transfixed, and then almost run over when the chorus line charges offstage.

Later, in my tiny top-floor room at the Hotel des Deux Continents, I'm urinating into the plumbing next to the bed as I've been doing for days. Pauline is appalled.

"That's not a toilet."

"I know it's not a toilet."

"Then why are you peeing in it?"

"Because the toilet is down the hall. This is way more convenient."

I'm standing there, still going.

"It's for me, not for you," she says.

"Women use the bidet to wash their private parts. Why do you think the little faucet points *up?*" she asks.

She swings those long legs off the bed, throws her hair back with both hands, and asks me to please step aside.

I'm going to get a demonstration. My lucky day. I want to tell her how good she looks, but I don't have to. I'm not thinking about the bidet.

"I can tell you like what you see," she says, teasing, dipping her head sideways. "You don't think we're done, do you?"

The next morning, we pack a picnic and ride the Triumph through back streets into the countryside west of Paris. We walk through open fields of wildflowers and lay out a blanket beside a stream. She wants to know all about America, what it's like, where I come from. Have I been to California? Texas? The Grand Canyon?

She's thinking after Paris maybe she'll go to New York, get a job as a showgirl on Broadway. Then maybe head to Hollywood and get into the movies. She's been learning a lot in acting class, and she wants to give me a little show. With the stream behind her, she's on her feet, reciting Shakespeare. I'm surprised at how she's saying the lines, as an Elizabethan might say them, in sync with the context. The deeper she gets into it, the more she seems to glow, saying her lines with professional ease, a natural.

I can't take my eyes off her.

She stops, her eyes wide and innocent, both hands palms up as if to say, what do you think?

"I'm impressed," I tell her. "I don't know much about acting other than what I see in the movies, but I think you're a natural."

"You do? You do?" she says, clearly pleased.

"I definitely do," I say. "Once you got into it, you had me."

She lets that sink in.

"Wasn't so good in the beginning, huh?"

"It's not that," I tell her. "Maybe I was a little skeptical. I'm not a big fan of Shakespeare. But I was watching you, listening to every word. I was thinking, *Pauline knows how to act.*"

After lunch, we open the wine and skinny-dip in the stream.

"I'm very happy," she says in my ear, wrapping her legs around me. "I appreciate so much what you said."

I glance up and catch sight of a boy on top of the other bank straddling a bike, looking down on us. I shake my head at him. He smiles and nods and after a moment disappears down the bike path. If this were America, the kid would be right back with all his buddies. But this French kid has seen it all.

When I wake up from a little nap, Pauline is staring at me.

"Hello, Green Eyes," she says very softly, her voice peaceful. "Your eyes are as green as the grass."

I can lose myself in those aqua eyes, even drown. I don't want to move, letting myself be drawn in. Maybe it's just lying here under an open sky and the shade of a tree or the stillness and intimacy or the wine, but I don't want this day to end.

"Do you know your eyes are the exact same color as the Piscine Deligny?" I ask, thinking maybe she'll laugh.

But she doesn't seem to hear.

She says, "When you go back to the States, will you miss me?"

"Of course I'll miss you," I say, without hesitation, a little surprised at myself.

But do I really mean that?

Am I falling in love or just happy to be here? All I know is, something has changed. I'm off balance. Even colors seem different, more electric. The scent of her skin is sweet, clean, deeply physical.

Is it love?

Suddenly she sits up and pulls her shirt down over her head and shoulders.

"Listen to me talk, will you?" she says, shaking out her hair. "It's much too early to be talking like this."

I lean back, my hands behind my head.

"What are you saying?" I ask.

"I'm saying this is wonderful, but we hardly know each other."

I can make out one cloud that looks like a crocodile. The jaw is widening, but the tail is dispersing.

"I'd like it if you'd come back with me. What do you think of that?" Even before the words are out of my mouth, I'm confounded. It's as if something has shut down my rational mind.

She gives me a skeptical look, pulls on her shorts, and walks down to the edge of the stream. I glance up, and the French kid is stopped again on the bike path. I wave. He smiles and gives the thumbs-up.

"What are you thinking?" I ask, curious now about how this conversation is going to end.

"I think you know exactly what I'm thinking. I think that if I'm not careful, I could fall in love. Right now, I don't want to fall in love, with you or anyone else."

She's talking to her toes in the water.

She's right. I know how she feels. Who needs entanglements? I've got thousands of miles and five or six months ahead of me.

But in spite of myself, I reply, "And why not? Why not fall in love?"

She looks at me.

"I don't have to be in love to come to America," she says, brushing the hair out of her eyes. God, she is so beautiful. "I don't have to be in love. I can just come."

"And what if I fall in love with *you?*"

There I go again. That seems to stop her.

I stand up. She doesn't move, not even a blink or a smile. She walks over, very slowly, never taking her eyes off me.

She rests her arms on my shoulders.

"Well then," she purrs, her breath on my ear. "We'll just have to see about that, won't we?"

We kiss for a long time, long enough to make us both want to come up for air.

"We'll also have to see about getting rid of that Manchester accent," I say, and she pushes me away.

"And *you,*" she says, "had better learn the proper way to go to the *loo!*"

For the next week, we let things go. We don't talk about love or falling in love.

We live together at my hotel, and I attend every show and acting class. She tells me one of the chorus girls is a Dutch lesbian who makes moves on the other dancers, whispers naughty things in the girls' ears in the dressing room, and once slipped her hand between Pauline's legs as they lined up to go onstage. She tells me she wants to quit smoking and that she has a standing invitation from a rich Greek who invited her to vacation with him on his private island in the Ionian Sea.

"You think you'll go?" I ask.

She gives me an impish look. "Well, that depends, doesn't it?" she says.

"Depends on what?"

"Depends on you and me, Green Eyes. Depends on whether we still feel the same way when we meet again."

We make a plan to reunite in Paris at the end of the summer. We promise to write, and we hold each other for a long time before I get on the bike and drive away.

I receive a letter in Rome and another in Madrid. She talks about how she misses me and still wants to come to America, perhaps as early as the end of the summer. But after Spain, it's radio silence. I send postcards but don't hear from her again.

BEER HALL

By the time I get to Munich ten days later, Pauline, to my surprise, has already begun to fade into the ethers like a dream, becoming more abstract with every kilometer I put behind me. So many other people to meet, so much else to see, so much to do. But her remarkable good looks and indisputable sex appeal is solidly embedded in my salaciously lupine, testosterone-driven subconscious, and I have every intention of following up with her at the end of the summer.

In the meantime, it's time to taste a bit of Germany in that most German of Germanic institutions, the hofbräuhaus. Munich's hofbräuhaus is an international destination of sophomoric excess that ranks second only to Pamplona and the running of the bulls. A perfect place for a lonely young American on a motorcycle to lose himself in a crowd and maybe pick up a few friends. Packed full, as it is most days, it's more like a rowdy political convention than a big saloon. Hundreds of suds-swilling Germans party it up night and day. Instead of cheering candidates, they quaff back vast quantities of foamy beer from tankards the size of toasters, cheering themselves senseless with drunken renditions of German drinking songs.

I can't wait to step inside.

Immediately, I'm swallowed by the push and roar of the happy crowd, and no one even notices me.

Everywhere I look, rows of people are packed on benches at long tables. Hefty, pigtailed *fräuleins*, big as linebackers, haul overflowing steins and giant pitchers by the fistful from table to table, keeping every patron topped off.

I spot a table of young people who look like students, so I ask if there might be room for one more. Sliding closer together along the bench, they ask me in English where I come from. I tell them I'm American, and they seem more than happy to fit me in. There are a few Germans and Austrians, a couple of Belgians, two Swiss, and the girls are pretty—nine in all. They tell me that I'm in luck because I've hit upon some kind of beer festival. They order a couple more pitchers, and I jump right in, downing the first stein without coming up for air. Pretty soon I'm singing right along, toasting with everybody, and looking forward to getting to know my new friends.

After an hour or so, everybody leaves the table nearly at once to go to the bathroom. It seems reasonable, since they were hard at it long before I arrived. But I'm the only one left.

After a few minutes, I wonder where everybody went and why no one has come back.

Finally, classic fall-guy, it dawns on me that I might be holding the bag. While I'm devising a strategy, one of the linebacker *fräuleins* presents me with a huge bill.

Nine drinkers, who knows for how long, and I'm only into my third beer. But I know the party's over.

With my rudimentary German, how can I begin to explain that this could not possibly be my bill—not that the fräulein cares in the least about anything I might have to say in any language. I can only attempt the lame truth—it must be the bill racked up by my new friends, who will be right back.

She gives me a look that says, "I've heard it all before, stupid."

What happens next unfurls in slow motion.

Two giant bouncers, who make the pork chop fräulein look petite, appear out of nowhere, pick me up like a battering ram, and hustle me horizontally toward the swinging doors at the back. In the chaotic instant before I crash through the exit, all I hear is a chorus of mocking laughter and howling derision.

I'm airborne over the alley, plowing headlong into a pile of garbage bags and empty boxes, ending up deep in the heap. Unhurt, except for wounded pride and the delayed shame that comes from realizing that I've been physically thrown out of a public establishment in front of hundreds of people.

Almost dreamily, I watch a rat amble across the wet alley. He freezes when he spots me, whiskers twitching, and rears up on his back legs, giving me a leisurely but thorough once-over. I hear a measly little squeak, then lots of squeaks, and the rat's head starts to go up and down.

I can see the raggedy little teeth, and I could swear the rat is laughing at me. I get the ludicrous irony, and now I'm laughing too. It's just the rat and me outside the hofbräuhaus in Munich, two shunned outcasts sharing a surreal moment to celebrate the comedy of the absurd.

I'm still contemplating my next steps when a young woman comes through the swinging doors and stops to light a cigarette. She spots me and walks over, exhaling a stream of smoke.

"*Haben sie dich verletz?*" she asks. Did they hurt you?

"*Nein. Alles gut,*" I answer, getting to my feet.

"You speak German?" she says.

"*Ein bisschen.*"

"Well, I probably speak better English than you speak German, so let's use English. So...you fell for the old trick!"

She nods knowingly, holding her cigarette off to the side.

"I didn't know about the old trick," I tell her, standing up straighter and brushing myself off.

"Obviously not." She chuckles.

"Maybe you are too trusting," she adds flatly.

"Obviously," I say.

"Don't be ashamed of that. It is better to trust, even if it's naïve. Today nobody trusts anybody—except Americans. Americans trust everybody."

"Really?"

"Come on," she says after a pause. "I'll take you to a quiet place where you can buy me a drink, and we can talk." I lead her to the Triumph TR6.

"Hop on."

At a nearby bar, I follow her into a large back room, thick with tobacco smoke and crowded with long-haired students.

As I look around, I lock eyes with one of the tricksters from the hofbräuhaus. He freezes until he sees I'm not going to present any immediate danger. He gives me a thin smile, a hesitant wave, and slowly approaches our table.

I'm tempted to coldcock him without a word, but I'm willing to see where this goes. He's one of the Belgian guys, and I already know he speaks English.

"No hard feelings?" he says, forcing a smile and reaching out his hand.

I ignore the hand.

"Why would I have hard feelings?" I ask him in a civil voice. "You only cheated me and basically robbed me. Why would I have hard feelings about that?"

He's not sure about the sarcasm.

I'm waiting, looking for an excuse to explode out of the chair. But he says nothing.

I'm about to introduce my new friend when I realize I don't even know her name. I notice he's glancing at her, and she's averting her eyes.

"Do you know each other?" I ask.

She looks at me, then at him.

"Yes, we know each other," she says. "Hello, Adrian."

"So…you were in on it?"

"No," she says. "I know him, but I was not in on it."

"Then what's this all about?" I ask, looking back and forth.

"I did not know he was here. But I should tell the truth…we used to be lovers," she says.

"No hard feelings," the Belgian interjects, this time speaking directly to her.

She just looks away.

Does this guy leave a trail of debris everywhere he goes?

"Why don't you just go back to your table?" I suggest to Adrian, suppressing another urge to whack him.

"I am very embarrassed," she says when he's gone. "I was surprised to see him here, and I am ashamed of what he and those others did to you."

"No, I'm the one who ought to feel embarrassed, no harm done. I just feel stupid. I should have figured it out."

"Yes, I think so!" she says, laughing. "I think you should have figured it out! What do they call it? A sucker! You are a sucker!"

I laugh. But only a little.

"So, if you knew what was happening, how come you didn't try to stop it?"

I already know the answer. Why should she have done anything?

But I'm just curious enough to ask.

"Because I wanted to laugh," she says. "And I did laugh! Why not?"

I like her candor.

"Yeah, I can see that," I concede, feeling relaxed and grinning. "I can see how it might have been pretty funny."

Then I tell her the story of the rat. And now we're both laughing.

After a moment I say, "You know, I don't even know your name…"

She flushes. "Oh my gosh!" she says. "My name is Hilde."

I introduce myself.

"A personal question?"

She looks at me.

"How did a pretty German girl like you get hooked up with a bum like that Belgian guy?"

"He was not a bum. He was just sexy," she says. "I like sexy guys. I like you too. I fucked him on the first date."

I think about that.

She puts a cigarette in her mouth and hands me a lighter so I can light it for her.

"Do you always fuck on the first date?" I ask.

"Yes. Unless he has bad teeth," she says, exhaling a blue fog.

"Otherwise you fuck…"

"Yes."

"So, you fuck a lot of guys?"

"Yes. A lot. Why, does that upset you?"

"No. But where I come from, the girls never fuck on the first date. And if they do, they don't admit it."

"In Europe it is different," she says. "It is more relaxed with the girls here. Unless they are in a convent—and then they would probably want to fuck even more!"

She laughs until she coughs.

Cigarettes.

I'm beginning to think of the possibilities.

"Let's have a drink and then go back to my place and fuck," she says, reading my mind.

When I wake up the next morning, I have no idea where I am. My head is reeling, and I'm trying to put it together. Sun is coming through the window, stabbing my eyes. I'm alone and naked, my clothes scattered on the floor. When I finally manage to pull myself off the bed, the room begins to pitch, and I have to catch myself on a chair, the only other piece of furniture.

That's when I notice the note.

I stumble into the bathroom, splash water on my face, rub my eyes, and read the handwritten note:

Dear Mister, it says. *I'm sorry we did not get to know each other better because I really like you. I know you probably don't remember a lot, but you were good in bed! Adrian (that is not his real name) and I want to thank you for the cash, which we will try to spend wisely. We could have sold your passport on the black market, but I left it because you are so nice. You are very trusting—maybe too trusting! Honestly, you should have known better! But that is why we love Americans! I hope the drug wears off quickly and that you have a good life.*

Love,
Hilde (not my real name)

Later, back on the road, I think how right she was.
    I should have figured it out.

CHECKPOINT CHARLIE

I t's a hot afternoon at Checkpoint Charlie in Berlin, and I'm nursing a Berliner *spezialität,* gazing through the window of a second-floor café that overlooks the Berlin Wall into East Germany. East German border police, the Stasi, look back at me through binoculars from guard towers along the wall.

Today is the first anniversary of the building of the wall, and I'm talking to my new friend, a young British journalist, about marking the occasion with a visit into East Berlin for the day. We've been watching the checkpoint for hours, and there's been no traffic, no cars, no people. The atmosphere is tense. American MPs and the Stasi glare at each other across the fifty yards of no-man's-land. We decide it's a perfect day for a visit. So we pay up and make our way downstairs and next door to the West Berlin gate.

An American MP not much older than I am gives me a curious, sideways look and demands to know what business I have in East Germany.

"No business," I tell him. "I'm just a tourist. Just visiting."

There's a pause as he shakes his head. "Do you have any idea how dangerous it is over there?" he asks. Then he says sarcastically, "In case you haven't heard, they don't like Americans."

"Yep, I've heard that," I say.

"Then I would strongly urge you to take my advice and forget about going over there," he says. "Once you are there, we can't do anything for you. You're on your own."

I look at my British buddy. "We've made up our minds," I say. "We want to go over."

The MP gives me an exasperated look. "I can't stop you. But don't say I didn't warn you," he says as he waves us into the border control office, headquarters of Checkpoint Charlie. Inside, we are greeted by two stone-faced officers seated at desks. They ask for our passports and hand us a stack of documents saying basically that we are exiting West Berlin under our own free will and knowingly venturing into a military-restricted zone and hostile government, against the advice and counsel of the US military. The documents also absolve the military and the American government of any responsibility should we meet with misfortune.

We sign all the documents, and an MP frisks us.

"Do you know what day this is?" the senior officer asks before we walk out the door. "This is the anniversary of the building of the wall. Maybe you've noticed that nobody is going into East Germany today. There's a reason for that. The East Germans are on high alert. It is not within my mandate to stop you or your friend. All I can do is give you advice and hope you take it."

We thank him. He gives us a long look, opens the door, and we step out into a strangely empty space. We're utterly alone now, in geopolitical limbo between two very different worlds, moving toward a frontier barrier and the unknown, from democracy to communism, from freedom to totalitarianism. Another MP raises the gate, and we step into no-man's-land. I feel eyes all over us. The next fifty yards seem to take a very long time. Now the Stasi barrier is rising, and we finally step across the line of the infamous Iron Curtain into East Berlin, where we are greeted by an East German soldier who smiles and ushers us up wooden steps into what looks like a makeshift office, much like the fifty-foot trailers you see at construction sites.

Having no idea what to expect, I'm ready for anything. But what we discover inside is a scene so ludicrously improbable that I never would have believed it had I not seen it with my own eyes.

I'm looking at a long line of a dozen or so smiling faces sitting behind folding tables that run the length of the left interior of the trailer. The first guy in line rises to greet me, reaching out his hand. He checks my passport and welcomes me to the German Democratic Republic in flawless English, which leaves me speechless. He's even got an American accent. This guy could be from Kansas. You'd never guess he was German. I notice he's the only one in uniform.

"Where did you learn to speak such good English—without a German accent?" I ask him.

"We know a lot about America," he says, giving me a knowing wink. "You'd be surprised!" It's like he's giving me a little peek under the tent.

Actually, I wouldn't be surprised. My British buddy has been telling me about a secret "American town" reportedly located somewhere in East Germany. East German spies and operatives are said to go there and live like Americans for months—speaking only American English, eating burgers and drinking shakes, watching American movies and TV, listening to jazz and rock 'n' roll, studying American culture and politics—total immersion. It's an idea they are believed to have gotten from the Russians, who are said to have their own "American village." I can only wonder, if this is true, why haven't all their spies converted? If they've seen for themselves how good it is in America, why haven't they all come in out of the cold and deserted to our side?

Maybe they can't get out of the cold, I'm thinking. But if they could, surely they would, right?

Now they're all standing, like a welcoming committee at a church social. Everyone else down the line is wearing a cotton shirt and slacks. One guy is even in jeans, which I have been told are very hard to come by over here. There are a couple of pretty young women too—both obviously Stasi—but they look like co-ed cheerleaders.

Folders and brochures are stacked on every table, and as we move slowly down the line, we are invited to have a look at them. The second guy is drawing my attention to a brochure that shows a happy family and some cows. He too speaks like "the guy next door" back home. Here's a pamphlet with lots of photos of industrial sites and workers smiling for the camera. One of the young women shows us a brochure all about the importance of sports in the GDR. It's full of color photos. She points out a big sports arena and an Olympic-sized swimming pool with GDR Olympic team members posing next to it. They all look superhuman. The males have waists like wasps and shoulders a yard wide. Some of the girls look like men. This Stasi lady is pretty cute though. She reminds me of an older girl I once had a crush on. She sees me staring at her and blushes, or pretends to. In spite of all the cuteness, I can definitely see something chilling in those pale, gray-blue eyes.

One brochure is a primer on the construction of the Berlin Wall itself, which circles all of West Berlin. The headline reads in English: "Antifascist Protection Rampart." The Russians and East Germans must think there are still a lot of Hitler's cronies left over from the war in West Berlin.

By the time we get to the end of the table, they're inviting us to be guests of the GDR for as long as we wish. If we'd like to think about staying on in East Germany for a while, maybe a couple of weeks or a month, say—well, they'd be delighted to make us comfortable and give us a place to live. Of course, it's just something to think about. If we tried it and didn't like it, then we would always be free to go.

My head is spinning. I look at the Brit. We thank our hosts and take our leave.

"Have a nice time," the guard at the exit says, opening the door. He speaks with a German accent.

"We'll see you later," we reply, and we step into another world.

THE VALKYERIE AND THE
INDIAN

I look around and realize that I'm staring at…nothing. Confronting us is a wall of gray buildings with their windows either boarded or blackened. Between us and the gloomy facade is a barrier of concertina wire, guard towers, and barbed wire with an opening to walk through. This is the death strip. If you run or make any kind of fast moves, you might get sniped by the Stasis. So we move slowly, deliberately. There's not a soul in sight or the sound of voices or even the usual background buzz of automobile engines and scooters you hear all over West Berlin.

It's as if we'd walked into a city of the dead.

But appearances here, as we've discovered, can be deceiving. Eyes, though unseen, are everywhere, and this neighborhood is anything but dead.

I see a flicker of movement out of the corner of my eye and look up in time to catch a face pulling back from a half-open window. We step through the hole in the barbed wire and turn up a cobbled street, empty of cars and people. There's no sound other than our own footsteps. After walking halfway down the block, I glance up and to my amazement see hundreds of faces looking down at us in eerie silence from the upper floors of what looks like an apartment building. They are all soldiers in green uniforms, and I realize this must be some kind of barracks. We're just couple of hundred yards from the wall. I remember what the MP had said back at the checkpoint, that East Germany is on full alert on this special day.

We are stunned by how strange each moment has been, right from the instant we stepped over the line. At first, it's a odd sensation, like free-falling down a rabbit hole into a kind of Wonderland. But we're about to find ourselves in a real-life scenario even more bizarre than the Mad Hatter's tea party.

It begins with a disconcerting growl that seems to come from nowhere and everywhere at once—an ominous, dangerous rumble like a sudden, unseen storm, with distant thunder getting louder by the second.

The street ahead is empty all the way down to where it bends to the left. The growl becomes an alarming roar that echoes off the buildings—what a flash flood loaded with rocks might sound like crashing through a narrow gorge. We're looking up and down, trying to figure out what's happening. I expect tanks or armored vehicles to materialize, but still the street is empty. Now the roar rends the air around us, amplified by the canyon effect, and we gape, transfixed, as a single figure on a large motorcycle suddenly bursts into view from around the bend and thunders in our direction.

Instinctively we stand back, away from the street, closer to the wall of the building on our left. As the figure draws closer, we both struggle to make sense of what we're seeing.

As the motorcycle fast approaches, we can see for the first time that the person in the saddle is a woman. And not just any woman, but a stunningly beautiful woman—Anita Ekberg on steroids.

She's big but not heavy, wearing a red bandana around her neck, a blue shirt open to the wind, which reveals the tops of substantial breasts, black leather pants, and leather jackboots. She's mounted on what looks to be a vintage 1948 American Indian, all yellow, chrome, and black. She wears no helmet. Long blond hair streams out three feet behind her, a vision of Nordic pulchritude moving past us now in a kind of dreamlike slow motion.

She's a flesh-and-blood Valkyrie on wheels, a Wagnerian wet dream. The soldiers are practically falling out of their windows cheering, apparently as surprised as we are. But their yells and whoops are all lost in the earsplitting shock wave of thunder. I can hardly believe my eyes, witnessing a German superwoman on an American motorcycle expressing her independence and freedom—behind the Iron Curtain, of all places, and in one of the most oppressive countries in the world.

In an instant, she's gone, disappearing up a side street, the roar receding, leaving us all in a state of stunned disbelief.

Who is she? Where does she come from? Where is she going?

In a surreal flash of noise and light, she's left me with an image of rebellious youthful freedom I'll never forget.

Later, after we cross back through Checkpoint Charlie into the familiar sights and sounds of West Berlin, I'm relieved that we managed to complete our little adventure without once being stopped or detained.

It's been a day to remember, and I'm still trying to take it all in. But in the end, the only thing that sticks in my head is the Valkyrie on the Indian.

ZERMATT

O n the narrow-gauge train that runs up the side of a mountain to the fairy-tale Swiss Alpine village of Zermatt, I look
into my cash belt and discover that I don't have enough money to
pay the fare.

The conductor is moving up the line of seats, and I need time to
think. So, I exit the car and step outside onto the narrow platform.

It doesn't look like anyone can see me from either car, so on
impulse I seize the moment and scoot up the ladder's steel steps.
On the roof, I crawl out to the middle and lie flat, congratulating
myself on finding a simple solution to bad situation. But before my
self-satisfied smile fades, the stupidity of what I've done suddenly
hits me. I'm amazed at my bizarre behavior. I would never do this
in the United States. What am I thinking? Switzerland is the most
inflexible, law-abiding country in Europe.

Contrite and ashamed, I start to make my way back to the ladder, intending to get down before I'm caught.

But a face is peering over the top of the ladder. A man is screaming at me in *Schweitzerdeutsch,* the Swiss German dialect.

"Verboten!" he shouts, deeply offended—as if a dog had just pissed on his leg. He demands that I come down immediately. There's no running away. Busted and sheepish, I climb back down the ladder, where I'm confronted.

I want to kick myself.

"Das ist verboten!" my accuser and the unhappy conductor shout at me at once. *"Man kann nicht so fahren!"*

I understand what I have done is forbidden. But when the accuser tells me in English that he's making a citizen's arrest and turning me over to the *polizei* in Zermatt, images of underground medieval dungeons flash through my head. In English, I apologize for my imprudent behavior and assure them that I intend to earn money in Zermatt to pay for my train ticket, and then some.

This only draws looks of pained indulgence, the schoolboy claiming the dog ate his homework.

"I sell original portraits of tourists to pay my way," I try to explain. I can see my words of assurance have little purchase with these two, who have pretty much made up their minds that I'm some kind of criminal.

"So, where are your art supplies?" my accuser wants to know.

"I buy new supplies whenever I come to a new place."

"But you say you have no money!"

"Then I use this," I counter, pulling a rolled tube of drawing paper and a box of pencils from my pack. I explain that it is harder to draw on rolled paper and that I only use it when I can't get fresh sheets.

"Are you English?" the conductor asks.

"Nein. Ich bin Amerikaner."

They both look surprised.

"Amerikaner? And you speak German?"

I nod.

"Americans all have money," the conductor says. "Why don't you have money?"

195

"Because I am a student." I tell them I've taken time off to travel in Europe, paying for my way by working as an artist. I tell them the work doesn't pay much but that I don't need much.

They look at each other, and I sense some of the tension has lifted. Does the news that I am American somehow calm their suspicions? Or do they like the idea that a struggling student is using a bit of resourcefulness to make a living?

They turn away for a brief chat, then the conductor does the talking.

"When we get to Zermatt, the authorities will be expecting you. However, this gentleman and myself, we are not going to press charges."

I feel a wave of relief.

"But you must pay a fine." One step back. "If you do not have the money to pay the fine immediately, you must spend the night in jail. That is the law."

My heart sinks. I rue my unwise decision to try to dodge the fare. But it's too late, and now stupidity has come back to bite me. I'm in trouble with the law, in Switzerland of all places. Nobody to blame but myself. Resigned to my fate, I thank both men. The conductor escorts me to my seat and instructs me not to leave until he comes to get me.

"Papers, please," the Zermatt policeman asks on the platform. He looks at my passport, which he does not return, then speaks briefly to the conductor and walks me across the street to the police station.

Inside, he spends the next thirty minutes typing up a report while I sit on a wooden bench, looking around the station's pale-green walls and admiring official state photos of the Matterhorn. Finally, he presents me with an infraction citation, a ticket for forty Swiss francs. I tell him that if he will let me go out and draw a picture or two, I can pay the fine in full before dinnertime.

He shakes his head. "Impossible."

I have no money. To get money, I need to go into the village and start drawing pictures. But if I'm not allowed to leave the police station, I can't get the money. I patiently explain the problem.

The cop is unsympathetic. Whether I can pay the fine or not, I'm getting the impression that he thinks I should do time just for going up on the roof of the train in the first place.

"In Switzerland, we don't do these sorts of things," he says. "If you do not have money, why would you get on the train to begin with?"

He waits to let that sink in, then adds, "And why didn't you first go to the ticket office?"

"I didn't have time," I tell him. "The train was already starting to move out of the station when I hopped aboard."

What good will it do to tell him that I didn't even realize I was out of cash? If he believes me, a weak excuse like that can only fuel his gypsy suspicions.

"You have my passport, sir. I can't leave without it. So, you know if you let me go to earn money, I'm not going to run away," I argue.

But it's no use. He's determined that I wind up behind bars, guest of the canton.

Then, suddenly, a brilliant idea.

"Dear Dad," I write from the wire office in the police station. "Have slight problem. Will explain later. Need money fast."

The rest of the day is a fog of suffocating boredom, punctuated by alternating pangs of frustration and regret. In the holding room, there's nothing to do, and nothing to read except for a bulletin board with long lists of regulations in German, French, and English. I wonder what it's going to be like spending my first night in jail.

After a dinner of soup and a roll, the night duty officer comes in and escorts me down the hall to my cell. He unlocks a metal door with a small viewing window. The cell is clean and white as a clinic, with a bunk bed, a side table, a small toilet that looks brand new, and it's more comfortable than the *jugendherberge*, the youth hostel where I had spent my last night in the valley. A large wooden crucifix hangs on the wall, a reminder, perhaps, that there is still hope of redemption for all sinners who enter here.

I'm curious to know if they've ever had any Swiss people in this jail, but I don't bother to ask.

Lights are out at 9:00 p.m., and to my surprise I sleep nine hours straight, waking to the sound of keys rattling in the door. I jump out of bed and pull on my pants.

A new policeman hands me a telegram, which I rip open.

"So do I," it reads. "Good luck. Dad."

MATTERHORN

I convince my jailors to let me rustle up some clients to earn my fine. That's how I meet Hans, an Austrian engineering student, and his girlfriend, Sigi. They ask me to join them on a hike up the Matterhorn to base hut. I tell them I have no climbing experience, and they tell me I don't need any. So, we pack a lunch of apples, cheese, bread, chocolate, and apple juice and set out in the brisk morning air. In an hour, we're above the tree line and already high enough to get a nice view of the cozy little village that Zermatters call the most beautiful place in the Swiss Alps. Early Alpine sunlight spills over the rooftops and into the streets.

Above us looms the great ice-tipped fang of the 14,700-foot Matterhorn, which I later learn has one of the highest climbing casualty rates in the world. I'm already huffing, grateful for the chance to catch my breath and admire the scenery. Hans tells me we aren't even halfway to the base hut.

It's not until almost lunchtime that we crest the final rise and see the cabin. It has a big observation deck, where a few dozen people have taken up every available space with tripod-mounted cameras and binoculars.

As we come closer, I sense something is not right. But I'm totally unprepared for the sickening scene that makes it clear why these people have their eyes riveted on the mountain.

Laid out on a broad canvas tarp on one side of the hut are the bodies, and parts of bodies, of climbers. I count three intact corpses, all male, battered and bloodied, unrecognizable, twisted like mannequins. I want to avert my eyes, but I can't turn away. Mesmerized by unexpected horror, I'm suddenly aware that I'm not unlike all those other ghouls and vultures waiting for the next young climber to plunge to a tragically early death.

"This is awful," I say to Hans. I can scarcely hear my own voice, subdued by a need to be unobtrusive and respectful so near to these dead age-mates who only a few hours ago saw the sun rise, just as I had done. But now they're corpses, killed by the mountain. And I'm alive.

"Yes. This is the worst season in many years," he says. "Already this week five people have died. We knew one of them, an Italian guy staying at the youth hostel."

Sigi turns around, crying. She walks away, her hand over her mouth.

Hans shakes his head.

"The people up there," he says, pointing to the observation deck, "they have come to see the show. Some are paparazzi. They will sell the pictures to the newspapers."

I hear my mother's voice: "Harry, a life without risk is no life at all."

"Why do so many climbers die?" I ask Hans. I've never seen dead bodies just lying out in the open before. In fact, I've seen only one dead person in my entire life. I picture Mike. Mike lying in his casket, looking like a wax dummy. Up close, I see his face rouged and powdered, hands crossed over his stomach. Mike, so far away and peaceful, taking an eternal nap in his best suit.

Then, I hear Hans speaking, gesturing toward the canvas.

"I don't know. Nobody knows. But these three were roped together. Something went wrong. The rock didn't hold. Or maybe the rock was wet, or maybe there was ice. Nobody knows. That's part of the tragedy; nobody ever knows what really happened."

A team of men in red jackets, carrying stretchers, tries to wave the crowd away. But the spectators seem transfixed, unable to tear their eyes off the scene.

One by one, the bodies are wrapped and placed on the stretchers. Body parts go in a bag hung between two men like a hammock. No one says a word as the red coats disappear down the mountain with their gruesome burdens.

One of the bodies, I learn later, belongs to an experienced Matterhorn guide. If there is such a thing as a Mountain god, today the god of the Matterhorn is definitely displeased.

MARSEILLES

After a hot day on the road, late afternoon dims to dusk as I settle into an empty chair in a sidewalk café in Marseilles, wiping dust and sweat from my face. Lengthening shadows slip like thieves across the waterfront plaza, stealing what's left of the sun. It's been a long ride, and everything still seems to be moving.

A waiter brings a demi carafe of cold table blanc and bottled water. I pour and swallow the first glass in one long gulp, then fill the glass again.

"You must be very thirsty," a voice says. French accent. I look over. A long-haired older man with a weathered face at the adjoining table is squinting at me. He's wearing a well-worn safari jacket.

"It's been a long day," I tell him. "I've been on a motorcycle."

"I used to have a motorcycle myself," he says. "There is absolutely nothing like a motorcycle to attract pretty birds. It's a vagina magnet. I used to tape a golf ball to the rear saddle and tell the *oiseaux* it was a safety device."

Doesn't take this guy long to confide intimacies to complete strangers.

"What? Are you serious?"

"Yes. I'm serious."

In spite of myself, I'm laughing. "I should have thought of that."

"It is really quite amazing what can happen." The man chuckles. Where I can find a golf ball in France? "Are you French?" I ask.

"No, Belgian."

"My name, by the way, is Conrad Goesse," he says.

We shake hands. "Harry Belmont."

"Are you a writer?" I ask, looking at his notepad.

He lifts a worn, leather-bound folder. "Yes. I'm trying to make a story from this old journal about my great-uncle, a master jewel thief, soldier of fortune, and slaver who spent a lot of time in Africa. Written in pen and ink, in French. It's full of amazing things."

"I'm very curious. I keep a journal myself. I'd like to see it. May I have a look?"

"I'll read you a passage," the Belgian says.

Goesse opens the journal and begins to read, translating French to English:

With a few other soldiers of fortune, I joined a band of Arab slavers in Mombasa without concern for the morality of it because at the time it was the only lucrative option open to me.

One day we raided a Kikuyu village and captured about a dozen eligible men and a few women. We Europeans then watched in horror as the Arabs murdered in cold blood the young and old of the village.

This was not what we had signed on for. We wanted out, and we wanted the Arabs dead. The answer, we decided, was not confrontation but management.

The Kikuyus have no equal as warriors in the art of stealth. Known as black ghosts, they are said to be invincible phantoms who strike with deadly skill. They are believed to practice a form of black magic that is the most feared weapon in Africa.

We negotiated with one of the Kikuyu men, leader of the captives, to gain freedom for his people in exchange for disposing of the Arab barbarians. He was the most extraordinary African I ever ran across.

"Now," Goesse says, pausing and looking up, making sure he's got my attention. "This is the interesting part..."

On the appointed night, I could still make out the Arab guard in the flickering firelight. I heard nothing, but he rose from his haunches, with his rifle at the ready, only to slowly sink back down to the ground in a single graceful motion. He seemed just to reposition himself on the ground, but his head was missing.

The guard's movement provoked the three other Arabs, who rose to their feet, pistols drawn. And as we watched—so help me God—their heads all vanished, as if on cue, in a grotesque choreography. Their bodies remained standing for an impossibly long moment, perhaps five or six seconds. Then they drifted slowly, almost beautifully, in an unworldly ballet that returned them to the very positions from which they had arisen a moment earlier.

As you can imagine, we had expected to see our Kikuyu collaborator and his warriors. But in fact, we perceived no sound nor other presence. It was beyond eerie. It was impossible.

Then, before we recovered from our initial shock, the missing heads suddenly reappeared as melting gargoyles in the smoke rising from the Arab campfire. The lips moved as if struggling to form words, the eyes wide in terror. As we watched, the heads fell without a sound into the fire.

I jumped up and raced over to the embers, but the fire was untouched, not a single spark disturbed.

We saw this with our own eyes. We were frozen in fear and disbelief. We could only watch as the women butchered the bodies of the

Arabs. They sang a chilling African dirge, more like a chant, that I know to be a prayer to the Ashanti earth goddess Agasa Yaa, who, according to legend, reclaims her children at death. The sonorous chant was unnerving and seemed to rise with the smoke. The women moved in a coordinated danse macabre, wielding their machetes and sickle-shaped mambeles *with incredibly graceful deliberation.*

Four of the women stepped toward the fire, cradling in their hands body parts that we all recognized with a primal shudder. Their chanting continued as they dropped the dismembered penises into the embers. The specter of bare-breasted African women carrying severed cocks put us Europeans on high alert for our own safety.

We were powerless to resist a pervasive sense of awful dread, surrounded as we were by a power far beyond the world we thought we knew. I was thunderstruck, for a few moments unable even to form words.

"What happened to the heads?" I finally asked our man, fighting to steady my fear. He answered that the heads had been sent to hetguage, *the nether regions, where they would remain in hopeless torment and despair for eternity, forever searching in vain for their bodies.*

Were the penises too doomed to wander forever in some kind of limbo, looking for disembodied vaginas? The wild incongruity almost made me laugh.

"I am leopard." he told me simply. "No white man can know obayifo.*"*

I know only that obayfiyo is some sort of invisible vampire creature from Ashanti legend that seeks human blood and that the leopard is connected with the concept of African royalty.

"Obayfiyo avenges the blood of the innocents, the children and old ones," he said simply, showing no emotion. "I fulfilled my part of the bargain, and you are safe—for now. What awaits you is life as a slave."

Goesse shuts the folder with slow deliberation and stares at me. After a long silence, he says, "What do you make of that?"

"What do *you* make of it?"

"I don't know. He swears he saw these things with his own eyes. But he never lived to see his journal published. It wound up on a shelf for fifty years. Africa is a puzzle within an enigma. I think we will never know."

"Did your great-uncle end up a slave?"

"The answer is yes, and to Arabs. But that is another story. In the end, he died a free man."

"When you were reading, I was thinking about a little experience I had with black magic myself a few months ago. In the islands."

I tell Goesse the story of Jama, the ebony torch vixen with her voodoo hex on Gordo and his vanishing prick. He laughs out loud.

"I believe it!" he says. "Never piss off anybody from Africa!"

REUNION IN VENICE

I t's a fine morning in the Piazza San Marco, and I've no sooner settled into a folding chair with my sketchbook than an elderly American woman comes over and asks me if I speak English. I put on my best Italian accent.

"Yes…of course," I say. "Would you like me to draw your portrait?"

"Actually, I would like you to draw my granddaughter's portrait," she says, and brings over a very pretty girl not much younger than I am. There's something about the girl that makes me look twice. But it's fleeting. I can't put my finger on it.

The girl smiles, and I smile back.

"Well, I'll leave you two alone and go feed the pigeons," the grandmother says, and she disappears across the piazza. I pull up another folding chair, and the girl sits down.

"Are you from America?" I ask, making conversation.

She nods. I prepare a page for the sketch and lay out my pencils.

"Where in America you come-a from?" I ask as I start drawing.

"I come from Philadelphia," she says.

Now she's got my full attention.

"Where in this-a Philadelphia you come-a from?" I ask, playing dumb and trying to get the right proportions of her face on the paper.

"I was born in a place called Chestnut Hill," she says. "But when I was little, we moved away." She's looking around, distracted, not really interested in making small talk.

I've lived most of my life in Chestnut Hill.

"Don't move-a you face," I tell her.

Then I ask, very curious now, "What kind-a place, this-a Chess-a-nut-a Hill?"

"It's a suburb," she says, acting bored. "It's very pretty. It's got lots of trees."

"I got a friend, he's-a been to Chess-a-nut-a Hill," I tell her, fishing now.

"Really?" she says, suddenly interested. "Chestnut Hill? That's a real coincidence..."

I'm having trouble getting the eyes. Hair, nose, and lips are easy. Eyes are always the hardest. Somewhere in the back of my mind, I'm thinking, why do I know these eyes?

"Yes, is very interesting," I say, concentrating on the eyes but not letting the conversation die. "He says he has a friend there."

I have no idea where I'm going with this. But she glances over, and I can see she's as curious as I am.

"A friend? An American friend?" she wants to know.

I'm nodding, working on the eyes.

Much better. It's coming together.

"Do you know where in Chestnut Hill this friend of your friend lives?" she asks, holding the pose.

"Is a place called Spring-a-field Avenue," I tell her.

"Springfield Avenue!" she shouts. "What a coincidence!"

I stop drawing and look up at her. She's staring at me with a look of complete surprise.

"I lived on Springfield Avenue when I was a little girl!" she says excitedly. "Isn't that weird? That is so *amazing*!"

Yes, it is amazing. And I'm the one who's even more amazed—because I grew up on Springfield Avenue, and it's all coming back in a rush. Could this be Cilla, the girl I had such a crush on when I was eight? The girl from the house right next door? Cilla, with the beautiful eyes, the eyes I fell in love with? Her hair was so much fuller and longer then, and the breasts...but the eyes...the eyes...

I drop the accent and put aside the pad and pencils.

"Cilla?"

She stares and furrows her brow, her mouth open.

"How do you know my name?"

"I have a confession to make..." I say, feeling the shame.

"You're not Italian, are you? *Who are you?*"

"Cilla, it's me..."

Her hand over her mouth, she stares at me.

"Oh my God!" she cries. "I didn't even recognize you..."

"How would you?" I say. "We haven't seen each other since we were kids."

"I can't get over this," she says. "Look at you with all that hair and that bandana. What's with the Italian accent?"

"It helps me get work and meet girls."

She laughs.

"Actually, I had a funny feeling about you when you first sat down, but I didn't recognize you. There was something about your eyes..."

She gives me a look.

"You're such a trickster!" she says. "What are you doing here? You're an artist."

"Just paying the bills. Gives me money for food and a place to sleep."

She asks where I've been and what I've seen and done. "And how about you?"

"I'm with my grandma," she says, pointing. "She's taking me all over Europe. She calls it the Grand Tour."

I look into her eyes. "Did you know I had a crush on you back then?"

I'm falling in love with those baby-blue eyes all over again.

She looks at me. "Did you know I had a crush on *you?*"

I didn't know. "What a waste," I say, sorting through the memories. "I wonder what would have happened if you hadn't moved away."

"I wonder," she says. "I've often wondered what ever became of you."

Now I'm beginning to wonder what might happen if we pick up where we left off, already trying to figure out how we can get some time alone. But the motorcycle is in a parking garage across the canal on the mainland, and the grandmother is hovering.

The grandmother walks up, looks over my shoulder, and pronounces the picture dandy.

"Grandma, guess what? This is my Philadelphia neighbor. We haven't since each other since I was a little girl."

The grandmother looks at me, puzzled. She's waiting for an explanation.

"Well…" I begin.

"You are not Italian?"

I stand up, introduce myself, and tell her the story.

"At first, we didn't recognize each other."

"Oh yes," she says, giving me a smile and a nod, but her eyes tell me she's not sure she approves of my little charade. "I remember you now. I remember once when I came to visit, you children were inseparable. You rode your bikes all day long."

I glance at Cilla. She turns to her grandmother.

"Grandma," she says. "This is the first friend I have met since we left home. We'd like to have a little time to catch up."

Cilla's spared me having to broach the subject. I want to believe she's feeling what I'm feeling.

"You can catch up all you want," the grandmother says, her eyes narrowing. "You know I promised your mother I would never let you out of my sight! So, don't you think for one minute I'm going to let you go off without me."

She keeps looking at Cilla.

I'm wondering if something might have gone wrong back home. Boy troubles, maybe? A scandal of some sort?

Cilla shrugs, making a sad face.

My dreams of possible romance in Venice are fading fast.

A young man walks up and the asks if I will draw his lady.

I'd be delighted.

"Well then," the grandmother says, reaching into her handbag and giving me the equivalent of ten American dollars. It's more than the price of the picture, and I suspect it's a precaution to keep me at bay. "We'll be on our way."

Before they walk off, Cilla gives me a hug. I keep her in my arms a little too long, and the grandma takes notice.

"I really want to see you," I say.

"Me too," she whispers. "We're staying at the Danieli. Nine o'clock? I'll be in the lobby."

GONDOLA

The rococo Danieli lobby, quiet as a London men's club, is a
study in subdued Venetian elegance: fine carpets, brass and
gold accents, polished cherry wood and mahogany, discreet smoky
mirrors, and offset amber lighting. Well-dressed people move
through dimly lit spaces. A concierge in tails escorts a tall, graceful woman in a black hat to his desk and seats her. An older woman
with a small dog in her arms steps into the elevator, and as she
does, Cilla steps out. She gives me no more than a quick glance
and walks straight through the front door.

I follow her.

Outside, she turns to me and smiles.

"I've escaped!" she says, her voice happy and relieved. "At least
we have separate rooms, which made it easier."

"Is this the first time you've busted out?"

"Yes! Let's get a drink."

The hotel bar spills out onto the promenade bordering the
Grand Canal. We grab one of the few remaining tables for two. A
waiter comes over, places a little vase with flowers on the linen top,
and lights a candle. We can hear the water lapping.

"Wow," Cilla says. "How romantic!"

She sits back and takes a deep breath. I'm admiring how truly beautiful she has become.

The waiter speaks English and returns almost immediately with a bottle of iced pinot grigio. He pours two glasses.

We toast, our glasses touching.

"Harry Belmont!" Cilla says, giving me a once-over. "Look at you!"

"And look at you...I've had a crush on you since we were seven. I never got to kiss you, but I've thought about it from time to time. I think I've still got a crush on you."

Is that a blush?

"Harry, isn't seven or eight a little early to be thinking about romance?"

"Maybe. But it actually started when I was five. I remember exactly how I felt. I think I was in love with you even then."

Now I'm sure she's blushing.

"But you are different now, that's for sure. Same eyes, but not the same girl at all."

"I hope that's a compliment."

"It is."

She nods, silent.

"Well, you're even better looking than that cute kid I had my eye on back then."

"Yeah, the kind of cute that only a mother could love!" I laugh.

"I remember your mother," she says, smiling. "She was a horse-woman, as I recall."

"Still is."

"We used to sit on the fence and watch her. She was a beautiful rider."

"Still is. How about your mother?"

"My parents are getting divorced. My mother's in rehab. Did you know she had a problem? And my father's in Brazil with a woman about my age whom I've never met."

"That must be hard for you. I'm sorry to hear it."

"It was a bit of a shock, but I have got used to it, pretty much. How about you?" she asks, taking a sip, clearly not wanting to talk more about that.

"I don't ride, but I have affection for my mother's horses. In France, I discovered they eat horses."

"*Eat* them? Who eats horses?"

"The French do."

"Well, I was there, and nobody told me. If I'd known, I might have tried it."

"Might have tried it? I thought you might have been revolted just thinking about it. I was."

"Not me. I love to eat! I'm up for anything!"

"That's good to know."

We're both smiling.

"I can't get over this," Cilla says. "I would never have dreamed. Do you believe in fate, Harry?"

"I don't know. Right now, I feel like the luckiest guy in the world."

"Maybe it was meant to be? Our meeting again?"

"Well, we're here to catch up," I propose, giving her a little salute. "So, let's catch up."

"That will require more wine!" she says, and extends her glass. I fill hers, then mine, and order a second bottle.

"Hoo boy!" she says. "This could lead to trouble!"

"I hope so." I laugh.

"Bottoms up!" she says.

"Bottoms up!" We clink glasses again.

"Oh, Harry, this is *so* much fun!"

"The night is young. You aren't worried about your grandmother?"

"Not in the least! She won't wake up until precisely seven o'clock. You can count on it—and I am counting on it!"

"You get along with your grandmother?"

"She's old fashioned and overprotective. But I love her, and we have a good relationship. She's always been there for me."

I think about my own grandmother, who's always been there for herself.

"Tell me more about your trip, Harry," Cilla says, getting comfortable. "I want to know everything."

I won't tell her everything. If I did, she might walk away. But I do tell her about my time in the pits and my man, T-Bone.

I tell her about the nights spent sleeping under the stars, the long days in the saddle, the repairs in little shops along the way, and my journal. She tells me about her school, her friends, and silly things that make us both laugh. Like the time she fell into the Christmas tree trying to put the angel on the top and when she set off a fire in the oven the first time she made cookies. And when the family dog pissed on her first boyfriend's leg.

"He was so sweet about it, I let him kiss me." She giggles and takes another sip.

After a while, I'm beginning to feel like we've never been apart.

"So…what would you think about meeting up again in New York?" I venture, wondering if maybe it's too soon to ask.

She looks at me and smiles.

"I want to show you New York. I'm so glad you asked—I was afraid to."

"Yes! Show me everything, because I'm going to live in New York."

"You are?" she says, sitting up straight. "That's so exciting! What are you going to do?"

"I don't know yet. But it will be something I like doing."

The waiter comes over with a small plate of olives, bread, green olive oil, and parmesan cheese.

"So, what do you like to do? What are your passions now?"

"Squash."

"Squash? Not tennis?"

"No, because with squash I thought I could compete and do well. There weren't many girls playing squash."

"It's a hard sport," I say. "Do you still play?"

"Until recently."

"And did you compete?"

"All the time."

"Really? Ranked?"

"Yes. All-American. Ranked number one in my age group. Very lucky...I won fourteen to eighteen when I was fourteen and kept on winning. Listen to me! I'm bragging. But...since you asked..." she says, taking another sip.

I can picture her on the court. Strong body and graceful speed.

"That's definitely something worth bragging about, a champion. I'm impressed but not surprised."

"There are a number of things about me that might surprise you, Harry, and a lot of things you don't know. But how could you?"

"I only wish I'd had a chance."

"Harry, we go back a long way. But we're basically strangers. Isn't that odd?"

I nod, fingering my glass.

She's grown pensive.

But then her eyes come alive.

"Don't you just love it here, Harry?" she says. "Everything is so new! And even with my grandmother watching, I feel so free! In this moment, I am happy. Are you?"

"I am. Another nice surprise though, to hear a girl from Philadelphia talk this way."

"I haven't lived in Philadelphia for years, Harry. I'm a New York City girl."

"No wonder then..."

"No wonder what?"

"No wonder you don't *sound* like a Philadelphia girl."

"What does a Philadelphia girl sound like?"

"Well, pretty shallow and uptight. They're not a lot of fun. I'd say they're more like your grandmother than you."

"Well, then, it's a good thing I didn't grow up in Philadelphia!" she says, with a wink.

I'm enjoying the wine, loving this girl, rolling with the buzz.

"I can't believe all these years later, we're together again—and in Venice! But here you are. I remember our races. You mostly won. Your beautiful blond hair streaming in the wind behind you. I've never forgotten that amazing blond hair. But now you wear it short?"

She looks down for a moment, then up, her eyes a little more lidded, and sets her glass on the table.

"Ah, yes..." she says, with a sigh. "It's a shame about the hair..."

Her entire demeanor changes.

What did I do?

"Harry, it's a lovely evening. And oh, I would love to see you in New York," she begins, subdued. "I didn't think...I didn't know whether it would get this far. But since it has, I think I have to tell you."

I'm alert, waiting.

"I'm not here on a grand tour, Harry," she says after a moment, showing no emotion.

"I'm here because I have cancer..."

The word takes my breath.

"...And that's why my hair is short and why I'm not playing squash now."

"But...you look great. You sound great. Everything about you is great!"

She shakes her head and looks into her lap.

I'm at a complete loss.

"I'd been getting headaches and losing my balance," she continues. "I even fell a couple of times, just blacked out. So, they sent me to Memorial. The doctors did some tests and told me they couldn't help me. But they also told me of a clinic in Switzerland that specializes in difficult cases like mine."

She pauses to take a slow breath.

"So…my grandmother and I have spent the last several months there."

I see a sad calmness in her eyes. But there's also acceptance in her face.

A hot, keening pang washes over me.

Is it compassion or love?

"I'm so sorry, Cilla" is the best I can do.

"No, Harry. Please don't. I'll know more in a few weeks. But I already feel better. I haven't had a headache in ten days, and I haven't blacked out since we left the clinic. In the meantime, we're touring Europe…I'm happy, Harry."

She looks away.

Is she?

"Your parents? Where are they in this?"

"They don't even know what's going on—and if they did, they probably wouldn't care."

"But your grandmother…your grandmother said she promised your mother…"

"That was just to keep you from getting your hands on me…"

I see a teasing little smile at the corners of her lips. How can so much loss and suffering hide behind so many smiles? I'm smiling back, relieved that her sense of humor is intact.

For an instant, I see Pauline's face, remembering the frightening story behind her smiles.

"How have your friends reacted? Have they helped you?"

"Well, I was engaged. But when he found out I had cancer, well…he stopped calling. Some people just can't handle illness, I guess. They don't know what to do. In any case, he just dropped out…so that's over."

Bastard.

It's painful to see the hurt in her eyes, this astonishingly beautiful girl who only a moment ago was so full of life.

I'm still in shock but deeply impressed by how steady she is.

"The good news, Harry, is that I believe in miracles. They say this clinic is a place of miracles—even better than Lourdes—but with some really good science mixed in with all the magic stuff."

She stops to take another sip, and I can see from the look in her eyes that she's determined to put a good face on it.

"Before I went to Switzerland, I met three people in New York who were cured of terminal stage-four cancers at this place, and they're now all very happy and very much alive," she continues. "Two of them have become good friends of mine. One is my age. Better yet, they've all changed for the better. Now they don't waste time on frivolous things. They have a purpose in life, and they want to help other people. Almost dying can be a very positive thing, Harry."

Her face is hopeful, her eyes tear bright.

I feel something moving in my chest.

It's building, this unknowable force that bows me to its will. Am I falling down the rabbit hole with a woman who may not live to see another birthday?

If she weren't so startlingly beautiful—or, ironically, so full of life—it would be easier.

Love?

"What…can I do to help?" I finally hear myself say, wondering if she can read what's going on in my dazed mind.

"How about your taking me for a midnight gondola ride?" she answers, with a laugh. "There's nothing in the world I'd rather do right now!"

Gino, the gondolier, welcomes Cilla with a big flourish. But he's nowhere near so effusive when he sees she's got company. Nevertheless, he declares in English, "I sing for the lovebirds!" and breaks into an aria from Puccini.

Even at this hour, the canal is alive with gondolas and water taxis. Quais and bridges strung with pearls of light cast graceful, fluid reflections into the black water. Another gondolier serenades his customers with an Italian love song. Silhouetted against up-lit palazzos, people on the bridges above us promenade slowly through the Venetian night like figures on a darkened stage.

"This is like a dream, Harry." Cilla snuggles close on the cushioned passenger bench, her head on my shoulder. "There is no better remedy. Isn't it beautiful, Harry?"

"Yes, it is."

Our lips touch gently, and linger. She moves into the kiss, and we embrace. Gino continues his serenade, no doubt convinced that his operatic talents have brought about this happy moment.

And perhaps they have.

"Bravo, Gino!" Cilla calls out to him. The gondolier amps it up. Night strollers on a bridge wave to us and applaud.

"Harry, this could be the best night of my entire trip," she says softly, leaning into me. "Or maybe even my entire life..."

I'm happy to have found her again, and I'm already worried about losing her.

But most of all I wonder what this brave, heartbreakingly beautiful love from my past must be thinking as an intoxicating panorama of life, riding on the wings of Puccini, slowly passes by.

From above, somebody shouts, *"Bellissimo!"*

GOOD-LUCK FOUNTAIN

I'm throwing a coin into Bernini's famous Fontana della Barcaccia (Fountain of the Old Boat) in the Piazza di Spagna, at the bottom of the Spanish Steps in Rome, when I hear a woman call my name.

I turn around and recognize an old girlfriend from back home.

"Suzanne? What are you doing here?"

She's running toward me. I jog toward her, lift her up, and spin her around.

"Harry, this is like a movie!" she declares, breathless, eyes dancing.

"My kind of movie," I say, putting her down. "What better place for a romantic scene than Rome on a summer morning?"

"Is that yours?" she asks, pointing to the Triumph.

"It is."

"Well, what are we waiting for?"

I take her on a little sightseeing spin. She wraps her arms around my waist, presses close, and I can tell she's happy to see me.

Suzanne's in Rome taking an art course as part of a college summer exchange program.

"It must agree with you, because you've never looked better."

Later, she introduces me to her friend, Christina, a stunning, twenty-five-year-old Italian countess. She's the daughter of an Italian count and an American heiress. The *contessa* is well connected. Suzanne says we'll meet interesting people on an excursion to the Festival of the Two Worlds in Spoleto.

I know about Christina. She's a controversial celebrity who recently gained international notoriety by posing nude for a famous photographer. The photos wound up in an equally famous fashion magazine. No surprise. This sophisticated European is sensual as a jungle cat, Etruscan beautiful, and bursting with sexual self-awareness. I love her Italian accent, and I can't stop staring at her.

Getting ready for the trip the next morning, Suzanne grabs my arm and pulls me aside.

"Listen, Harry, I would appreciate it if you weren't quite so obvious," she chides, not bothering to conceal her jealous irritation. "It's hard enough for me around Christina, and you are *my* date."

"Oops. Sorry. I'm all yours."

She knows it's a lie.

Sporting white capri pants and sandals, Suzanne ties a red bandana around her head and rides behind me. Christina's at the wheel of her yellow Alfa Romeo convertible in a see-through mini-dress that hikes up to her pink panties.

We motor north three hours through a golden landscape of olive trees and Cyprus to Spoleto, a storybook medieval town in the Umbrian hills.

Two of Christina's hip Italian friends join us for dinner at a sidewalk trattoria. Paulo has an abundance of slick black hair, wears dark sunglasses, and looks like a movie star. Francesca, a tall blonde from Milan, models for Dior. Shortly, another friend, Maria, a film-school student and apprentice costume designer from Genoa, sits down next to me. She has glowing black eyes and luscious, full lips. I can't get over the lips. Every girl at the table is a knockout.

We're on our fourth bottle of red when Paulo starts playing a guitar. One of the girls sings a popular Italian love song, and everybody joins in. I'm having a great time and pouring myself another glass when Suzanne says, "Come on, Harry. We've got to go now."

What?

"I can't go now, Suzanne, Maria's in the middle of a sad story about how she just split with her boyfriend."

"*Harry*!" Suzanne is emphatic. "We want to show you Christina's apartment."

She gives me a coy look and leans down and whispers, her voice heavy with innuendo, "If you don't come now, you'll be *sorrr-ryyy*! You know what I mean, don't you, Harry?"

I don't know for sure what she means. But her look is enticing enough that I bid a reluctant *ciao* to my new friend from Genoa.

When we walk into Christina's apartment, there's only one bed, an unmade queen size.

"Well, now, ladies. It's late, and I see there's obviously not enough room for three, so I'd better find a place to bunk down before it gets any later," I announce, just in the off chance I got it wrong.

But the gods are still smiling.

"No need for that!" Christina puts in, giving me her top model look with the smoldering, lidded eyes. "We can all sleep right here. The bed's big."

"Great idea!" I practically shout, feeling I am a very lucky man but also feeling the wine and trying not to show my growing excitement.

"This is the best ganja money can buy," Christina says, as she rolls huge reefers for all three of us.

These things could be cigars.

"I don't know, ladies. I have almost no experience with marijuana," I tell them, sounding hopelessly sophomoric just when I want to sound cool.

"Don't worry, Harry. This is the best stuff on the planet. You'll love it."

Both girls suck in great lungsful and hold their breath until they burst out laughing. I can't hide that I'm a novice, so they make sure I inhale deeply with each drag so as not to waste a single puff of the pricey joint. They find my innocence and ineptitude hysterically funny, cracking up each time I cough. I'm laughing too, when suddenly I notice the girls are naked.

"Whoa! You took your clothes off! How could I have missed that?" I chuckle, reaching out to caress first one, then the other.

They're giggling and pulling off my shirt and pants. I want to help, but I seem to have lost control of my arms and legs. Everything is slowly spinning. But I couldn't be happier. I know I love these giggling girls, maybe more than I've ever loved anyone in my whole life. I'm flat-out crazy in love, and I can't wait to show them how much.

The last thing I remember is the three of us rolling around in a tangle of limbs and laughter. I've never been so happy.

But in my journal, I note that night as one of the great tragedies and regrets of my life. Not because I drank too much and smoked dope like a fiend or because I indulged myself to excess and must have behaved like a drunken fool.

The reason is that I spent the entire night with two beautiful, willing women, and with few exceptions, I don't remember any of it.

CLEOPATRA

S unday morning. Market day. Suzanne and Christina have gone off to do some serious shopping and check out the art in af-riend's gallery. I park the bike in the piazza in Spoleto to have a look around.

It's a good day for the market—clear skies and not much heat in the sharp, metallic morning air. I can smell ancient stones warming slowly in the sun. People wander among stalls with net bags, studying produce, feeling tomatoes and melons, and haggling with the vendors, most of whom spend a lot of time in one exasperatingly fractious minidrama after another, looking indignant, dismissive, trying to cut a deal. Hands are all over; you'd think they were talking about life and death. But in the end, everybody's happy. The money's coming in; the goods are going out.

More people show up, and the place is getting busy. Vendors announce their wares like town criers: flowers, fresh fish, eggs, fruit, vegetables from the local farms, pots and pans for the *cucina*, racks of hanging salamis of all sizes, and fresh bread. The butcher hawks live chickens, beef, veal, and pork chops. One woman is knitting children's sweaters. There's a cobbler who can make you a pair of custom leather sandals right on the spot for a dollar. It's worth the dollar just to hear him sing about his shoes. Under a red awning, a man and woman are selling fine leather goods. I wander over and take a look at the wallets.

I'm about to move on when someone says, "Excuse me." I turn, and here's a woman in enormous sunglasses, her hair hidden under a white scarf. She's wearing a blue-and-white-striped gondola shirt, white clam diggers, and blue espadrilles.

She's almost petite, but there's a lot of bosom under the shirt.

"Excuse me," she says again. "Is that your motorcycle?" The voice sounds familiar—slight British accent?—but I can't place it.

"That one?" I ask, pointing in the direction of the bike.

She glances over. "Yes, that one."

I nod. "Yes, it is."

She gives me a big smile. I want to ask her if we've met. But I keep my mouth shut because she might take it the wrong way and think I'm on the hustle. I don't want to chase her off.

She amps up the smile.

"Would you be a dear," she says, "and give me a ride?"

Why am I not surprised? Everybody loves the Triumph TR6. I'd be happy to give her a ride.

"Are you ready to go right now?" I ask.

"The sooner the better," she says.

We walk over to the bike, and I ask her, "Have you ever been on a motorcycle?"

"Only scooters," she says.

"This is different," I tell her. "On this, you've really got to hold on."

"What do I hold on to?" she asks, looking at the seat.

"You hold on to me," I say.

She nods. "Okay. Let's go."

I lower the footrests and fire up the engine, and she climbs on. Because she's short, she has to negotiate her legs and fanny to get up on the saddle. She grabs my shirt on both sides, and I tell her to let go of the shirt.

"Put your arms around me," I tell her. "Hold on tight, and don't let go." She wraps her arms around my waist, and we're on our way. As we accelerate out of the market, she gives me a squeeze, and I'm acutely aware of those remarkably warm breasts pressing against my back. Now she gives a little extra jerk, and I know she is surprised by the sudden surge of raw power between her legs. We pass under an arch, the sound of the engine slapping off the walls, and then up a narrow street and onto the road heading out of town. I'm thinking we'll take a ride up the mountain to Christina's place.

Within seconds of leaving town, we're blasting through the wind, and she lets out a whoop. We've got the cypress-lined tarmac to ourselves, except for a white car that appears a hundred yards behind us in the rearview mirror.

"Faster!" she shouts. We're topping sixty, ripping across open country. Now we're breaking eighty. I glance at the mirror and see the white car is gaining. I can see it's a Rolls Royce.

"Faster!" she shouts again, this time more urgently, giving me another squeeze. We're blowing down a winding black ribbon that takes us through fields and olive groves to the foot of the mountain, where we slow and turn onto the mountain road. The Rolls turns too and continues to follow us up the mountain.

"Who is that guy?" I shout over my shoulder.

"Richard!" she yells.

"Who is Richard?" I'm shouting. But before the words are even out of my mouth, it dawns on me. Richard? Can this little lady breaking my ribs with the big boobs, babushka, and giant shades be...the world's most famous movie star? How can she be? Elizabeth Taylor is *a lot* more beautiful, for one thing...

"Don't let him catch us!" she shouts.

But now I can see it. There was a rumor they were coming to Spoleto after filming ended on *Cleopatra* in Spain.

Am I part of a game? Is she playing with me? Are they both playing with me?

Are they playing with each other?

Am I in some kind of trouble?

I have no idea.

But I give her the ride of her life up the switchbacks.

"Oh my God! *Oh my God!*" she screams.

The Rolls is barreling around the hairpins like a drunken beluga whale, and I wonder if the Rolls might roll. I'm putting distance between us, but it keeps coming. The road ends at Christina's, so I'm not sure what I'm going to do when I get there.

I'm nipping the sharp turns tightly. The Rolls has dropped out of sight in the mirror. Just a few more switchbacks, and we'll be at the top.

But then what?

Finally, we arrive at Christina's and the end of the road.

She slides off the seat, removes her sunglasses, and rips off the babushka, and I can see she is who I think she is. She's flushed and almost gasping, as if she'd just had sex, and those famous lavender eyes are flashing right into my own. In an instant, she grabs my face and kisses me full on the mouth.

I'm speechless.

"My God, that was *fun!*" she cries. "But you've got to *run!* Run! Run! Run! Get out before he comes!"

"Why?" I ask, flustered, curious to know how bad it could be.

"Because he might hit you!"

Now I'm angry. "I'll hit him back!"

"No!" she says, grabbing my arms. "He's just jealous. He's *always* jealous. It's not about you. It's about me!" she shouts, shaking me. "I don't want him to do something he'll regret, so get out of here *right now*, while you can. I'll take care of Richard."

She pushes me toward the garden gate of the villa. I'm surprised at her strength.

"Go in there. Don't let him see you." We both hear an engine racing and look to see the big white whale swinging around the bend, straining up the last bit of road.

I pull the iron latch, slip through the gate, and lock it behind me, disappearing behind the bougainvillea-decked villa walls.

"Don't come out until he leaves," she says, shooting me a quick glance through the little iron-barred window.

The Rolls slams to a loud stop seconds later, fat tires grinding hard into gravel. A door slams, and I hear a man shout something. Right away, even without looking, I can recognize that distinctive Welsh growl. I peek out the little window, and there he is, Richard Burton, all in white: white sweater, white trousers, white Italian shoes. Even the frame of his sunglasses is white. He looks like an Elvis wannabe—all in white but clearly in a black mood.

"What the hell do you think you are *doing*?" he sputters, scarcely able to contain himself. His face is red.

"Richard..."

"You're not a woman; you're a hellion! A harridan!" he rages. Then, looking around, he says, "Who the hell was tht man? Where is he?"

"Oh, you old *drunk*!" she shouts. "He's just a harmless boy! A boy! I don't even know his name!"

"Where is he?"

"I made him go. I made him go because you're so crazy you might even try to kill him!"

"I will kill him!"

"It's not the *boy*, Richard; it's *me*! Look at me! The boy has nothing to do with it. I want to have *fun* for a change, Richard, and you're behaving like a jealous *fool*!"

"Damn you!" he bellows, his voice like a lion. "You think this is fun? Racing around on motorcycles with perfect *strangers*? You could get yourself killed!"

"Oh, fuck off," she says, deflated, as if the wind had suddenly gone out of her. "Sometimes you exhaust me."

"Get in the car," he says.

"No. I don't want to get in the car."

"You want to stay here then? You want to stay here with that cowardly boy who's too afraid to show his *face*?" This last part he shouts out in all directions.

He walks around to the passenger side of the Rolls and opens the door.

"Get in, and we'll talk about it in the car."

"I don't want to talk about it," she says. "I just want to have a little *fun!* I don't want to sit around all day and watch you drink!"

It's like they're acting in a scene right out of a movie. What a shame I'm the only audience.

I wonder if this is what celebrities do when they sneak away and spend romantic time together out of the prying eyes of the paparazzi. I've heard that they fell in love in Spain filming *Cleopatra*. It's only been a few weeks since shooting ended, but they're already acting like a couple of brats who have been married for years, two prickly hotheads under the same roof. I can only imagine what it must be like at home.

If this is love, maybe I'll take a pass. For an instant I think of Pauline.

There's a pause, and Cleopatra glances in my direction.

"Is that where he is?" Marc Antony says. "Is he behind that wall? Are you behind that wall, boy?"

"Behave yourself, Richard," she says. "Can't you simply try for once to behave like a grown man?"

"That's precious, coming from you," he snaps. He gives her a fierce look, and they stare at each other in silence.

For a crazy moment, I want to step out, just to see what might happen. I'm wondering what he might do. Would he try to fight me, challenge me to some kind of a duel? Or would he relax and shake my hand?

I feel intimidated. But I really want to know. So I grab the iron handle to open the gate, ready for anything.

But while I'm indecisive and daydreaming, she suddenly walks over to the car, says something to Burton, blows a kiss in my direction, and gets in. He closes the door, walks back to the driver's side, gets behind the wheel, and turns the car around, and they drive away, leaving me to ponder what had just happened.

The fragile wires that bind the world's most celebrated couple have frayed almost to snapping right before my eyes.

I step out and watch the big white Rolls disappear down the mountain.

The only time I ever see either of them again is in the movies.

SARAH

A magnificent Florentine palazzo hidden behind a tall hedge catches my eye. The big brass gate is wide open, and before I know it, I'm drawn onto the gravel driveway, attracted by a force beyond my powers to resist.

The villa looms into full view in all its Italianate splendor—five stories of Renaissance extravagance, festooned in crimson bougainvillea. Gardens are in full bloom, surrounded by a manicured lawn. Beyond, I can see the famed golden hills of Tuscany rolling into the distance. Then suddenly there's a motion to my left. I look over, and for a moment I can't believe my eyes. Three girls in bikinis are waving. I can see the pool tucked away.

Now I count five more girls.

I wave back, "*Buongiorno!*" Then in English: "I know I am trespassing!"

I turn around as if to leave.

"Don't go!" one of the girls shouts. A couple of them are hurrying in my direction.

"Are you American?" the tall one with the long blond hair asks.

"Yes," I say. "Are you?"

"*Yes!*" The girl fairly shrieks. "You are the only other American we have met since we've been here. Over a week now."

Now I'm off the bike, and we're all shaking hands. The other girls are coming over, curious to see what's going on.

I can see they like my motorcycle.

"What is this place?" I ask.

The tall one is also the prettiest, and I end up talking mostly to her. Her name is Sarah. She grew up a surfer girl in Manhattan Beach, California, and thought about becoming a professional volleyball player. But she's no ditz: copresident of her high-school class, straight A's. She explains that they're all students at a top New England women's college, and this is the summer campus of one of the cultural exchange programs. Several times a week, chaperones drive the girls into Florence to see the sights. The rest of the time they take art-appreciation classes in the villa.

The girls invite me to have a swim. I change into a suit and dive into sapphire water, resting on the bottom, giving thanks for this unexpected windfall before stretching out on a chaise to dry in the sun.

A few of the girls cluster around, asking questions. Why am I in Florence? What am I doing in Europe? Why am I on a motorcycle? Where have I been so far? They're all happy to be in Florence. And so am I.

"They keep a sharp eye on us around here," Sarah says. "We don't get out much."

"I can imagine. So...you guys want to party?" I ask.

Sarah looks at the other girls, then back at me.

"Do you have any friends?" she asks.

"No," I tell her. "It's just me."

She looks at the girls again. They've gone back to reading books or sunbathing. Two seem to be asleep.

"Well, then," she says. "That's probably not going to work too well."

"What's not going to work?"

"Eight of us and one of you."

I nod. "But just the two of us might work."

"Exactly," she says. "That's what I'm thinking."

"What about those chaperones you were telling me about?"

"Not a problem." She tells me the two American female chaperones, both faculty members, were discovered in bed together just the night before last. So now there's an understanding. We won't tell on you—and you won't tell on us.

"You don't have to worry," Sarah says. "These girls are going to be just fine tonight, and every night."

Over a simple pasta dinner and a bottle of red, I quickly discover Sarah is not the sort of girl you meet every day.

"After high school, what was your plan?" I ask her.

"Well, I thought I was a hot shot, so I applied to Stanford for a scholarship. But they turned me down. Guess I was just a big fish in a small pond."

"So, then what happened?"

"I ended up in Boston instead."

"Do you like it?"

"Can't surf in New England, so I ski now."

"Stowe?"

"Yes, you know it?"

"Yeah, on vacation, I teach for free, so I get free lift tickets."

"You're a ski instructor?"

"Not private lessons. Just beginners and kids."

"That sounds nice."

"It is nice. So, what are you studying?"

"I have a double major, Chinese history and Russian literature."

"Mind if I ask why?"

"No particular reason," she says, taking a sip of wine. "But I think the way things are going in the world, it might be a good idea to understand China. And Russian literature is *the* best—if you have the patience to read it."

"I tried *War and Peace*—too dense for me. I had no patience at all. You need a who's who to keep track of all the characters."

She laughs. "That's true. Actually," she says, "I'm thinking about graduate school in engineering."

"An advanced engineering degree? That has nothing to do with humanities."

"No. But in my family, undergraduate school is for experimentation and exploration. Engineering is professional, but it's just another option. I test well in physics, and I might want to get a job designing rockets and spacecraft. My dad works for Northrop Grumman."

I watch her.

"All pretty girls are dumb. Especially blondes—haven't you heard? Did anyone ever test your IQ?"

"Yes."

"Are you going to tell me?"

"No...but I'm not as dumb as I look."

I'm staring directly into the restless intelligence lurking behind those lovely blue eyes.

"Believe me, you don't look dumb."

"Well, I'm very happy you get it, Mr. Belmont," she says, toasting me with her glass. "Because I date a couple of guys in Boston who don't. Intellectual snobs who wouldn't credit a good-looking girl with brains if she hit them over the head with a book. Which is what I feel like doing sometimes."

"I've got a couple of guys like that in my own family. Neanderthals with women," I tell her.

"So how did you escape being a Neanderthal yourself?"

"I was terrified that's where I was headed back in Philadelphia. So, I just left. Seeing if I could find something better."

"I'm glad you found me," she says.

After coffee, we take a little motorcycle ride through the night-time streets of Florence, eventually ending up at my pensione.

Sometime in the early hours of the morning, I wake up, summoned out of a restless dream. The room is suffused in a silver glow flooding in from French doors that open out on quiet streets. Sarah's standing there naked, fine surfer body bathed in platinum, staring out at a full moon the size of a dinner plate. I get out of bed and go to her. Without turning, she says, "Beautiful..."

Full moons always bring good things.

I don't think I've ever seen a bigger one. I tread gently, not wanting to interfere with whatever spell is weaving its magic, the kind of magic that comes only in the night under the moon.

"You are beautiful" is all I can manage to say.

She turns to look at me.

"Thank you," she whispers, touching my cheek. She shifts her gaze back to the night sky.

Talking only seems to spoil the mood, so we stand silent and motionless, somehow humbled, side by side in the platinum light, lost in our own thoughts. Adam and Eve naked in the Garden of Firenze, sensing now some ancient, unknowable dreamlike thing. We're aware we share a rare instant, full in the knowledge that we'll probably never see each other again.

"What are you thinking?"

After a pause, she says gently: "That this...this is a moment neither of us will ever forget..."

She looks at me again, eyes searching. We're locked in the wonder of the huge moon, somehow reduced to our most vulnerable, primal selves, back to beginnings, at the mercy of an all-seeing silent witness that hovers above us like a god.

"Yes...that's exactly what I was thinking...which means I will never forget you."

And I never do.

THE ASPIRING PROFESSOR

One month later, on a beach in Santander on Spain's north coast, I sit near a beautiful woman, pushing my toes into hot sand. She glances over—relaxed, smiling—and our eyes meet. I don't need to tell her I'm not Spanish. She speaks to me in perfect English, and now she's talking about her two boys who have gone to Barcelona to spend the summer with a great-aunt. The oldest boy is seven. She is a teacher, she tells me, but when school is out, she is a prostitute.

A prostitute?

She says this without the blink of an eye nor hint of a blush, as if she were talking about the weather.

I look into her flashing eyes, summer sun painting a stripe of molten copper across her tanned shoulders. I can already see myself with her, and maybe she can see something in my eyes, read my mind. She smiles, waiting, her eyes curious, a grown woman with the fresh face of a teenage girl, luxuriant black hair catching the light. We talk about life. She laughs and draws a doodle in the sand with her finger, rubs her foot against mine, and then we leave together.

After, we take a long walk on wet sand. I hold her hand, and it's almost like being back home. She tells me both her boys play the guitar, and she is working on her master's so she can teach in the university.

Does she have a husband? I never ask because I don't want to know.

Instead, I ask, "If you do teach in the university, will you still be a working girl in the summers?"

She turns and gives me a mischievous little smile.

"Maybe," she says. Then with a wink, she adds, "Because I always like to work…"

This is a conversation I would never be having in Philadelphia.

Out on the water, a sailboat slowly makes its way back to a cove among the rocks. The last of the sun licks the tops of the hills, and a pregnant moon starts to inch over the edge of the sea, which gets me thinking about an early start in the morning.

But just then she says, eyes closed, "Harry, will you stay with me tonight?"

I look at her, then at the moon. Is it already full again? In my mind, I flash on Sarah, good memories. But I'm mindful about trying to get an early start in the morning.

What is it about full moons?

"It will be a beautiful night, almost a full moon, *a luna llena.* Can you imagine? I have a terrace with a view."

"You know I have to leave…"

She touches my hand.

"I know. But I'm lonely, and I would love the company. I will cook us a traditional Spanish paella."

Moments later, we hop on the saddle, and she wraps her arms around my waist. We stop at a bodega to buy fresh bread, olive oil, and a couple of bottles of local red. At another place, we pick up shrimp, clams, squid, and fresh fish right off the boat.

The apartment is five flights up, but it's clean, comfortable, well worth the hike. You can see the little harbor all strung with lights. The moon, higher and brighter now, casts a shimmering pewter path on the Med.

"Maybe you can teach me how to make paella?" I say, as we empty the bags in the kitchen.

"Do you cook?"

"No, but I like to eat."

She laughs.

"All men like to eat," she says. "But not all men like to cook."

"I love paella."

"In Spain, many men cook. The big chefs are all men."

"How did you learn to cook paella?" I ask.

"Every family has its own recipe," she says. "I'm going to cook my mom's recipe, which she got from her mom."

My mom's mom couldn't find the kitchen in her own house.

She puts me to work cleaning shrimp and assorted minor pantry duties, while she prepares rice, chops onions and parsley, and crushes garlic.

There's a long silence while we slice and dice.

"Would you like to know my name?" she asks.

I look up, a deer in the headlights.

Oh God…

She looks at me steadily, awaiting an answer, her knife hovering over the parsley.

"Yes," I say, ashamed. How is it possible to be with a beautiful woman and never even ask her name?

"My name is Pilar," she says. "And I don't sleep with men I don't like."

"Pilar. That's a beautiful name."

She smiles and resumes chopping.

"I'm glad you like it, Harry. I thought you'd never ask."

"I'm sorry," I say.

She nods.

"Have you never heard the name Pilar before?" she asks.

"Do you know John Wayne?"

She looks at me as if I'm five years old.

"John Wayne, the American movie actor? The big cowboy? I love John Wayne. Of course I know him. I would sleep with John Wayne. I would never ask him to pay me."

Her little verbal slap puts me down another peg.

"John Wayne's wife's name is Pilar," I tell her.

"Yes, Pilar," she says, as if remembering but trying to place the face. After a pause, she adds: "Harry, I would like to give you your money back."

Another surprise.

She's reading my eyes carefully.

"I don't want it. You earned it. Think of your boys in Barcelona. I'm just happy to be here tonight."

"Thank you," she says, still holding my eyes. "Thank you, Harry."

We don't eat until ten o'clock, in the Spanish tradition. She lights candles on the terrace. The food is good, even better with the luscious local rioja that she tells me comes from a tiny vineyard just up the road. With every sip I can smell the iron-rich, musky Iberian earth and taste ancient limestone. I like it so much, I keep pouring more. We eat slowly and talk into the night. I'm surprised how funny she can be. I sense that if I were not on a mission, this could turn out to be something very good indeed.

When we finally blow out the candles and head to bed, it's almost two. The moon is arcing down to the far side of the earth. The night is hot. Tired from a long day, we drift off, naked under a ceiling fan. It's our only night, but I feel as if we've known each other a long time.

We don't make love until the sun wakes us.

After, over café latte and buttered bread on the terrace, I realize I can't pull myself away.

"Would you mind if I stay another day?" I ask, finally, surprising myself. "I don't want to leave. Not yet."

She looks at me, tipping her cup to her lips.

"I like you, Harry," she says. "I don't mind at all."

That night, we make plates of tapas and eat out on the terrace under the stars. The next morning, I slip away early and drive alone mile after mile through endless olive groves, struggling to shake off conflicting pangs of longing and an inexplicable sense of loss. What is this new thing? Why should I feel loss? I mean, what have I lost, and what have I got to lose?

What, then? Is it guilt?

I try to focus all my attention on the road ahead.

As the miles roll by, I get to thinking once again about the stunning contrast between where I come from and where I am now. Where I come from, the notion of a young woman working in any job is unheard of, almost unthinkable. Never mind prostitution.

With the exception of a few entitled matriarchs like my grandmother, my world is strictly a man's world built on privilege and entitlement. Enterprising, independent-minded girls are viewed with suspicion. Girls go to finishing schools. They attend elite colleges—usually all-girl colleges (where you might find the family name on the library or gym), mainly because it's a chance to meet other WASPs. Each girl has her own debutante party. It may be the most important event of her life. Husbands come and go, but a deb party is forever and will forever define who you are. Most of the time she will marry other WASP money. Everybody talks a good game about romance, but no one seriously expects anything as pedestrian as love to get in the way of a good social match.

Maybe Spanish aristocrats might have a like view of how things ought to work. But I suspect that If I tried to explain any of this to Pilar, she would simply gape in puzzlement, as if hearing for the first time about the strange cultural rites of some exotic tribe. And if I tried to explain Pilar to the debutantes back home, they would practically faint in disbelief.

TRAFFIC COP

In a village outside Barcelona, it's siesta time. Ahead, the single-lane cobblestone road leads to a whitewashed cluster of red-roofed houses and shops. A man sits in a folding chair near the only traffic light. When he hears me coming, he stirs like a melting puppet in the shimmering heat. I can see he's a policeman, rising now from his chair, pushing a button on a light pole. The light changes from green to red.

Not another soul in sight, not a car, truck, or bus, not even a goat or a dog. Just me and a melting cop in the middle of an empty Spanish afternoon.

I pump the handbrakes. The front tire loses purchase. I notice too late the cobbles are slick, maybe from a car accident or a spill from one of the mule-drawn carts you see everywhere in the provinces, hauling olive oil.

Both wheels slide. The bike slaloms and falls hard, hurling me into the gutter, where I scud twenty feet like a rag doll, finally coming to rest in a heap.

I struggle to my feet, no apparent broken bones. The helmet has a black scar where it hit the pavement. I immediately turn my attention to the bike, a broken toy in a jumble of upturned plastic furniture in the corner café where the policeman had been sitting.

I can see the bike may be totaled, and I'm thinking I'm stuck in Spain with no transportation and next to no money.

Besides some pain and shock, I feel rage. I imagine that the cop changed the light only because he had nothing else to do on this sultry, dog-ass day. Or maybe he did it in hopes that I'd run the light and he could collect a cash fine, which, of course, he would pocket. The jacket has held, but when I look down at my leg, I can see blood leaking through a rip in my pants.

The cop is walking toward me, shouting and gesticulating, as if I were to blame for this mess. As if the crash were an insult to his person. I'm pumped, shouting back in English. Together we raise an angry babel that seems to wake the entire town from afternoon torpor.

Window shutters fly open. I'm still reeling as a crowd of young men materializes. They all seem to be taking my side against the cop. In seconds, they're carrying the bike carcass back into the street. Several people show up with tools. Within minutes, they're swarming all over the wreck like a pit crew, straightening the wheels, aligning the bent mainframe, checking for fuel and oil leaks, everybody talking at once.

Somebody brings me a cold glass of sangria. The work is hot. It's almost a hundred degrees in the shade, and they're all sweating through their clothes. Nobody seems to mind, and they won't let me pitch in.

The cop has disappeared, probably so he won't have to help.

A woman in black shows up with bandages and iodine. She steers me out of the sun, sits me down under an awning, and does her best to clean up the leg. The sangria is delicious. It goes down smooth as iced tea, but kicks in with a satisfying flush of awareness that I'm not dead or dismembered.

A close call, but in fact no more than a setback.

I close my eyes and find myself drifting down to a shadowy, uncomfortable place where suddenly I see Mike's face gazing at me out of the gloom. He seems to be smiling.

"Buddy," he says. "It's not your fault."

Not my fault?

Then I get his meaning.

Startled, I force open my eyes, squint into the summer glare of old Spain, and shake of Mike's ghost. I still hate myself for leaving him on the floor that night, for letting him die. In my mind, I see him flying off that other motorcycle to his death. I try to stand, as he had tried to stand, but my head goes light, and I fall back. I wonder if I might faint. Now he's standing near the stricken Triumph, giving me a thumbs up, telling me everything is going to be all right. Somehow, I know he's also telling me that he too is okay.

I want to believe it, and I silently thank him for his forgiveness.

After a couple of hours, I begin to feel whole again, healed in important ways I can't comprehend. Only a little worse for wear, I thank my new friends with embraces all around, mount my restored bike amid a chorus of *adios* and *vaya con dios*, and ride into the late afternoon.

This is how I say good-bye to Mike. And my guilt.

SURPRISE ENDING

Low overcast hangs above Paris when I finally return in early October.

Dead leaves skitter in eddies, little ghosts dancing briskly around my feet. Squadrons of black grackles perch on naked branches. People are walking around in sweaters and scarves. But I walk straight into a sandbag.

I go to the Folies and rap on the stage door. The goon recognizes me and lets me in. I walk down the cramped corridor, looking to surprise Pauline.

An accented voice comes from behind me. Is it German? Maybe Dutch?

I turn around.

"Hello, Green Eyes, I'm Wilhelmina. We met, but you probably don't remember—we all look alike." The tall dancer with the throaty voice laughs, gesturing me toward an empty dressing room.

"My friends call me Wili," she says. "I have to get ready. But let's sit down."

I'm about to open my mouth when Wili says, "Pauline told me all about you. She was very fond of you, always talking about her Green Eyes…"

"Where is she?" I ask.

"It's complicated," Wili says, lighting a cigarette. "I'll be truthful with you. Pauline and I became friends, and then, we became lovers."

She pauses and takes a drag on her cigarette, looking to see how I'll take the news.

"I'm sure you did not expect that. I did not expect that," she says, squinting through the smoke.

The words suck the life out of me. We sit in silence.

"I'm not sure what to make of that," I say finally.

But I'm thinking—Pauline? Can't be true.

"So why are you telling me this?"

"I'm telling you because we're in this together, Green Eyes. Look at this," she offers me a handwritten note.

I read it out loud. "Dear Wili. Please forgive me. I've gone to Greece for a vacation. I don't know when I'm coming back."

"I know where she is," Wili says. "She's with that rich Greek on his island."

"Did she say anything to you about me before she left?" I ask. "Did she say anything about coming to America?"

Wili looks down the corridor toward her dressing room. The dancers are filing in. Everybody's laughing and talking at once in German, French, Dutch, and English.

"I've got to go, Green Eyes," she says. "All I can tell you is, that girl is a mystery. She talks about dreams of Broadway and Hollywood, and I fall in love with her. Just when I think it's real, she disappears in the middle of the night and runs off with a rich Greek. What can I tell you?"

She gives me a sad look of exasperation.

"Maybe she'll find you, and you can both live happily ever after."

I stand up. "Or maybe she'll find *you*."

Wili reaches out and strokes my cheek gently with her hand.

Then she turns on those long cancan legs and strides, like a goddess, back to her dressing room.

REVELATIONS

Under the dripping awning of a fashionable shop in the chic Paris suburb of Neuilly, I close the umbrella and pull from my pocket a folded piece of paper to recheck the name of the fancy restaurant where I'm supposed to meet my father. He's in Paris on business and wants to see me.

The last time we'd seen each other, I had announced my plans for the future. That did not go well. So, I know today could spell trouble. But the lure of a lavish French dinner with expensive wines—everything free, courtesy of Dad—overrides the cautious little voice in my head.

On the way, the wind picks up and rain goes horizontal. I arrive wet as a river rat, my best and only travel outfit soaked. The old tweed jacket—that once belonged to my father—smells like sheep urine, and the drenched khaki pants look like they just came out of a duffel bag, which they did.

Inside, out of the rain, I glance down and see a little puddle already pooling around my waterlogged bike boots on the spotless black-and-white tiles.

The maître d' takes one look and keeps on looking, waiting for me perhaps to realize that I've accidently stumbled into an establishment way out of my league.

Instead, I turn my attention to the elegant room to locate my father. After a brief scan, I spot him comfortably ensconced at a window table.

He could pass for a French aristocrat. Candlelight dances off a flute of what I have no doubt is very fine champagne. As he sips, he's reading *Paris Match*, a French newspaper.

"May I help you?" the maître d' says a little too pointedly, in French, letting me know it might be best if I go right back out into the rain and stop fouling this Michelin two-star's carefully crafted ambiance of class and impeccable taste.

"Yes. You can take me to my father there, Mr. Belmont," I answer in French, gesturing. "And I would appreciate it if you would take this and put it where it can dry," I add, handing him my umbrella.

"Monsieur Belmont!" the maître d' effuses, now alive with fawning good will, eager to quickly redress the unfortunate misunderstanding and to assure me that everything is now quite all right.

"*Mais oui! Absolument! Suivez-moi, s'il vous plait!*"

I attract only a few quick looks of disapproval before we reach the table. Most of this well-fed crowd is far too busy experiencing every nuanced bite while taking extraordinary care to make certain no one gets the wrong impression that they're actually having a good time. Such a public display of indiscretion in a shrine of fine dining, and in this particularly exclusive corner of haut-Paris, would be inconceivable, positively bourgeois.

But I have a sudden, impish vision of a loud posse of couples from Omaha or Fort Wayne whooping it up, drinking way too much of the cheapest wine in the house, having the time of their lives and emptying the place faster than a conga line of wild monkeys. French patrons would be falling all over themselves trying to get to the door.

"You're late," my father says, folding his newspaper and rising slowly.

I step forward to give him a quick buddy squeeze, so we can get the uncomfortable business of hugging behind us. Holding his hand up, he says with a little smile, "You're wet."

I step back, almost relieved.

"Sit down," he says. Then in French: "Andre, another bottle, please."

"The same, monsieur?"

"*Oui. Merci.*"

Even I'm impressed. Here's my father—or a clone of my father—decked out in a custom-tailored, midnight-blue suit and blue silk tie, crisp custom white dress shirt, and bespoke, bench-made English leather shoes, black and shiny as the old Rolls that still sits in our garage back home. Slick as a blade. Dad, the suave and elegant man of mystery, the movie star. I have to hand it to him. He looks pretty good. Reinvented, you might say, as a continental bon vivant.

Which makes me wonder, have I been missing something? Is this all an act? If it's an act, why? Does it have anything to do with me?

"Sit down," he says again, gesturing to the other chair.

"Sorry I'm late," I say, as a waiter positions the chair and seats me. Then, moving like a matador, he artfully drapes across my lap the impeccable linen napkin that an instant before had looked to me like a white rabbit.

"You look awful," my father says, smiling.

I have to laugh.

"Got caught in the rain. But you look good."

Andre appears, opens a new bottle of champagne, and fills our flutes.

"To the traveling man," my father says, raising his glass. The flutes touch.

"Where are you staying, Dad?"

"I'm staying at the Ritz."

"Really? Kind of expensive, isn't it?" I say, putting the glass down. Think you can afford it?"

I am only half joking.

"Business trip, remember?" he explains. "Expense account covers a lot."

"So, we're having a business dinner?"

"Actually, I met with someone earlier. Head of the Paris office."

"What's his name?"

"It's a she, actually," he says, relaxed, taking a sip. "Her name is Monica Sanders."

I look carefully at him.

Has my father been cheating on my mother?

"This is some business trip," I offer.

"Now, don't jump to any conclusions," he says, still relaxed. "Not everybody in business is a man. If I were having an affair, do you think I would sit here and tell you I was meeting a woman?"

I think about that.

"So...?" I go on, curious now. "What's with all the..."

I don't know how to describe it.

"All the what?" he asks innocently.

"How come you're so dressed up?"

He gives me a puzzled look.

"Dad, I don't think I've ever seen you so...dressed up," I try to explain. "I mean, let's face it, you look pretty sharp."

"'Sharp? You think I look sharp?"

"Yes."

"I would like to believe that sharp is not the best choice of words," he counters. "You've often enough seen me in black tie, Harry. And I always wear a suit to the office. I don't know what you're getting at."

When I say nothing, he continues.

"Are you suggesting…that I'm making some kind of special effort for Mrs. Sanders? Yes, you heard me correctly. It's *Mrs.* Sanders. She's married. So, you can relax."

I nod.

But I'm not satisfied, thinking of mom back home all alone in that big house in Philadelphia.

He can see my question in my eyes.

"In serious business there's an unspoken code, as you may someday discover yourself—if you don't first starve to death struggling in some garret as a writer or actor," he adds.

"There's a dress code in the States. But in London, Paris, or Milan, it's much more theatrical and unforgiving. Style can often trump substance. Following the rules opens doors in business."

Smug and self-satisfied, Dad's educating the clueless kid and loving it.

"Perhaps even more important is to be able to converse comfortably anywhere, anytime, with anyone—preferably in several languages. Essential for life and career."

I remain silent for a moment.

"And how do you think you're doing in life and career, Dad?"

"I meet that higher code in every detail, Harry," he replies, without missing a beat, "and always have. Which is something you might want to give me credit for. If you don't meet the code, you don't meet the customer. If you can't get in the door, you can't make any money. I can get in any door in the world."

Pleased with himself, he empties the flute and holds it for Andre to fill.

"That's pretty impressive," I tell him after a moment. "I never would have guessed."

There's a pause.

"I see," he says a little flatly, perhaps not appreciative of my bland response.

"Monsieur?" Andre asks, moving toward me, the bottle poised in his hand. I look at my father, who nods to Andre, then to me.

"Sure, why not?" he says. "We have a lot to talk about."

Andre fills the flute and disappears.

"So," my father says, placing the flat of his hand emphatically on the spotless linen tabletop. "We don't seem to know one another very well, do we?"

Now I see where he wants to go, and I'm ready.

"Well, who's to blame for that, Dad?" I ask, without emotion. "I mean, you've always been pretty busy with…whatever you do."

He nods. "Touché!"

"I mean it's fairly obvious. You've always had your own world, and that's fine. I'm not complaining."

"I like to think it's never too late," he says.

"Too late for what? You've got nothing to apologize for. I've been pretty much on my own for a while. And I'm doing just fine—even though I may not look it."

"So, how *is* your little experiment going?" he asks.

"You mean the trip? Just great. The last time I saw you, you didn't like the idea. You threw me out of the house."

"Well, we didn't agree on whether it was the right thing to do or the right time to do it, did we? I didn't throw you out of the house, by the way. I threw you out of my office."

I take a sip of champagne and settle in.

"To answer your question, I had one little bump in the road, so to speak, in Zermatt, as I'm sure you recall. I loved your telegram. I'm still laughing."

He smiles.

"Did everything work out okay?"

"It did."

"I knew it would."

"And in Spain I had an accident."

"Accident?" he says, putting his glass down. "You didn't tell me about that."

"Never mind. It wasn't serious. I got a little roughed up, and so did the bike, but in a couple of hours I was on my way."

"Were you hurt?"

"A few scrapes, but the helmet and gear helped. A little village outside Barcelona. Skidded on some oil in the road and slid into a ditch."

Neither of us speaks for a moment.

"So, what do you think now?" he asks.

"About the trip?"

"Yes. Do you still think it was the right thing to do?"

I give him a long look. I'm sure he already knows the answer.

"By far the best experience of my life."

He takes another sip.

"You haven't lived very long," he says, giving me a "you'd better wise up" wink.

"Well, what have you learned?"

"I've learned it's a big world out there." I smile.

"I mean, lessons in life," he says. "Have you learned any lessons in life?"

"Well, I found out I can take care of myself. I wasn't so sure about that."

"And your future? Your career? Have you thought about that?"

"I have confidence in myself, Dad. So, I'm not worried about that. That's all going to take care of itself."

He shakes his head.

"That's another example of the naïveté that worries me about you," he says, having another sip. "That's not how life works. Things don't just take care of themselves."

"What I mean, Dad, is that when you have a plan, things *do* take care of themselves."

"How would you know?

"I'm working on it. It's a work in progress."

"What does that mean?"

"I know what I want."

"People twice your age don't know what they want. People my age don't know what they want."

"But that's what this trip's about. I'm trying to find out!"

"So, what have you found out?

I stare at him. "Let me tell you again what I don't want. I don't want to be on the perpetual party circuit. Do you get that much, Dad? Do you finally understand that part?"

He nods solemnly. "Go on."

"I want to spend my life doing something I like. You, above all people, should understand that. I have confidence that I can design and navigate a life of my own. I'm sure I'll be good at whatever I do. And I have no doubt I'll make money at it—without, I might add, a penny from you. I'll go as far as I have to, for as long as it takes. That's the plan, and I'm sticking with it."

I feel energized. But he seems nonplussed.

"How is this plan going so far?" he asks.

"It's already starting to work. It may surprise you, but I've been getting pretty good at art and making money at it. And I'm keeping a journal, which I hope to turn into a book. Sure, it's a dream. You may call it a pipe dream. But that's the kind of thing I'm talking about.

"It's not that I don't respect you, Dad. I do. But I just don't want to go the traditional route and pretend that what I end up with is a good thing, telling myself I did the right thing, when I'll know until the day I die I did the wrong thing."

"Instead," he says, jumping right in, "you'll go somewhere and be a street artist? Or a ski bum? Try to write screenplays in some Hollywood dump? Why don't you go down to Mexico? Be a beach-bum surfer dude smoking dope for the rest of your life? Get real, for Christ's sake!"

I'm amazed at how he sees me.

"Surfer dude? What's that all about?" I shoot back. "You want me to give *you* credit? Give *me* some credit! Obviously, you're not listening. You have no idea who I am."

"All right, all right," he says, backing off. "I'm listening. Tell me how I got it wrong. Tell me who you are—since I can't seem to figure it out for myself—and what you want."

"I don't want to sell out. Like you did. I know about the two best-selling books. You were *this* close to being a literary figure, a famous writer. Instead, you went into advertising."

"Ouch!" he says, wincing. "I can see you're out for a little blood."

"Not blood."

"So, everybody can relax because you're going to have it all? Do I understand *that* part? May I remind you it is I who have two best sellers to my credit?"

"I just want to understand," I say.

"Actually, it's very simple. I did it for the money."

"You did it for the money?"

"Sometimes, for all your self-righteousness and quickness to judge, Harry, I do think you can be pathetically naïve," he says, giving me a cutting look. "The life of a writer in those days was hard, just as it is today. You had to be prepared to risk everything—total failure—and make next to no money doing it!

"I had to provide for my mother and two sisters because right about then my father died. And that's when I took a steady job with the agency. I couldn't risk failure as a writer. I did it for the money."

"But then you married Mom. So you didn't have to worry about money."

He looks at me.

"That's where you're wrong. It was your grandmother who controlled the money, and to make sure she held on to her power, she never gave your mom a dime. That's why things turned out for me the way they did. I was still the breadwinner, only now there was my wife, used to fine things and social position. And my own family whose welfare I am responsible for still. Yes, I think that's when the boozing began too."

"So...that's why you sold out. That's why you didn't go back to your writing, or music? Or those terrific cartoons you sold to the *New Yorker*. You really couldn't, after you married Mom?"

"Call it what you like, but make no mistake. We loved each other. And still love each other. Your mother is no fool. When she teased that I was a gold digger, I never denied it. Instead, we both laughed. Otherwise we wouldn't have been able to joke about the money. In fact, after she inherited, it was her idea to buy a piece of the agency. That's why I'm a copywriter, yes. As I say, it's all about the money."

When I say nothing, my father adds: "So, I married into money. You can take that any way you want. And I hope it doesn't come as a great disappointment to you, because it has given you the good life—even if you seem to have your doubts."

He raises his glass in a little toast.

"And, by the way, I'd do it again. I have *no* regrets."

That's an outright lie, but I feel only sadness and remorse for him.

And what about my mother's life?

"No regrets?"

"In fact, I've decided to tell you something you may not be expecting. Something I've been thinking about and wanting someday to tell you, to try to explain to you."

Andre comes over to ask if we'd like to order. My father waves him away.

"I've never really felt the time was right," he continues. "But somehow, here in Paris, far from the world we live in, I think it is time."

Good God. What's this? The man has never confided anything to me, nor revealed himself in any significant way. Though, in my mind, he's no different from any other father I've ever met. What could he possibly tell me now?

"Well, go right ahead then."

He looks down at his hand.

"Do you remember growing up and sometimes I wasn't around?"

"I remember that very well."

"Well, I never admitted it to you, but—like you—I had a yearning to travel, to feel free. Frustrated when I was young, but later I used to disappear for weeks. I told your mother I was on business. And sometimes I was. But most of the time I was here, in France. And business had little to do with it."

I say nothing, waiting for more.

"You see, there have always been two of me," he continues. "But you've only known one."

"Have I?" I interject. "Right now, I'm not sure I know even one."

He takes a sip. "Touché! But…unlike you and your trip, I can't remember any of it."

"What?"

"That's right. I remember nothing of those times."

"How is that possible?"

"Oh, I remember bits and pieces," he says. "I used to drive a sports car around the Riviera. I used to laugh a great deal and drink a lot of wine and eat magnificent meals. And yes, I can remember lots of girls. But I don't remember their names, and I don't remember where I was or what I did. In fact, it's all a blank to me."

I'm having trouble getting past the "lots of girls" part. "And this is what you've waited all these years to confide in me? This is the fatherly talk you've always wanted to have with your son? How many girls are we talking about?"

"I don't know, and it's not important," he says.

"And why not?"

"Because I'm an alcoholic."

I can only gape, giving these alien words time to make a controlled crash in my head.

"Alcoholic? I don't think I've ever seen you drunk."

"You have," he says. "You just didn't know it."

My mind reels back over the years.

"I guess not," I say. "You must hide it very well."

"Nobody hides it better."

"But how?" I want to know. "How can I not have known?"

"We all remember what we want to remember, and most of the time I didn't give you much to go on," he says. "These things are called benders. If I didn't seem to be in touch, or communicate, it's probably because I was drunk. So maybe to you everything seemed perfectly normal."

"So...you were drunk even in the daytime?"

"Yes."

"At work?"

"Sometimes."

"Are you drunk now?" I ask.

"A little. Normal for me. But it would not be normal for you. I function very well, where most people could not."

"Does Mom know?"

"I don't think so. I've never told her."

"Surely she would smell it."

"No, the magic of vodka. But you see, alcoholism is a chemical as well as an emotional dependency."

"How did you allow yourself to become an alcoholic? Why would you want to be shitfaced, unaware of everything around you, out of it, instead of in it?"

"Oh, I'm aware," he says. "But I get your meaning. Actually, I rather like my world. It's mellow, less stressful."

"Like when you threw me out of your office?"

If my father's a happy drunk who appears to be sober, why should I bother to reason with him? He has a point. He seems to suffer no ill effects, and he's comfortable in his world.

I think of all the kids I know who smoke pot.

I drink down the whole flute, gratefully, replacing it carefully on the table.

"So why," I ask slowly, "are you telling me this now?"

There's a long pause.

"Good question," he says. "I don't know, really."

Another pause. "I think because I am ashamed...and because it was all such a waste. And it could have been so good. The adventure. The travel. But today it's just a cloudy patchwork of days lost forever. And I can never get them back."

The conversation is at a standstill, and both of us are at a loss. Andre sweeps in, rescuing the moment. The sole is fresh from Normandy, so Dad orders that, and a Bordeaux bottled before I was born. But I order steak frites, solid bistro food, and a side of mâche.

"So, enough about me," my father says reasonably.

"Your mother is here. Do you know that?"

"What?"

"Yes."

"What's she doing here?"

"I don't know."

"Why didn't you tell me?"

"I didn't know."

"How can you not know?"

"She didn't tell me. She just showed up. This afternoon."

"Didn't you ask her why?"

"Yes. She said she just wanted to be here. And wanted to see you."

"Why didn't you ask her to join us?"

"Because I needed to see you alone."

"Why? So you could tell me you're an alcoholic?"

"Yes, that, and more. I hope I haven't made a mistake in telling you."

"So what's she doing now?"

"Taking a nap, I think."

"Does she know I'm in Paris?"

"Yes, of course. Maybe that's why she's here."

"We should go back."

He seems to consider that.

"Where are you staying?"

"Over on the Left Bank."

"Get your things. Come to the Ritz. The suite has four bedrooms."

THE RITZ

Two hours later, a bellman opens the door, and I step into the suite. The living room is ablaze with light. I can smell fresh roses. Down the hall, I hear contentious, angry voices.

I pause outside an open bedroom door.

My father and mother are arguing.

"All these years go by, and now you're telling me you're an alcoholic?" My mother's voice is stretched tight as a wire. "Does Harry know?" she nearly yells.

"Yes, he does."

My father sounds contrite, defensive.

"When did you tell him?"

"Today."

"Did he already know?"

"No."

"How did you hide it from him? Why did you hide it from me? How can anybody hide something like this for so long?"

"I can hide anything."

"Is that a boast? I don't think I ever saw you drunk. Where did you drink?"

262

"I left home. I came to Paris, and other cities, to escape. It's not uncommon."

"Oh, so that makes it okay…all those times away, nearly every year? It wasn't just business?"

"No."

"I felt so sorry for you! All that traveling. How could you do that to me? Over and over."

There's no answer.

"Were there women? Is that why you did it?"

There's a long pause.

"Sometimes."

"You cheat! You bastard!" I hear a sharp slap.

"You shouldn't have done that," my father says, his voice thin, menacing.

"You deserve it."

"No! I don't deserve it."

"You're a grown man. With responsibilities and status. It *is* your fault."

"It is *not* my fault…because I don't remember…"

"What do you mean, you don't *remember*?"

"I was *drunk*, for Christ's sake!"

"That's no excuse! You played me for a fool. You walked out on me! You lied to me! What a fool. A naïve, lovesick fool! I allowed my father to ruin my future. And now this! You've become more like my father than my father! What did you expect me to do? I needed you to rescue me. But it was never about me, was it? It was only about *you*!"

There's a pause.

In a quieter voice, she says, "I look at us now and wonder, how I could I ever have loved you?"

"*I have* always *loved you!*" my father roars defiantly.

Her voice rises again. "Then why do you drink? Why do you want to hurt me? What have I ever done?"

Silence.

The anguish is palpable. Standing just outside the room, I try to comprehend their entangled grief. All the years unraveling.

"See? You have no answers!" she spits. "Here you come to Paris, and I find out you're meeting Harry. You didn't even tell me, didn't even invite me. You can't leave me out! He's *my* son!"

"He's my son too."

"Not really! You don't understand that boy. And never did! And now, too late, you want to steal him from me, win him over—and ignore me. I won't allow it! Pathetic! You are a pathetic man! Harry's the only really good thing that's ever come out of our marriage!"

There's a heavier slap—and a thud.

I rush into the room, rocked by the sight of my mother crumpled on the floor.

My father stands over her, chest heaving.

My God. Is she dead?

I kneel and cradle her in my arms. My strong and beautiful mom so suddenly, frighteningly vulnerable.

She stirs and sobs.

I look up, fighting an urge to kill.

All I can do is ask, "What have you done?"

My father stands back, staring down, choking on his tears.

For a gasping moment, no one can speak. My mother's eyes well, infinitely sad. My father, strangely still, struggles to say something but can make no sound.

I begin to feel a strange, overwhelming calm.

"Mom…Dad…we need to get out of this room. Let's go into the living room. Come."

As I lift my mother to her feet, she puts her head against my chest.

My father nods assent.

Slowly, we make our way to the living room. I sit with my mother on a sofa, still trying to comfort her. My father raises his eyes to some faraway place, deeply distressed, his fists gripping. My mother seems totally unaware of his presence in the room.

I put my arms around her, pull her close.

"It's all right now, Mom…deep breaths. It's okay."

She's shaking, leaning into me. I can feel hot tears on my chest.

"It's my fault…" she sobs, her voice an unfamiliar cry of emotion.

I try to soothe her. "We will all get past this."

She nods but doesn't speak.

"I was so cruel to him," she whispers, shaking her head, grasping me tightly. And then, as if awakened by years of pain and sorrow, the words pour out in a rush.

"So cruel! I was so cruel! I wanted to hurt him. I just lashed out. I shouted. But it's not his fault. It's *my* fault. I was so angry, not just at him, but at my whole life…I was angry at my life. I took it all out on him, told him he was to blame. He had just settled. Settled for a life I never wanted. It all came out at once…It's so, so sad…"

She struggles, gulping air.

"But I wanted to hurt him," she continues, after a moment. "I told him all I really ever got out of our life together was you. And now I feel like I'm losing you too. Oh, Harry!" Her voice rises to a wail.

"I'm jealous. I'm just jealous…afraid he will take you away from me. That's why I came to Paris. I thought he was stealing you and leaving me out. I'm so scared. I don't want to lose you, Harry. What am I going to do?"

Now I feel my own tears begin to well.

"Mom, you can never lose me."

"I told him I never loved him. I can't believe I said that…is it true? No, I know it is not true. But I screamed it over and over, and he hit me." She fights for a breath.

"I don't blame him for hitting me…"

I sway her gently, like a baby.

"It's okay, Mom, let it go…he didn't mean it. I know you didn't mean to hurt him…and I know he didn't mean to hurt you. He's crying too…"

She opens her eyes wide, brushing away tears, wanting to believe. "You think...he didn't mean it?" she says. "Do you really think so?"

"Yes, I know so. All that matters now is forgiveness," I tell her, glancing at my father, who sits, his face buried in his hands. I can hear stifled sobs.

"We all need to forgive. You need to forgive Dad, and he needs to forgive you."

Shock tremors gradually dissipate, but I can sense the dismay, the unbearable lingering weight on her heart, the weariness and resignation, the fear and confusion.

I turn to my father. He's gazing at us, eyes red, a look on his face of unbearable calamity. He turns to me. His eyes begging for help.

There's a long silence when I wonder if he might just get up and walk away. But then, for the first time in my life, he speaks his heart.

"I...don't know...what happened in there," he says, wincing. "I am not a violent man." Bewildered, he just stares.

"It was very wrong...what I did..."

He wrestles with the pain of revealing so much, especially to me.

But he's clearly also speaking to himself.

"I am a little frightened," he goes on, "because...I didn't know... I didn't know I was capable of such a thing. I didn't know this... part...of me. I've always...always loved your mother...I've always loved her.

"But the sad thing," he says, trying mightily to speak, "is that she said she felt I've let her down...and maybe I did. But I...tried my best...I...really did..."

The silence is agonizing. Finally, my father wipes his eyes with his handkerchief, and my mother brushes away her own tears.

Dad looks at me directly.

"Harry," he begins, "do you remember that day in my office when you told me your plan for the future?"

I nod.

"The first thing that came to me was that I wanted to take off too—just like you."

He pauses and looks away.

"I have come to realize that I wanted to *be* you. But I didn't have the guts to own up to that. Instead, I was gripped by some kind of twisted guilt...or was it envy? I thought if I didn't put my foot down and keep your nose to the grindstone—as my father did with me—I would somehow fail in my fatherly duties. I told myself that the risk for you was too high."

He shakes his head.

"Sadly, I didn't recognize the truth until after you were on your way. Then, I let myself off the hook. It makes me even sadder that I could see myself in you, but I hadn't allowed you to see yourself in me."

I'm about to speak, but he holds up his hand.

"No. Please..."

I remain silent.

"If I had any hope of starting over, Harry, it meant I had to face my drinking problem, and tell you," he continues. "Then I was forced to tell your mother. But now look what I have done!"

He extends his hands toward her as his face contorts and tears stream down his face. I see not my cold, smug father but a lost soul staring into the abyss.

"I feel...feel such...shame," he says, his voice uncharacteristically weak, "but I know that shame won't make it better...I know I can't take it back."

Then he gets up from his chair, arms still extended in supplication, and takes a tentative step toward my mother.

"Alexandra...I am so sorry...so very, very sorry. Please...please, forgive me...please *help* me..."

She hesitates but then stands. After a long moment that fills the room with unbearable silence, she takes an uncertain step toward him.

They move closer.

"Charles…" My mother extends her hands, inching forward, until their fingers touch. They say no more, but in a moment, all four hands are locked. Without another word, my father walks my mother to the door. Neither seems to notice me.

After they're gone, I exhale, wander over to the window, and with a long sigh gaze down on lights coming alive in Paris.

How did that happen?

I've become the parent, and my parents, the children.

In the distance, floodlights switch on, illuminating the Eiffel Tower in red, white, and blue.

I'm smiling. A wave of bittersweet love and loss washes over me. I see treasured family scenes, faces from my trip—Sarah, Pilar, Cilla. I see Dom, T-Bone. My coach. Priceless moments. I feel love and sadness, a song without music. Redemption. I don't know whether to laugh or cry.

In the darkened glass, a familiar young man with hard, unflinching eyes stares at me. I stare back.

"Everything's okay now, buddy," the man in the glass says. "The ball's in your court."

I high-five my reflection.

"Yes, it is," I tell my hard-eyed self. "Let the games begin."

GOOD NIGHT

I close the journal, glance at the dog, hoping for a sign. The dog watches with interest, ears slightly cocked, head atilt, expectant. Liquid eyes and the suggestion of a dog smile give reassurance that all is well in our world.

Outside, the light is gone. The fire, reduced to sputtering embers, glows cherry red in encroaching darkness. The peace that surrounds us in this cozy den reminds me just how lucky I've been. I stuck with the plan, wound up with my own consulting firm, three best sellers, grown kids off starting their own families and careers, grandkids on the way, plenty of money, no debt, good health.

Where is the strife in my story? The conflict? The devastating collisions of life that make for spellbinding drama?

How did I manage to dodge all that?

Could it be, as they say, that luck is everything?

God knows I've been blessed with more than my share.

In some ways I feel like the old prizefighter who went the distance. But that's only because I never got knocked out. And almost all my punches have been lucky.

Not so, for so many others around me. I've seen friends succumb to booze, greed, folly, tragedy, loneliness, heartbreak, dis-
ease, and just plain bad choices. I've seen troubles at close hand
that I may never have been able to endure myself. Some of the sorrow I witnessed you could lay down to bad luck. But most of it was
just a ton of self-inflicted misery.

Jack, who ditched his wife of twenty-five years for a younger
woman, only to get ditched himself—but not before his kids turned
against him—wound up getting taken to the cleaners by the gold-
digging bitch of a trophy wife and had to go back to work for a
former employee just to make ends meet. He took to drinking,
and the last I heard, he'd moved into an apartment in a downscale
neighborhood.

Lots of stories like Jack's.

And a few more that were truly tragic. All self-inflicted.

Andrew. Courtly, upright Andrew, who lived like a king for
years by screwing all his friends blind in a huge Ponzi scheme that
crushed dreams, ruined countless lives, and rained shame upon
his unsuspecting wife and two kids in college. When he wound up
broke, the family moved out. The trial made national news. The
day before he was scheduled to report to federal prison to serve a
thirty-year sentence, he took a swan dive off the Brooklyn Bridge.

And then, of course, there was old Gordo. Had he lived, he
would have been very old Gordo. But Gordo, not surprisingly, fell
in with some bad characters in a get-rich scheme. Gordo, who
didn't really need the money, which made his story all the more
tragic. Old Gordo, who did eventually get busted by narcs, wound
up dead of a heroin overdose in prison at age twenty-seven.

If it could happen to Gordo, it could happen to anybody.

The only difference between Gordo and me is choices.

Of course, I've hit a few bumps of my own. Watched Cilla finally die of cancer back in New York. Almost died myself of pneu-
monia—twice. Lost my first child in a freak accident. Spent almost

a month in a hospital after surviving a private plane crash. The bumps of life. But not one of them self-inflicted.

Then, of course, there's Mike. There will always be Mike. Mike's death is a big bump, and the one that won't go away. The only reason he's not here right now is me. Even today, half a century later, the memory haunts me. Had he lived, I think we would have still been best buddies. I can see him now, over in the big leather chair that used to belong to my father, fat, with white hair or maybe no hair, still a Giants fan, drinking a very cold beer, talking to the dog.

Would he have taken over his dad's plumbing business? Or made it all the way to the NFL? Or taken the money route on Wall Street? Or maybe been a teacher or coach, or even an entrepreneur?

He died too young to give it much thought. But I think about it all the time.

Was Mike's death self-inflicted too, a result of a fatally unforgiving choice?

If so, all the more reason why I shouldn't have left him lying there.

I pour myself a little glass of whiskey, put a couple of logs on the fire, stare into the flames. I sip the whiskey, strong brown stuff that puts warmth in my chest and lingering fire on my tongue. With a rising sense of well-being, I put aside Mike, pour another glass, sink into my chair, listen to the logs crackle, and admire the dancing flames.

I take another sip, swallow the burn.

Maybe I'll never get over it.

"So, how does it feel to be old, buddy?"

It's Mike, Mike's voice in my head.

He won't let it go. I won't let it go.

Without thinking, I reflexively glance around the room, half expecting to see Mike's ghost.

The dog gives me a puzzled look.

"I'll never be old," the voice says. "That's the good thing about dying. You never get old. You stay young forever."

"What's it like over there?" I ask, going along with it. Is it the whiskey? Or am I losing my mind? The dog looks anxious.

"You meet a lot of interesting people."

Interesting people.

"Like who?" I can't believe I'm speaking out loud, as if he were actually right here in the room.

"I've become friends with a philosopher, guy by the name of Friedrich Nietzsche," Mike says.

I never heard of Friedrich Nietzsche until my last year of college. Nietzsche's aphorisms.

"Did he tell you any of his aphorisms?" I ask.

"He did."

"So give me an example."

Did I really say that? Am I talking to the dog?

"How about this: 'The golden fleece of self-satisfaction protects against blows but not against pinpricks.'"

How strange. I haven't heard that one since I was a student. Where did it come from? Did it come from Mike?

"You saying I'm elf-satisfied?"

"I am."

I stare into the flames.

"But it's all right," Mike says. "You have reason to be. I might have been the same myself."

"So you're sticking pins?"

"I am."

The dog, giving up on this unfathomable repartee, sinks back on the rug and closes his eyes.

It's true. My story is not a story of woe. It's a story of affirmation. If you want it, and you know without a shadow of doubt you can get it, then it will come. If it doesn't come, then you give it a push and *make* it come. It's not a trick or a special gift. Anybody can do it.

If you believe that, then maybe sometimes there can be happy endings.

But the self-satisfaction part is not so good.

"I'm sorry, Mike," I say. "Satisfaction. I'll take it. I'm glad of it and grateful for it. But self-satisfaction…you're right."

"Don't get me wrong," Mike says. "I'm happy for you. It all happened because you made it happen. But don't knock yourself out trying to pat yourself on the back."

"You think I could use a little humility and introspection?"

"I do. But don't knock yourself out with that either."

I laugh out loud.

"I miss you, buddy," I say, and then to my amazement, I can feel my eyes well up, and the tears start to come.

I can't believe my good fortune. But Mike wasn't so lucky.

"Mike…oh, fuck."

"No, no, it's okay," he says. "It's always been okay. And I've been right there on the sidelines all along, the whole time, rooting for you. Don't let it go to your head, boyo, but you played a pretty good game."

"You've been here?"

"I've always been here. You could have done something dumb and I gave you a little nudge and you never knew."

I'm fighting back the tears.

When was the last time I saw Mike? Saw his ghost? Was it back when I had that motorcycle accident so long ago in Spain?

"Fifty years…has really it been fifty years?"

"Not for me. For me, there is no time. Right here, and you never knew. I'm your guardian angel, boyo!"

When I can't speak, I take a breath.

"I knew it. I always knew it," I say. I'm confused, talking to my-self. Ridiculous. But it feels good to say the words. "You know how sorry I am. So sorry. Look at me crying like a baby…"

Talking to an empty room and a dog that doesn't give a shit.

Another sip of the brown, and I close my eyes, try to wipe away the tears.

"Hey, it's not all bad," he says. "I'm still eighteen."

"Mike, I can't talk."

"Before I go," Mike says. "I want to say…I like happy endings too."

That's when I feel the big hand patting my shoulder. My eyes snap open. I look behind me, all around the room. What's going on? Am I utterly delusional? Have I lost it, really lost it?

The dog sits up, gives a little bark, seems to look past me, barks again, walks over, puts his head on my lap.

"Mike?"

Silence. No more voices.

But the dog looks up at me with those sleepy eyes and nods, not once, but twice.

I've always suspected that dog could read my mind.

AUTHOR'S NOTE

This book could not exist without the extraordinary contributions of Edith Bjornson (Edee), my editor and counselor, muse and strategist, who kept the project on course, thinned my words when they grew too fat, and kept characters in character. For her valued insights, sharp eye, treasured expertise, commitment, and so much more, I am forever grateful.

Made in the USA
Columbia, SC
02 July 2018